Alpha Farm

Facing Your Demons

A Prepper Chicks Series

By Annie Berdel

ANNIE BERDEL

For information contact:

AnnieBerdel@yahoo.com

www.AnnieBerdel.com

DEDICATION

This one was for me.

A purging of the Soul.

Let life begin anew.

ANNIE BERDEL

ACKNOWLEDGEMENTS

There are certain people who come into your life that you allow the opportunity to either destroy every dream possible, or they take the opportunity to cheer you on from their balcony in your life.

To all those who said I couldn't… I did.

To all those who threatened… Bring it.

Abba ~ j'adore!

Mark. My partner in crime. Thank you for your patience.

To my children ~ because I want more for you.

To Dixon ~ because I am your human and that makes me happy. Still.

Hristo ~ No words. You see my soul.

Pauline Nolet ~ for seeing me without my makeup on and only making my words better! Your insight is much appreciated!

Sandra Parker ~ the voice of Alpha Farm! So glad you are back!

To all the beta readers ~ YOU STILL ROCK

ANNIE BERDEL

1

It felt like her soul was being ripped from her body. Strand by strand, it was being unwound and exposed.

Is this how death feels? she wondered. *The moment right before you die… Is it really this excruciatingly painful?*

Her legs gave out and she fell to the floor. Demons—long hidden within the catacombs of her mind—screamed out.

This can't be happening, she thought.

She curled into a ball on the cold linoleum floor to try to protect any innocence she had left. Her heart shattered into innumerable pieces. Her body began to shake with the fierceness of a spring thunderstorm… violently trying to remove her pain.

The blackness of her mind drew her deeper and deeper into the unknown, a place few people survived. Clawing at the smooth surface beneath her, she gasped for breath... Her sanity dripped from her nails like fresh blood drawn from a mortal wound.

She felt the sticky goo beneath her fingers... pulling her farther into the darkness. Flashes of white cut through the darkness as her mind remembered. She felt the lifeblood of her beloved Dixon attaching itself to her skin. Yanking her hand away from the pool of blood that now covered a good portion of the floor, she inadvertently smeared the red stain across her shirt as she clutched her fist tight to her chest.

He was gone. Possibly forever. Her best friend... her husband... her Tommy. The one person she counted on to always have her back. She was alone. One. The cord of three had been broken.

Her body gave birth to the bitterness, the fear, the ugliness of life until the exhaustion took over and rocked her to a stillness.

"God, why?" She whimpered through leftover tears.

She faintly heard His voice... calling to her through the darkness.

"Help me," she breathlessly whispered.

She lay there in silence. Her breathing slowed. Her mind drifted. She heard Him again calling to her, but He was so far away... so far away.

"Please help me," she begged ever so quietly.

The sweetness of peace started to slowly pour into her soul. She took a deep breath, wiping the matted hair from her face. "Please hear me," she whispered.

Raising her head, she began to sit up, but her strength failed her. The demons returned and angrily taunted her soul, leaving white scalding hot fear where love once was. A fear so real and honest it shook her innermost being. She had no control over her own body, her own emotions. Her body pulsated with such an intensity, such a fierceness that she cried out to God for death to be quick. But He never gave in to her pleas of release. He stayed with her until little by little the peace started to return.

With all the strength she had left, she dragged herself to the wall and propped herself up. With her head in her hands, she started to weep. Raising her face to the heavens, what was left of her tears flowed from her heart, mixing with the now smeared blood across her cheeks.

Her soul, trying to escape, pushed against her human form so hard she couldn't breathe. Sobbing took over as she rocked herself back and forth against the reality of what had happened.

"God help me!" she cried out, running as fast as she could from denial.

Drawing her legs up to her chest, she rested her head on her knees as peace once again drifted in like the waves of the ocean.

Cupping her head in her hands, she took a deep breath. Silence. She needed the silence. The quiet. It was soothing. Her mind was a mix of a multitude of thoughts, but the silence drew her closer.

Taking a deep breath, she was afraid to move. Afraid the fear would return and torment what was left of her soul. Taking another deep breath, a tiny grain of peace entered. Then another. Her breathing was returning to a normal rhythm... but her mind... her thoughts... she wanted to stay in the quiet. Reality was teasing though. Little snippets were trying to break into the silence. She frantically kept trying to swat them back into the darkness. She had to keep them away.

It was so hard to stay in the abyss. One by one the memories started to sneak in... slowly at first. But like a mountain stream after a soaking rain, the memories started to flood into the cavities of her heart ripped wide open by fear.

Lifting her head in defiance, she cried out to God with such intensity that she felt the heavens quake. Rocking up onto her knees, she approached her God with such intensity that all fear hid.

"I'VE HAD ENOUGH!" she screamed. "How much is one person supposed to handle in one lifetime?"

Placing both hands on the fabric created in her mind, she tore open the inner curtain and approached the very throne of God with such blatant arrogance that she thought for sure she would be stricken down. But He allowed her to release her fear, her pity, and her mistrust until all were gone... and gently, He began to rebuild her...

Slowly she crawled to the sink. Her mouth was like the Sahara desert, arid and parched. Her face was matted with hair, snot and filth from the last few hours. Reaching up a hand, she managed to pull herself up to the faucet. Not trusting her legs to hold her, she threw her shoulders farther over the edge of the counter and balanced on her stomach. Turning on the spigot, she splashed water on her face, allowing it to quench the tightness of her parched lips and tongue. Scarlet swirls filled the sink, memories of long ago, of her past that she had to accept.

Her mangled hair hanging down around her face, she allowed her fingers to rest under the stream of cool liquid, concentrating on the ripples. It simultaneously was feeding her soul. "God," she moaned, knowing that He alone knew what she needed just then.

Placing more of her weight onto her legs, she knew she had to turn around and face her destiny. Her knees slightly buckled as she felt those little bastard demons of fear clawing again at her insides. Exhaling with force, she stood still, holding onto the side of the sink. Taking one hand, she raked the hair away from her face.

"Okay, chicka," she breathed out. She took a deep breath and held onto it as long as she could.

Releasing the now stagnant air with force, she drew in another breath and closed her eyes. "Help me here," she asked of God. Turning slowly, the blood now streaked across her face like a warrior's paint, she faced her demons.

2

Michael stood in the open doorway of the cabin. He hadn't felt a zephyr in ages, or maybe he hadn't slowed down long enough to notice, but it felt good to be back home with the only family he had left. A slight grin spread across his face as he remembered the look on Chloe's face when he introduced her to his sister, Emma. He enjoyed the look in her eyes as he saw the wheels spinning in her head. Her mind could go a million miles a minute if she didn't gain control of herself. He had seen her take one mundane comment and spin it in so many ways that somehow she almost solved world peace from the epiphany she conjured in her mind. Or worse, destroyed the planet. With zombies or, even worse, with bugs. Big crawly bugs that made his insides weak. If there was one thing he took from combat training, it was his distaste for the nasties. You could only have so many in your diet before it was time to move on, and when forced to eat them day in and day out, forget it. Giving a low chuckle, he decided that he would have to come up with a few more epiphanies to keep that glint in her eyes.

Breathing in the cool crisp night air, Michael needed to sort out his feelings for Miss Chloe, he realized. Out of obligation to his sister, he had traveled across the country to make sure this "precious jewel," as Emma referred to her, would make it back to the farm safely.

There's got to be a story there, he thought.

Emma would not have risked his life for just anyone. Knowing his sister, he knew she wouldn't just tell him, or she would have already.

Pulling the cigar that Tom had given him back at the main house from his shirt pocket, he snipped the end and lit it with a wooden match. If there was one thing his brother-in-law had taught him, it was how to enjoy a truly fine cigar, and what better time than when you were trying to clear your head.

His eyes squinted as the flame from the match danced before him. Drawing in his breath, he felt the smoky taste invade his mouth, teasing his lungs. Flirting with the end of the cigar with his tongue, he withdrew it and exhaled. Against the moonlight, the vapor delighted his external senses as the tension within his body began to subside. He could relax here, one of the few places on earth that soothed his soul.

Chloe. His mind recited her name over and over in his head, teasing his long-fought plan of aloneness. He had a blueprint, damnit. One he had been working on all of his life.

Is it time to settle down? Man, staying in one spot? Growing roots? Monogamy? Holy hell!

A shiver ran up from the base of his spine, tingling as it nestled into the base of his skull, making his hair tingle above his shirt collar.

Damn.

He had been running his entire life. On his own and no worries about anyone or anything except maybe Emma. But, hell, she took care of herself. He would check in with her occasionally because he knew she worried about him, but if there was a woman who could handle herself, it was Emma. Maybe that was part of his problem. Wait. Problem? Now this was a problem?

"FUCK," he muttered under his breath.

Taking a long inhale, he paused, keeping the demons captive in his chest.

CHLOE, her name echoed from the trees.

Puckering his lips, he slowly released the smoke. Rolling the cigar on the railing of the porch, he carefully laid the burnt tip over the edge of the floorboard. He would get back to it later. A fine cigar you just don't throw away. Right now though, he needed to talk to his sister.

3

He pulled Nina's cold, lifeless body from the back of his truck. The blood from her neck wound had started to seep through the tarp he had wrapped her in. Emotionless, he picked the bundle up and threw it over his shoulder. For once he was glad she wasn't a large woman.

He had known Nina for a good number of years, being assigned to duties at the White House. Senator Varga had ended up being under his care once the new president had assumed office. Well, not really his care. More like under his watchful eye. His gut told him to stick as close to this female as he possibly could without throwing suspicion or making their relationship questionable.

Sean Kissler, lieutenant general in the United States Army, now had the task of returning Senator Nina Varga's body back to Washington, DC, along with a plausible excuse for why she had a gaping hole in the side of her pretty little neck. Seemed easy enough just to tell the truth, but he wanted to think that notion all the way through to the end before he told anyone. No mistakes. Too much had already been lost, and if there were any more screwups, let's just say that people who could make Nina look like chump change would start getting antsy. They would already pick apart what the hell happened with the senator, he didn't need them sticking their nose into his business any more than that.

Laying the bundle down on a table in the medical tent, Sean picked up a folded blanket from the shelf underneath where Nina now lay. Dreary green, the blanket seemed to absorb the emotions in the room and amplify them. Throwing the wool cover over the corpse, he reached back down under the table and pulled out a plastic packet. Ripping it open, he gently placed the lifeless cadaver into the body bag, being careful to tuck the blanket in around her. He still cared about her, and as idiotic as it seemed, he wanted some comfort, a sense of humanity left with her.

Tired, he would kill for some shut-eye, but he needed to get his men packed and get the hell out of here. He was done with this farm and done with the idiots who lived here. He wanted nothing more than to get back to his normal existence in Washington and get some R & R, but knowing the occurrences in the world currently, that wasn't going to happen. Too much was at stake, and the hand that was dealt had to be played out until its end. Who survived wasn't his concern, but making sure the plan was fulfilled was.

Stretching his tired back, Sean leaned back and tilted his head towards the ceiling of the tent. Closing his eyes for just a second, he ran his fingers under his hat and gave a quick scratch. He had been meaning to get a haircut, and then the shit had hit the fan and his hair was forgotten about. One of the first things he needed to do when he got home was to whack this crap off his head.

He needed a new plan now. His ass was on the line with this one, as he was the ranking officer. Reaching down, he pulled the zipper up on the body bag, making sure not to catch anything. He made sure everything was tucked inside as best he could. The teeth of the ligature had slid as far as Nina's chin when Sean paused. Staring down at her now lifeless face, he realized she wasn't as glamorous as everyone had thought she was. Take away all the makeup and fancy hair and she looked quite manly. A faint hint of a mustache was creeping on her upper lip. Figuring it part of her Hispanic heritage, he hadn't really paid much attention to her attributes before, but this definitely caught his attention. Sean ran his finger along her cheekbone and down to the corner of her mouth. Sliding his finger into the corner of the corpse's mouth, Sean pushed against her teeth to try to get her mouth to open. Something wasn't quite right, and he could feel it in his gut.

4

Emma reached out to grab him, but he faded from her vision. Again and again his apparition tormented her. If only she could touch him. Save him. The hazy confusion taunted her. Was he real? She felt the pain that now resided in her chest, like a fire burning her from within. Her soul being ripped from her body left little doubt that she was still alive. Crying out, she heard her voice be carried off into the night with no response.

Her legs failed her and she crumpled, rocks digging into her knees as she hit the ground. The palms of her hands caught the full weight of her upper torso and buckled her elbows out, but she held her head high enough so it didn't touch the dirt. Her hair, now matted from sweat and grime, dangled from either side of her face, shadowing her from seeing what was beyond.

GET BACK UP! she yelled from within.

She had to find the strength to find him. Tomás was her life. The images of him lying on the kitchen floor, blood matted in his hair, his cheek turning shades of blue and purple... his lips swollen beyond recognition.

She reached up and touched her own lips, the memories haunting her. His lips. She must have kissed them a thousand times. She would lie in bed and stare at their perfection as he slept, her husband unaware of her unwavering infatuation. She adored him. She adored every inch of him. He was her everything, and she would willingly give her own life to protect him.

Droplets of water fell past her lashes and mingled with the dirt and blood staining her pale face.

"LORD!" she cried out. It was all she had left. One simple word. All the Bible verses she had spent countless hours remembering failed her now.

"Lord." It was now a low murmur deep within her throat. She was so tired. Exhaustion begged her to just quit. To lie down and give up. The battle was over and she had lost.

The breeze tormented her as it spread its fingers along her cheek, brushing it ever so lightly.

Tommy?

He used to caress her face as she was falling asleep, such a peaceful feeling. Reaching up, she could almost feel his hand beneath hers, locking fingers as they had done so many times before.

Her head jerked up as yet again the demons danced against the darkness of the night. Placing her hands on either side of her, she lowered her head and raised herself to her feet. Standing, her mind began to spin. Perspiration broke out across her forehead as she fought to stay upright. Raising her chin, the determination she was unaware of moved first one leg and then the other. Her weakness triumphed as she collapsed back to the cold, hard ground.

"EMMA!"

Her eyes widened. He was alive! She could hear the faintest cooing, calling her to him.

"EMMA!"

She heard his voice again! But from where? Her chest heaved as she used every ounce of strength she had left. Pushing up, she slowly got to her haunches. With both hands still on the ground to steady herself, she paused, her head so dizzy it made her close her eyes.

Come on, girly girl, you can do this, she moaned inwardly.

With every ounce of strength she had left, she pushed off the ground and stood up straight. Her chin jutting outward in sheer determination, she kept her eyes closed as she gave her full attention to balancing on her limp legs.

"EMMA!"

He was behind her! Her eyes snapped open as her body had already begun to turn in his direction. Excitement driving the pivot, she was spinning entirely too fast. Her face now a phantom white, her eyes were failing her as the outer edges of her vision started to dim. Her knees were giving way from the weight of her body as she finally realized she was going down and needed whatever help she could find.

"Tommy," she mumbled.

Reaching up to her temple, she tried to get her eyes to focus like there was a magic button on the side of her head. Emma felt herself fall against his chest. Nausea started to creep up into her throat. Every ounce of bile from her stomach was inching up her esophagus, looking for an escape. Clinging to him like a moth being ravaged by a summer night's thunderstorm, she felt his arms encircle her just as her sight went totally dark. She shivered. Her weary body succumbed to the bowels of hell as the demons enveloped her soul. She collapsed into the murkiness, not caring anymore.

5

I'm glad I bought these boots before all hell broke loose, Mike thought to himself as he stepped over a fallen tree branch. He had always been picky about his footwear. If there was one thing he took away from his military service, it was to always keep your feet dry. He had seen guys march for miles in wet footwear just to find the skin of their feet still ensnared in their socks after they removed their boots. Once that image was burned into your brain, it was hard to forget it.

A twig broke beneath his foot, giving him pause.

I must have lost my touch, Mike thought to himself.

Chuckling, he decided it was time to hone his skills. Riding a motorcycle across the country to rescue a damsel in distress didn't exactly afford him the luxury of flexing his ninja skills, but now that he was back at the farm, he intended to take full advantage of the downtime. Heck, maybe a couple of his nephews would enjoy some maneuvers. He stopped dead in his tracks as Emma popped into his head. Emma with that look she had when she didn't agree with what you just did or said. He had better include the nieces too, or Emma's eyebrow would rise ever so slightly, but he'd figured out long ago what it meant: that the gates of Hades were about to open if something didn't change right quick.

Stopping at the edge of the clearing, he paused. Something was wrong. Crouching to his haunches, he slowly backed up, allowing the edge of the field to envelop him. His eyes small slits now, he scanned back and forth, looking for an anomaly. He could feel it in his gut; he just couldn't see it yet. Slowing his breath, he inhaled deeply through his nose and released it through his mouth until his pulse quieted. Closing his eyes, he listened.

A low, plaintive, broken sound was coming from the direction of Emma's house. Waiting, he tried to dissect the whimpering. That big white dog? Chickens didn't sound like that. It almost sounded human.

Zoning in on the area toward the house, he skimmed over the landscape. Damn it! Why couldn't he see anything! Back and forth his eyes darted as his pulse quickened.

Two things he was sure of: something was wrong, and he wasn't going across the field with no cover. Slowly he crept farther back into the woods. He would circumvent the pasture and come out on the other side where the tall pines were. There was enough underbrush there to keep his cover in case, well... in case something was wrong. Thinking that something was wrong at the house hit him hard in the gut. Emma was his only family. And family you defended with your life.

All muscle memory and instinct kicked in, and Mike was back in survival mode. He quickly found himself flat down on the other side of the clearing, with his face in the pine needles. All of his senses were on high alert as he reassessed the situation.

Scanning the area, he noticed a decrease in the noise that had enveloped the house earlier when they had arrived. Generators had been set up to power much of the equipment the military had brought in; huge lights were being used around the encampment so the dozen or more people could work late into the night. The hum of radio communication along with an occasional command, quickly followed by a "yes, sir," was absent. Could they all be bedded down for the night? It would be a first since they had arrived, if they were. Now? Now it was eerily quiet. It was abnormal, and he was trained to notice the anomalous.

He heard her before his eyes found her. His ears locked on her location. The anguish emitting from the dark form made Mike sick to his stomach. His first instinct was to put it out of its misery.

Slowly the creature rose and tried to stand. Even in the darkness, the agony this person was in vibrated on the breeze and made Mike glad he hadn't approached it. Reaching down, his hand slid gently down his side until he could feel the cold hard grip of his Glock. Calmly, his index finger found its target and pressed in ever so gently, releasing the firearm from its captivity. With one quick jerk, Mike removed the firearm from the holster and brought the gun towards his torso, keeping it in front of him. His finger now alongside the trigger, Mike looked in the direction of the wounded human, habitually aligning his sights for full impact.

Mike caught his breath as the clouds parted overhead. Luminosity from the moon caught the gold strands in the woman's hair before him. "Oh my god," he muttered under his breath.

Emma?

Cautiously, Mike made his way up onto his haunches. He needed to get down there to Emma but didn't want to risk being blindsided by whatever had attacked her. Keeping his firearm at the ready, he traced his way along the line of trees until he could see clearly behind her.

Nothing.

She was trying to say something, but Mike couldn't make out the words. He walked out of the safety of the trees and stood still. She looked directly at him with a horrifying glassed-over glare.

"Emma?"

She heard him. From her body language alone, he knew she had heard him. Taking a step closer, he paused and checked out the area. Still nothing.

Mike took another step closer. It was like she was seeing straight through him.

Taking a deep breath, Mike skirted the tree line quickly and came up behind her.

Weird, she didn't even move, he thought.

Peering into the night, there was no other movement, no other sound but himself and his sister. He walked up behind her and just stood there. The hair on the back of her head was matted with what looked like blood. Her clothes were disheveled.

"Emma!"

Emma spun around so fast that she lost her balance and collapsed into Mike. Her face pallid, he watched as her eyes rotated so that all Mike saw was the bloodshot sclera. She tried to say something, but he couldn't make out the words.

Catching her in his arms, Mike stared in horror at her appearance.

What the hell!

6

"Just calm down!" Johnisse said to Tiffany. "Let me try to figure this out!"

Tiffany paced back and forth across the floor. "Honey, we need to get out of here! Something very wrong is going on out there."

"You don't think I know that?" Johnisse spat back at her.

"Listen, I'm sorry, but I need time to think. We don't know what's going on, and from the sounds of it, whatever happened wasn't pleasant. It's been quiet for a while now though."

"FINE!" Johnisse screamed with frustration as she made her way to the door.

"Hello?" Johnisse spoke to the door tentatively. No sound.

"Hello?" Her voice now carried more bravado.

"There's no one there, Johnisse, just go!" Tiffany blurted out.

Johnisse tried the handle, locked.

"Now what?" Tiffany asked.

"I don't know," Johnisse said, as she was clearly frustrated. "Emma would have made a way out somehow," she replied as she began feeling along the door frame.

A slow mischievous grin crawled across Johnisse's face as her fingers lit upon the small metallic object.

"Damn that girl!" she whispered as she pulled the key from its hiding place.

"What's going on?" Tiffany asked.

"Long ago, Emma told me about a secret door, or a way to build a door so you never get locked inside a room. She told me that we should put them in our house, kinda like a safe room but with a twist. The safe room should have a secret exit. I guess they did this kinda stuff back when this house was part of the Underground Railroad."

"Seriously? You're talking to a black woman here. Give me that key!" Tiffany smirked and grabbed it from Johnisse's hand.

Looking around the room, Tiffany was looking for any clue as to a secret doorway. She walked over and knocked on the walls, felt along the window, checked under the bed and popped her head into the closet. She was obviously perplexed, from the look on her face.

"Well, my gorgeous black woman, can this black woman give it a shot now?"

Tiffany looked at the key and willingly handed it over to Johnisse. "Hurry, I need to tinkle," she quipped.

Exasperated, Johnisse clicked her tongue, grabbed the key and walked away. "Okay, let me try to remember what Emma told me. Geesh, it's been years."

"Jay!" Tiffany screeched.

"Oh hush, let me think," Johnisse replied.

Feeling along the door frame, Johnisse found what she was looking for. Sliding her finger into the faint groove, she pressed inward and instantly heard a pop. Pulling gently, the fancy detailed frame of the door swung outward.

Tiffany stood watching in dismayed shock. "I would have found that if I had more time."

Johnisse looked over at her with disbelief beaming from her eyes. "Oh really?"

"Just hurry up, baby. I still need to pee!"

Following the door frame down to level with where the doorknob was, Johnisse pressed against the wall. Surprisingly, it gave way. Johnisse could now take the key and unlock the door.

Tiffany was about to rush past her when Johnisse grabbed her by the arm.

"Hold up! We don't know what's going on out there. Give me a minute to check it out."

7

Chloe stretched in bed as she rolled over. Grabbing anxiously at her calf, she winced as a charley horse took control of her muscles.

Ooh! That smarts! she thought.

Flexing her foot to try to speed the muscle spasm away, Chloe heard her stomach grumble.

Wow! Is there any part of me that's not having a problem?

Sitting up, Chloe felt the pressure behind her eyes and a headache creep in.

"No, I guess not."

Looking around the room, she needed to find something to put on, as she wanted to make her way down to the kitchen. Some aspirin and a glass of milk sounded like the ticket to feeling better.

I should have gotten my bag out of the RV, she thought as she opened the closet door. To her surprise, it was full of clothes. Luckily the decision was easy, as hanging on the back of the door was a bathrobe. And not just any robe, this was one of those big furry grandmother-type bathrobes with the big flowers stained onto the fabric.

"This will work just fine," she cooed.

Chloe slid it on over her bare shoulders and folded the comfort around her naked body. *Delicious*, she thought. *I can understand why old ladies wear these all the time.*

Catching a glimpse of herself in the vanity mirror, she had to give a chuckle. Her punk hair with the robe was far from a fashion statement. If only her johns could see her now.

A bit of regret crept across her heart. Life was different now. There was no going back to the way it was. This was her home now, and no one ever had to find out about California. If there was a god, she would beg at this point to make sure her previous escapades were long forgotten.

How would they even find her now?

She shuddered at how naive she was being. These men had money, and lots of it. They also had the determination not to stop until they got what they wanted. Was that her? Was she what they wanted? She was quite close to several, about as close as a prostitute and a john could get, but there was one… one in particular that made her heart beat faster. Feelings were an enemy in her line of business, but this man had the power to drive her demons deep under the wall she had built around her heart. He knew her. He knew every inch of her. He knew how to manipulate her body to surrender to his demands. She had tried to fight him. He had made her look like a schoolgirl with her first crush.

"Oh, Chloe," she cooed.

She was taken aback at the emotion surfacing against her struggle. She would miss him? Yes, the cat-and-mouse game they played she would definitely miss, but would she miss the man behind the mask? Possibly.

She glanced down at the floor with an enormous amount of shame as Mike entered her thoughts. Could he offer her the tease that she craved between two lovers? Was he worth the effort if he couldn't? He did have other traits that could come in handy. Eye candy, yes. Intelligent, of course. Trustworthy? Ohhh, she breathed out. That one took her aback. Trust. What was trust? She had never needed it before but now? Now it teased her like the sticky strands of cotton candy against a child's face, just far enough out of reach of her tongue.

"Miss Chloe, what have you gotten yourself into?" she murmured beneath her breath.

Opening the door to the room, she headed out to find the kitchen.

8

Not sure what exactly was going on, Mike wanted to take every precaution in the world to keep his sister and himself as safe as possible. It wasn't like Emma to go traipsing off after dark with blood all over her, so something was obviously seriously wrong.

Slowly lowering her to the ground, Mike gently cupped her head and rested it on the dirt beneath them. Quickly walking around behind her shoulders, Mike slid his hands under her armpits and tugged as tenderly as he could. He wanted to get her out of view in case someone or something was still out there.

"Sorry, sis," he whispered as he dragged her limp body to the tree line. Emma started to stir, so Mike knelt down beside her.

"Emma?"

His voice teased at her senses... pulling at some unseen string still connecting her to reality.

"Em..." Mike groaned as he started to assess his sister's condition.

"Damnit, what the hell happened between last night and now?" he muttered under his breath.

Taking a deep breath, he peered around. Nothing. He couldn't see nor could he sense anything or anyone. History had proved to him that if he sensed something, whether he could see it or not, he'd better pay attention. Tonight there was nothing but emptiness drifting on the wind.

"Emma," he said with more authority.

Gently tapping her cheek, he watched as her eyelashes fluttered briefly.

"Emma!" This time he barely caught himself from yelling at her. He gave her cheek a solid smack and backed up a bit. Wouldn't surprise him one bit to have her come up swinging.

"Damnit, Emma, wake up!" He was shouting now, having grabbed hold of her chin and shaking her skull back and forth.

Emma let out a low moan.

"Come on, girl, come back to me."

"Tommy?" The name tumbled off her tongue.

"No, honey, it's Mike," he gently said as he brushed her hair back. Trying to be patient, he waited for her to come around more into reality, as it was obvious she was still incoherent.

"Mike?" Her lips mouthed his name as she fought to wake up. Her head moving slowly back and forth, she tried lifting her hand to her head. Missing it the first time, her arm thudded quickly back to the ground. Lifting it again, her hand made contact with her eyes.

"Mike? Wha…"

"Shh," Mike said. "Give yourself a minute."

Bending her leg at the knee, Emma tried rolling to her side. "Mike, Tommy," she sputtered as she tried to roll to a sitting position.

"Hey, slow down a bit." Mike's command fell on deaf ears as Emma was now raised up on her elbow and trying to sit up. "Okay, well, since you aren't going to listen to me, what the hell is going on?"

Emma tilted her head to look at her brother. Tears rimmed her eyes as she tried to speak. "Tommy," she stuttered.

"Yes," he drew out. "What happened to Tom?"

"They… they…" She tried, but her tongue was being held captive by images returning to her mind.

"Emma, take a deep breath. I really need to know what's going on," Mike stated.

Emma again tried to gather herself to a sitting position. As she was falling over, Mike gathered her and sat her against the nearest tree. Taking her chin in his hand, he held her gaze. "Emma, what happened?" he said with a gentle intensity that seemed to help calm her.

"They… they were here. Dixon. God!" Emma started to shake uncontrollably, but Mike continued to hold her chin.

"Emma, tell me again. Why were they still here?"

Tears danced down her cheeks, intermingling with the dried blood still there.

Using both of his hands, Mike held her face between them and focused her gaze. "Emma?"

Taking a deep breath in through her nose, Emma mentally allowed the cold air to circle her mind and chase out all the cloudiness. Pursing her lips, she slowly blew all the demons from her mind.

"They had Tommy in the basement. He beat him pretty bad. I'm not even sure if… if…" Her voice trailed off as the severity of what had happened nestled into her soul. Tommy could be dead for all she knew. "Mike, they took Tommy. He's dead, hanging in the kitchen."

"What? What do you mean? Who is hanging in the kitchen?" he asked.

"Can you help me back to the house now? We really need to get back to the house."

"Of course, but we're going to take it slow. Okay? Emma? Okay?"

"Yeah, sure," Emma responded, but Mike already knew he would be trying to keep up with her.

9

Johnisse stopped dead in her tracks as she entered the doorway to the kitchen, causing Tiffany to run right smack into her back with a thud.

Chloe let out a gasp as she crossed over the threshold.

All three were standing there as the knob turned and the back door opened.

Six eyes were fixed on the door and wide with horror as Mike entered.

Mike just stood there looking at them with a quick glint of curiosity.

Turning his head, he saw what had caused the frightened look on all their faces.

Hanging from the pot rack in the middle of the room was one of the most grotesque scenes he had ever encountered.

Six eyes followed his gaze.

"Go in the other room," he commanded. "Open the front door so I can bring Emma around so she won't see this again." He pointed towards the front of the house.

"Again? Emma saw this?" Johnisse asked.

"Yeah," he responded, lowering his gaze.

"Let's go," Johnisse said as she grabbed Chloe by the arm and herded Tiffany before her.

Johnisse turned and glanced at Mike before she left the room. She saw the raw emotion burned into his face. Taking a deep breath, she realized that the days ahead were not going to be one big happy party.

10

Ridley walked into the room with amazement and a newfound respect for her mom. All these ladies, actually. How did they manage to pull this all off?

Before her were shelves of supplies. Everything she could only imagine that at a time like this would be hard to find.

Running her fingers along the front of the wooden shelving, she mentally took inventory.

Turning, she looked at Mountain Man and smiled. "Any idea where a girl can get some paper and some kind of writing instrument?"

"Yes, ma'am! You really think you can save her leg?"

"I'm sure going to try," she said with a faint smile. "I want to get my thoughts down on paper first. Then make a list of things I'm going to need. But first, I want to knock her out cold and examine her leg in detail. Any idea what's all in here? Some of these totes are closed tight."

"Oh sure! Shelby kept a detailed account of everything in here. We weren't even allowed in here without her permission. First time one of the kids wandered in here being nosey, I thought she was going to cause an earthquake herself. She was mad. Never seen that woman that upset before," Mountain Man replied. "When do you want to get started?"

"Yesterday?" she replied as she walked past him out of the room.

Mountain Man watched the determined young woman walk away. Turning, he pulled the heavy door shut and locked it tight. Resting his forehead against the door, he took a deep breath. Tears glinted at the inner corners of his eyes.

Straightening his back, he turned to leave only to find Ridley standing a short distance off, watching him. Locking eyes, an unheard exchange of trust and hope floated on the musty air.

Turning, Ridley led the way back out of the lower half of the barn and into the sunshine. The air losing its strong scent of mold, Ridley took a deep breath. Laying a hand across her stomach, she told herself to be more careful about what she was doing. It wasn't just about her anymore. She would need to discuss possibly moving the supplies out of the barn now.

"Hey, Jeremiah?" Ridley queried. "What happened?"

"Bella stepped on her leg. I thought you were told that?" he said, looking puzzled.

"No, no. What happened out there?" she said, pointing out past the barn.

"I wish I knew," he said as his eyes followed the imaginary line traced in the air by Ridley's hand.

"Best guess," Ridley quipped.

"Well, guessing, I would say it was some kind of localized nuke."

"NUKE? Why are we standing out here, then?"

"My guess is that it was an airburst, so less fallout. Most fallout hits the ground within twenty-four hours. And don't forget, we are northeast, more north than east, of where the burst happened, so the jet stream hopefully carried most of that towards, say, Georgia." Raising his hand to shield his eyes from the sun, he continued. "I haven't even seen much Bikini snow this far north, so we'll take our chances. Plus, Shelby. That woman has an oil or herb for everything out there. We just need to get her better."

"Bikini snow? Tell me about that over dinner, m'kay?" Making a mental note to check if Shelby had iodine tabs somewhere, Ridley entwined her arm in Jeremiah's thick meaty limb and tugged lightly to get him headed back towards the house. Still entangled when they reached the house, Ridley turned so she could see Mountain Man's face. "I'm gonna save her. I promise."

"Listen, I need to go check on a couple of things towards town. Think you could keep Shelby distracted for a while?" Jeremiah asked Ridley.

Looking a bit perplexed, Ridley agreed with the condition that the Mountain Man tell her all about his adventure when he returned.

"What are you going to be doing?" she asked.

"Just looking for answers," he replied with very little information, as was his habit.

"Okay, yeah. Prepare to talk a lot when you get back. I want all the details."

Ridley released her arm from Jeremiah's and quickly disappeared into the house. She had a lot of work to do and needed to get started while all this was still fresh in her head. She wanted to get it all down in written form and tear it apart. Then tear it apart again. She had one shot at saving Shelby's lower leg, but there was a good chance, with all that had happened, that Shelby's life was in danger. Dysentery was no joke and the number one cause of death after a down-grid.

People prep food because it's a comfort. People don't prep medicine and sanitary items because it's something they don't want to let their minds slip into. They expect their rider on a white horse to rescue them. What they don't expect is to die because someone took a dump in their water source.

Ridley also wanted Doc Scott to be involved in this. While he wasn't a doctor of humans, he did have a lot of knowledge that carried between species. Cold hard facts needed to be weighed and evaluated. What made the best sense considering the situation they were in? And then there was time. Something they had very little of. Too much time had already passed, and with each minute erased, more damage was being done internally.

Giving a low giggle, Ridley remembered how shocked she was in medical school the further she got into her studies. Humans and beasts. Not a lot of difference in dealing with the basics. It was the emotions that made it tough.

Laying a hand gently on her stomach, Ridley smiled. She had made a choice, this time based on her emotions and not on fact. Would she regret her decision down the road? Was she being selfish?

11

He sat in his office, feet up on his desk, chair tilted back and a waft of smoke drifting from the stolen cigar between his lips. He needed to regroup, rethink his plan, but for the life of him, he couldn't get that damn woman out of his head. He should have killed her right then and there in her kitchen, but the torture that seeped out of every pore in her face was worth it. It also felt real good to finally beat the living shit out of that spic of a husband of hers. He wished he could see her face when they found his body. By spring the maggots should have done their job, that was if the wolves or whatever demon beasts that roamed her property didn't have at him.

A low chuckle escaped from his throat as he interlocked his fingers on top of his head and tilted his chin upward.

Lifting an eyebrow, he needed to find a way to stay entrenched in the good graces of Nina's posse.

Too bad the little cunt won't be around anymore, but that's life. Live and let die. And the more that die, the better for me, he thought.

He had been a bit grossed out seeing her pretty little neck ripped to shreds, but it gave him a sense of justified vengeance to finally get rid of that damn dog of Emma's. Call it a lover's retribution. Yeah, he liked that. Retribution. Had a good ring to it. He could play the fuck out of this, his loyalty to Nina. Hell, he might even worm his way into the White House.

Swinging his legs down from the desk, he needed to get busy packing. He had a trip to take, a funeral to attend. A house to visit and stay in as a distraught fiancé. Oh hell yeah, this was going to go quite well for himself. Fuck this small town. A new sheriff was coming to Washington.

12

"Come here, honey," Tiffany said as she took hold of Emma's arm. Slowly Tiffany, Johnisse and Chloe moved Emma into the living room and in front of the fire that Johnisse had built in the hearth. Nestling Emma in the recliner, Tiffany grabbed a blanket and tucked it in all around her.

"Thanks, luv." The words were so quiet that Tiffany wasn't sure if she heard them. Glancing down at Emma's distraught face, she gently flicked Emma's bangs to the side and placed a kiss on her forehead.

"Just rest, honey," Tiffany whispered. A faint smile crept across Emma's face as she drifted off.

Tiffany looked at Johnisse and then at Chloe. "What do we need to do?" she asked, wringing her hands.

"Well," said Johnisse with a sharp exhale of breath, "someone needs to stay in here and keep an eye on her." She pointed her chin towards Emma. "You want to do that, Tiff?"

"I can, but what else needs to be done?"

Chloe flicked a finger up towards the kitchen as Tiffany's gaze followed.

"I'll stay in here with Miss Emma," Tiffany said as she pulled a chair over beside Emma. "I'm just going to sit right here in case she wakes up and needs something. Go on about your business, I have this covered."

"Well, let's just get this shit done before she wakes up, then," Chloe spurted out as she turned and walked towards the kitchen. Quietly, Johnisse followed her with her hands tucked deep in the pockets of her cargo pants. This was not something she was looking forward to.

Mike was already at the sink when Chloe and Johnisse timidly crossed the threshold into the kitchen. Physically he was there with them, but his mind was a thousand miles away as he remembered how lucky he thought his sister was living here at the farm. The last time he had visited, he stood in this very spot, watching Emma's grandkids through the big window above the sink. They were playing follow the leader with the goats across the field, laughing without a care in the world. Everyone even back then thought life was hard.

Now, he bet they all wished they were back then again. Even as hard as it seemed, it was still better than now.

"Mike?" Chloe broke the silence first.

Turning, he saw them both there waiting. For what he didn't know. The look of helplessness written across both their faces.

Are they waiting on me? Mike questioned himself. *Well, of course they are. Shit. How am I going to do this with these two?* He had to get the dog down, he just wasn't sold on having both of them in here helping him.

Taking a deep breath, he motioned to both of them to come closer. As quietly as he could, he relayed the plan to them, this small squad of champions trying to protect their heroine. Emma didn't need to see this. They could have a proper burial, but she just didn't need to see the torture this animal had endured. Demons taunted the flesh hanging from the ceiling, making the tissue cry out with droplets of scarlet tears.

Mike motioned for the girls to move the cloth tarp over alongside the dog. Mike took the hilt of the knife still in its body and yanked it upwards and out, letting the paper note float to the floor. Walking over, he picked it up and stood reading it for a moment before he gently placed both into the sink.

Taking a kitchen stool, Mike placed it near the tarp next to the body. Effortlessly, he climbed upon the top and stood up. Motioning to the girls, he moved them to each side of the dog. Grabbing his multi-tool from his pocket, he began to saw at the rope securing the dog to the pot rack.

"Be ready," he whispered.

The rope cut through as the dog slumped from its captivity. Both girls grasped at the corpse, but with the lack of fur, the cadaver slipped from their hands and onto the floor.

Everyone froze, ears perked for the slightest sound from the living room. Waiting for a few moments, Mike gave the nod to continue as he climbed down from the stool.

All three of them maneuvered the dog onto the tarp. Reaching over, Mike grabbed the pile of snow white fleece and laid it gently by the underbelly of the animal.

Bringing both ends of the tarp inward, they covered both the dog's face and rear. Then, as respectfully as they could, they rolled the dog over and over until it was completely sealed within the tarp.

Mike had grabbed a skein of clothesline, and as the girls helped, he wrapped the cord around the bundle, securing it.

In perfect unison, the trio picked the bundle up and moved it to the back porch.

Back inside, they quickly swept and mopped away any evidence they could find.

In silence, the three stood in the middle of the floor. Tears started creeping down Chloe's cheeks. Mike encompassed both of them in his arms and allowed the emotions that they'd kept so tightly constrained to be released. Mike closed his eyes as his body absorbed the trembling these two women had controlled to help him. His respect—he owed them this. His life—he vowed to protect them at all costs.

13

He couldn't sleep and ended up wandering into the kitchen, hoping to find a shot of whiskey or at least make a cup of tea to help him doze off. Both together would be perfect. He hadn't been in there long when he heard someone either sleepwalking or being scalped coming down the hallway. Either way, they were making a lot of noise trying to make it into the kitchen. Standing back out of the light, Scott shadowed himself against whoever was shortly going to intrude into his much-needed space.

Scott watched as Angie looked around the kitchen, rubbing her eyes, trying to wake up. She knew the big black thing was what she needed to get hot to cook on, but damn if she could kick herself for not paying attention to Emma when she had used hers. Her red hair was tousled by the little bit of sleep she had gotten, and Scott thought she looked like an ethereal spirit who was having problems drifting through dimensions.

"I love you."

The words stopped her in her tracks. Turning, her eyes filled with terror as they met Scott's.

He was pulling a chair back to sit at the kitchen table. Walking over and still shaking a bit, she knelt before him on the floor, resting her chin on his knee.

"Life can change in the blink of an eye, can't it?" he asked.

"Yes, it can." The words drifted off her lips with memories of times past. So much had happened recently that it made both their heads spin. Angie laid her head down on Scott's knee, obviously deep in thought. Running his fingers through her hair, Scott realized the simple motion was just as calming to him as it was to Angie.

She didn't say it back.

Trying to cover his disappointment, he drew a deep breath and belted out a little louder than he anticipated, "Hey, we got this!"

"Think we'll make it home?" The question had bounced around both their heads for a while now. Asking it out loud was like admitting defeat. It was a given that they would eventually start back to Ohio, but now that the words had been thrown out there, they both knew it was a possibility it might take a long while or might just never happen.

"Don't know, sweets, but we will make home wherever we happen to be. I think it's time we sit down and actually address the issue, though, as it's been on both our hearts," Scott replied.

"I know, it's just, things are so different now. There's no way to go back. And it's not that I even want to, but there's still this sadness of times and people lost, if that makes sense," Angie replied.

"It does." Scott's head bounced quietly up and down in agreement.

Angie made motions to stand. "I need some coffee," she muttered halfheartedly.

"Coffee? At this hour?"

"Believe it or not, it helps me sleep," she replied.

"Need some help?" he asked.

A faint flush crept across Angie's face.

"I'll take that as a yes," he chided. "Listen, if we're going to make life pleasant, we need to communicate a little better than this. I get that there are a lot of things you don't know how to do off grid, but please, let me know if you need help. I may be very talented, but mindreading is something I still struggle with," he said with a little bit too much of an imperious tone.

"I'm not a child. You have no reason to reprimand me!"

"I'm sorry. Come here," he said as he patted his thigh. "Listen, things are a little stressful, and I'm sorry that sometimes I don't keep myself in check better. Especially when I'm tired."

Angie crawled up onto his lap, wrapping her arms around his neck while she nuzzled into his collar. "And I'm sorry that I don't show more patience, especially when things are so stressful," she responded. She was safe here, maybe not for forever, but for this moment. Closing her eyes, she felt the stress in her muscles start to relax.

"I love you, Angie."

Her lips barely moving as her breathing became heavier, she said, "I love you too."

He felt the words against his skin before their reverberation surrounded his heart.

Giving her a few more moments to ensure she was fast asleep, Scott effortlessly lifted her and walked the few steps into the living room. Laying her down on the sofa, he pulled the quilt down from the back and covered her slumbering body.

Interesting, he thought as he looked at the pattern of the quilt. *Where have I seen this before?*

14

The blanket of darkness was pulled back as the sun peeked its head over the horizon. Emma stirred, stiff from being in a chair all night. Turning her head slightly, she saw her brother across the room, stretched out on the sofa. *Nice. He gets to be comfortable. How did I get the short end of the straw and get stuck in a chair?*

Her brows furrowed together as the fogginess faded from her mind. *Why am I sleeping in a chair?* Memories of the previous night flooded her with panic.

"Tommy," she whispered to no one.

Lifting her arm to remove the blanket, she tried to lean forward and get out of the chair. Trying to restrain the moan escaping her mouth, she decided it was in her best interest to slow down her escape from the room. Looking around, she fought back tears as she secretly reminisced about the years she and Tom had been married.

Across the top of the fireplace mantel were pictures of their children when they were little. It was almost time to start decorating for Christmas. Would she put up the nativity scene this year? Tom had bought her the little white marble figurines depicting the birth of the baby. Who would be left to celebrate that baby's birthday this year?

She sat in Tommy's recliner, his humidor on the end table beside her. Reaching over, her fingers trailed the smooth wood lid that held his favorite cigars. What she would give to once again know he was close by the smell of that distinctive smoke in the air. Where was he? Did Nina's men take him?

Details. She needed to remember the details from last night, but so much was still a blur. Laying her head back, she closed her eyes and tried a trick she had learned long ago to try to remember. Focusing on her breathing, she inhaled slowly in through her nose and released it through her mouth. Breath after breath until she felt her pulse slow. Next she concentrated on her chest. With each breath, she envisioned her lungs expanding and decreasing. Over and over until she felt herself start to relax. She moved on to her stomach. Each breath, each movement. Zeroing in on only that area. Drifting back, she began to relive last night.

Nina flashed before her. Not the person but the passions emanating from her memory. Hatred, jealousy… Emma's pulse quickened as she absorbed the emotions. *Breathe. Focus.*

Taking a few moments, she concentrated on her breathing. Taking a deep breath, she felt the air rush into her nostrils and fill her bosom. *Release the demons.* She envisioned all the hatred escaping on the tendrils of her breath as she exhaled.

The night. The dark. She was back watching Dixon defend her as Nina tried to dig the knife into her flesh. His teeth grabbed Nina's arm as she stabbed him in his side. She saw Nina's hand reach into her boot and draw another blade to be used. Nina's arm came back as her chest filled with evil force. With the quickness of a stalking cheetah, Nina brought her arm down towards Dixon. The blade found its target. The dog released a high-pitched squeal as the knife dug into his lung.

Time stood still for Emma. Her white knight lay dying and she couldn't move. Scenarios played out in her mind like an old movie reel. Staring in horror, she barely heard the scream escape from her lips. Everything had slowed down. Was she stuck in a lapse in time? Her mind was still spinning, but any movement, any sound was like she had changed speed on an old record player to 33 rpm when life was normally 45 rpm.

She felt them first, the souls that built this homestead, their essence painting on her soul the markings of a warrior before battle. She felt the power start to pulse through her veins as she saw the silhouette emerge from the tree line.

Emma saw Nina on top of Dixon, digging the knife into his side. Deeper and deeper she pushed as the dog winced in horrific pain. Running over, Emma grabbed the back of Nina's hair and yanked as hard as she could, practically throwing the petite woman away from the dog. Unfortunately, Nina still had a firm grip on the knife, which yanked from the dog's body with the woman's thrust backwards. Kneeling down, Emma placed both hands on Dixon's wound and pressed as hard as she could, the blood staining his white fur crimson.

Emma knew the entity was near, she felt its soul mingle with hers. A feeling of unspoken recognition was exchanged. Not realizing that Nina was behind her, watching, Emma kept her hands over the wound of her beloved dog. Closing her eyes, she started to pray.

The creature paused behind the woman standing with the knife in her hand. Its beautiful ashen fur masked her deceptive spirit. She recognized the warrior within Emma and fought beside her. This wolf, a part of this land as much as Emma was.

Nina raised the knife to strike Emma in the back, and the wolf did not hesitate. With one swift movement, the beast had Nina on her back. Digging its teeth into Nina's neck, the wolf raised its jaws, ripping the tender flesh from the woman's collarbone. Raising its muzzle towards the moon, the wolf cried in retribution.

DIXON!

Emma woke from her trance with such force that her screams woke Mike. With years of living the life he had, Mike was on his feet, gun drawn faster than Emma could get the damn blanket off herself.

With every ounce of strength she had, Emma stood up. A faint trail of perspiration starting to bead across her upper lip, Emma fought her own will to just collapse and give up.

"I've got to get to Dixon," Emma exclaimed to Mike.

"Honey, Dixon isn't here."

"I know!" Emma said hurriedly as she looked around herself for something to hold onto.

Mike grabbed onto her elbow to stabilize her, a look of distress on her face.

"Emma, sit down. Please," he demanded.

"No, I need to get to Dixon," she pleaded.

"Emma, please." He was begging now. He knew she needed to stay put.

"Mike, we need to go."

"Go where?" he asked.

"To Doc Scott's!"

"What the hell for?" he asked.

"Mike, stop asking questions. We need to go now." Practically yelling, Emma was already walking out the front door. Running his hands through his hair, Mike was at least glad she didn't go out the back door. Grabbing his hat, he followed her.

15

Scott backed up against the counter, coffee cup in hand. Shifting his weight, he leaned back and watched as Angie and Ridley set the table. It was these little things that were really making the difference right now, this sense of normalcy. It would have been just as easy for all of them to grab a bite and run off to attend to the ever-mounting chores, but having everyone sit down at the dinner table each night to discuss the day's events helped. It also kept them connected. Well, except Shelby. Ridley did not want her moved around, but they did move the table as close to her bedroom door as they could. They also made sure she ate at the same time as everyone else, and they made sure they occasionally yelled out for her opinion on the current topic floating around the table.

It still had to be hard. This being alone. She had sternly insisted that her husband and kids join the rest of the group at the table, which left her alone in her room.

"Rid, you have this fixed in your head yet?" Scott asked Ridley.

Ridley, stopping long enough to glance up at him as she placed the silverware, nodded briefly. "Can we talk later?"

"I am at your disposal, young lady," Scott replied, giving her a quick smile of assurance and turning as he placed his now empty cup in the sink behind him. "Ladies, what can I do to help?"

Strolling over, Angie slid her arm around his waist and gave him a quick squeeze. "If you want, you can go round up everyone. I think we're about ready in here," she replied.

Placing a quick kiss on the tip of her nose, he pulled away and started to make his way to the back door. Turning, he glanced over at Ridley. "Hey, Rid, you want to step outside for a minute?" Scott asked, looking at Ridley with such an intensity that she dare not decline the offer.

Looking over at Angie, Ridley set the knife down and came around the table without taking her eyes from Scott. Why did she feel like she had just been sent to the principal's office without knowing what she had done wrong? Damn flashbacks of high school made the hair on the back of her neck stand up. The walk of shame down that long, highly polished hallway always gave her pause to rethink some of the decisions that she had made, but once inside the office, sitting before that big desk, being spoken down to like she was an idiot made her rethink that shame part. She began to see her callings as more of a source of pride where the indoctrination had not taken hold. Tell her what to do? No way! She had her own mind and thoughts and views on how she was going to impact the world. It surprised many when she decided to go to medical school. More school. Eight more years to get all the pieces of paper that she needed to make the impact she wanted. Until this happened. This world now.

She walked past Scott, who, being the gentleman that he was, was holding the door open for her. Still not taking her eyes from him, her head followed his eyes as she strolled past and turned to finish the way backwards. Scott walked out, letting the screen door close with a thud behind him. Standing face-to-face with the young female, Scott put both his hands on his hips like he was about to unload.

"Give it up, missy."

"What?" Ridley asked, perplexed.

"You've been keeping a secret from all of us. Spit it," he said.

"What! I honestly don't know what you're talking about!"

"You feeling okay?" he asked.

Ridley felt the color rise in her face, betraying all the hard work she had done of keeping her secret. "Damn," she muttered under her breath.

"What was that?"

"Nothing," Ridley replied a little too fast. Backing up, she twirled around and walked over to the old wooden banister separating them from the yard full of fall leaves. Hitching a leg, Ridley pushed one buttock onto the top of the railing and stretched her other leg out in front of her to keep her from falling forward.

"How long were you going to keep this a secret?" Scott asked.

"Again, Scott, I have no idea what you're talking about."

"Oh stop, Ridley. You might be able to fool all them," he said as his arm motioned in the direction of the house, "but you aren't fooling me. You're pregnant," he said matter-of-factly.

Looking Scott straight on, Ridley went to open her mouth when Angie came bursting through the back door.

"Come quick!" Angie exclaimed.

Ridley came down off the banister and made her way towards the door but not before Doc could raise his finger towards her face. "We will finish this conversation later, young lady."

Ridley had the feeling he wasn't kidding either. Gulping, she finished walking through the doorway with Scott hot on her heels, both following Angie into the living room and nearly running Angie over as she stopped abruptly, blocking the view into the room.

"What the…" Ridley started before catching the slur of profanity about to escape her mouth.

"Ang, you want to tell us what's going on here," Scott said as he stepped around Ridley and farther into the room.

Angie moved to the side as both Ridley and Scott looked at the visitors sitting in the room.

"Momma!" Ridley sang out with the excitement of a six-year-old on Christmas morning. Running across the room, she swung into the older woman with such velocity that she almost knocked the woman down.

"Ridley!" she replied with the same excitement at seeing her daughter.

Apple Jack, Ridley's father, was standing next to his wife, watching the reunion with a grin on his face. Walking over between both of his girls, he wrapped both his burly arms around them and gave them a big bear hug. His family was together, and the man's heart was obviously overjoyed. Some men had the coldness to walk away from their families when things got rough. Not looking back, starting a new life. Not this man. Apple Jack was all about his family. A true man's man who would walk through the fires of hell to save his own. They didn't make them much like Jack anymore. In all the terror and upheaval going on outside right now with the unknown, it was good to see that beauty would rise from the ashes if one placed value on the important things in this life. Family.

16

There was literally nothing in the room except for a fluorescent light in the ceiling and a switch beside the door on the wall. No windows. No air vents. No chairs, nothing. The four men just stood there, arms in various poses, waiting for the fifth man to speak. They knew why they were there. The original plan was now trashed, and they needed their new orders. Each of them had spent the last couple of hours wondering where this unanticipated fork in the road would take them. How much the unforeseen incident would cost them.

They all had spent a lengthy time serving their country. At one time or another they each had questioned who or what they had actually taken an oath to. The words they each recited were to defend the Constitution of the United States of America, but sometimes it seemed like it was more to preserve the lifestyle of certain elitists. The country had changed, of that they all agreed. Time and again they watched as the rights of the people were stripped away. Greed reared its ugly head as backroom deals became the norm until you weren't sure if anyone knew right from wrong. It really just came down to how much currency was exchanged over the wires. Hell, it wasn't even Federal Reserve notes or gold. Currency now had become cold hard commodities or, in some instances, soft, warm bodies.

Breaking the silence, Sean cleared his throat. "Men."

Each now straightened his back, all eyes on the brutish man who demanded their attention.

Handing each of them a pale yellow folder, Sean opened the last file he had left in his hands as the rest of the men followed suit.

Each man lowered their head to read what was written on the pages they held.

"Are you fucking kidding me?" Lieutenant Tim Eklund burst out.

"Tim, contain yourself," Sean muttered without looking up.

The silence resumed as the men continued reading. What lay before their eyes was the framework for a total dismantling of the country they had loved.

"Nina knew about this, didn't she?" Lieutenant Miles Cottner asked, his eyes drilling into Sean, looking for any sign that he was wrong.

Commander Sean Kissler had been Senator Nina Varga's confidant, her sounding board, yet he knew nothing about this. "Yes, I believe she did."

"So, I'll pop the white elephant in the room. Think she was using us?" Lieutenant Commander Sam Benteg asked, looking for any sign of emotion on Sean's face.

Keeping his eyes diverted, Sean's head came up. He needed an answer for these men. Did Nina use them for her own purpose? What was going on that he wasn't aware of? Was he a fool?

"I don't know, yet," Sean replied.

"Damn it, General, you were with her all the time. What do you mean, you don't know?" Miles asked.

"I don't know means I don't know!" Sean blurted out.

Silence pierced the air as the four men looked at their commander. The same thought weaved its way through each of their individual scrutinies. *If Sean didn't know, then what the hell was really going on here?*

"What are we going to do now?" Miles finally asked.

"If, and I say, IF any of this were true, Nina has information somewhere hidden," Tim broke in.

"Probably," Sean replied.

"Okay, well, let's go to her house and look around," Tim threw out.

"Which one? Miami? DC? Not as easy as it sounds. Besides wouldn't that be the obvious place to look? Was she that dense? Nah, it's somewhere else," Sam said.

"Fuck," Sean muttered.

"What?" Miles asked.

"Her kids," Sean replied.

Fidgeting nervously, the men looked at each other like they each were afraid to draw the short straw. They already felt bad about what had happened at that homestead, and none of them wanted to be responsible for a couple of kids under these circumstances. Besides, there was no proof that the kids were the answer. Problem was, they knew Sean. No stone would be left unturned until he figured out exactly what was going on. And that might mean a trip back to the farm.

"You boys up for a trip to Hanny's?" Commander Scott Jeffries asked, looking at his peers one by one.

He was met with a strong silence, yet Sean understood. They hadn't been back in DC long, and this meant more time on the road while all the interesting shit was going on here. Each of these men were now independent contractors, Black Water as the media called them. Since early retirement thanks to President Walker, it was about all that was left for someone with their skill level. It wasn't like they could go down to the local pizza joint and get a job. These men were trained mercenaries compliments of the US government.

Hanny Beaver Airpark was just a blip on a map between Pittsburg, Pennsylvania, and East Liverpool, Ohio, but it housed one of the most intensive underground military operations on the east side of the Mississippi. It put Cheyenne Mountain to shame in sheer size, as the base itself extended beneath Lake Erie. Masked by the salt pit operation on the north side, the base extended down under the lake by two thousand feet at points. A legitimate operation funded by the government, it housed one of the five largest salt-excavation businesses in the county. Behind all the crystals resided a network of tunnels that would eventually bring you to Wheeling, West Virginia. In between, the only way in or out was through Hanny Beaver Airport.

The area was named after what the Delaware Indians called Amockwisipu, or Beaver Stream. As the tale would tell, a soldier was helping to construct Fort McIntosh back in the seventeen hundreds. Building a cabin southwest of the fort itself, the soldier met and fell in love with a young Indian girl that he affectionately called Hanny, meaning God has favored me.

Hanny became the code word for any trips near the area that needed to be more than discreet. It was a base of operations that was used by the United States military that few had knowledge of. It would become the base of the government if a crisis arose.

17

Jeremiah wanted answers. He had a family, friends and a community to help protect, and he would be damned if he didn't do everything within his power to make sure they were safe and had a chance at life. Packing a small backpack, his intention was to walk over towards Memphis to see what he could find out. Basing his decision on destination as to where he witnessed the blast coming from, he figured it was a direct hit on the city, if not close enough to do heavy damage. But what was it, and better yet, who caused it?

Making his way towards Wellwood, the largest town near his family farm, Jeremiah stopped occasionally just to look around. He was safe walking through Wellwood, as it was so large that it had never been included in the census, and that was just how Jeremiah liked it. You didn't just stop by on a Sunday drive out here. It was in your best interest to know someone mighty important before you headed into the territory Jeremiah had lived in all his life.

He was seventy-five miles from Memphis on a good day, but that was going straight down Interstate 40. Today was not a day he felt comfortable walking so exposed on a major interstate, so he detoured his plans a bit north. He figured he would skirt south of Brownsville and then head over towards Stanton. If he made good time, he might be able to make it to his uncle's farm in the Mason area. What used to take half an hour in a car would now take a brisk ten hours to walk, and that was with no issues along the way. By Jeremiah's calculations, his uncle's farm would put him about forty miles outside Memphis, which was about as close as Jeremiah wanted to get unless he had to.

Noah and Hannah Bontrager lived on an Amish dairy farm outside Mason, Tennessee. They still held to the traditional ways of living, so when the explosion happened, they didn't notice much of a difference on the homestead other than the ramifications of the blast. Trees and outbuildings had taken the brunt of the explosion, but no livestock was hurt, and Noah could find no injuries to any of his family still living on the farm with him even though they had felt the downdraft afterwards.

"Jeremiah!" Noah shouted as he walked over to meet his nephew halfway down the dirt path they used as a driveway. The dogs had alerted him to an intruder, but Noah was pleasantly surprised when he saw the stature of his sister's son. Six feet seven, he was colossal compared to other men in the family. At the age of seventeen, the outsiders called him Mountain Man and treated him with the respect of someone who could easily impair their movements, but the man had a heart of gold. He was the gentlest soul and so misunderstood that he had given up long ago trying to convince people otherwise. He stayed to himself and his family, so it was a bit of a surprise to see him today.

Grabbing the large man's hand, Noah placed his other hand on the back of the man's elbow and shook with a mighty grip.

"Uncle," Jeremiah replied as the handshake turned into a bear hug.

"Oh, it's so good to see you out and about on this fine day. What brings you?" Noah asked.

"How are you and the family?" Jeremiah asked.

"We are well. I am assuming you know about the explosion?"

"I would flatter you by saying that I missed you all, but yes. I came to seek answers."

"Come to the house, then. I know Hannah would love to see you and inquire of your family. We have much talking to do," Noah replied, guiding his nephew by the elbow towards the house.

Kneeling beside the debris, Jeremiah ran his hand over the smooth gray finish. Nine inches of black and white wires that had obviously been severed in half lay limp out of what was once an arm of a machine. More of the same wreckage was placed on a tarp in the utility shed of his uncle's farm. Jeremiah tried to picture the contraption in his head, and all he could think of was a spider.

"There any more of this out there?" Jeremiah asked.

"Not that we have discovered yet, but it took us a bit to gather all of this together. It was scattered quite a distance," Uncle Noah said as he lifted his chin and aimed it towards the mess of metal and plastic. "What are you thinking, Jeremiah?" He could see the wheels in his nephew's head spinning, knowing he was trying to put all the pieces together. He had seen the boy build just about anything, including his own farmhouse, so it would come as no surprise if he had an idea of what all the parts created.

"Nah, nothing yet. I have some ideas, but, man, it's hard to tell," Jeremiah replied as he stood up and walked farther around the pile. "Any of you see anything before this happened?"

"One of the neighbors over towards Taylor's Chapel was talking of a blue light over the city. Not much else. We don't see much odd out here, so this stuck out right quick. You think it's connected to what went on over in Memphis?" he asked.

Bending over and picking up a small piece of what had been the outer skin of the object, Jeremiah turned it over in his hand, his mind being etched with each small detail. Engraved on the side was half of a five-pointed star.

"You see this?" Jeremiah asked his uncle, handing him the piece of debris.

"Nope, but I didn't handle it any more than getting it in here. We were more concerned with outsiders coming in once we realized what was going on, so our attention was on perimeter patrols and securing the homestead. What do you think this was?" he asked, handing the hard plastic back to his nephew.

Jeremiah, lost in thought as he was digging through the rest of the clutter, all but ignored his uncle. Noah, recognizing the glazed-over look, decided to head back up to the house and let Jeremiah have his space. He didn't need a thousand questions by an old man who hadn't ventured much into the outside world, and Noah knew if anyone could figure out what had happened, it was his nephew.

Six hours after the rest of the family had gone to bed, Jeremiah wandered back into his uncle's house. His head was aching from the amount of concentration he had given the inanimate object lying in the barn. Being as quiet as he could, he made his way into the living room, where his aunt Hannah had said she would make up a bed for him on the couch. He was surprised to find his uncle still awake and waiting on him since the man had to be out in the milk house in a couple of hours.

"Jeremiah, you figure anything out?" Noah asked, obviously tired.

"I have some theories," Jeremiah responded.

"Please, share and put this old man's mind at ease."

"I'm not sure how peaceful these answers may be, and don't forget, I'm just guessing here," Jeremiah shot back.

"Just amuse me. Knowing what it is, is sometimes more beneficial than knowing nothing, no matter how frightful something is."

"Okay, I'll give you that," Jeremiah began. "From what my mind was trying to tell me, that thing out there could be, and I say could be because without putting it all back together I just don't know, so could be some type of small drone. Kinda like those small planes that you complain about that fly over your fields looking for illegal crops. Anyone else know about this?"

"Yes, several people do," Noah replied.

"Really? You talked about this? I'm surprised at that. You usually don't like to talk about your business."

"I don't, but there have been more of these objects found in the area. Two that I know of. This one seems to be the farthest from the city."

"Any descriptions of any of them? Same color?" Jeremiah asked.

"Pretty much all sound 'bout the same. Why?"

"Anything else match? What about that blue light that Hannah saw? Anyone else see it that has one of these?"

"One other did say they saw a light. Why? Where are you going with this?"

"How much of the area was burned around where these were found?" Jeremiah kept going with the questions, his mind spinning faster and faster.

"Whole area is burned up. Big hole where this thing came down. Why, Jeremiah? We all thought it was because of the blast. Couple of the young men tried to get close to Memphis but stayed out, as they said it was pretty much leveled. We waited for fallout like we had been taught, but quite honestly, we haven't seen much of anything at all. It's like everything was damaged but us unless you got caught in the fires or the quake mess. Us out here farther away are just dealing with the downed trees and such. Even the cattle are fine," Noah explained.

"Listen, I need to get headed back home at first light, but would you mind if I take a couple of these pieces back with me. I have some outsiders staying at the house I would like to show these to."

"They won't be messing around here after, will they?" his uncle asked, concerned to have outsiders on his farm.

"Not without me, but I may bring one or two down to check out some things. And I may have misspoke. I also need to tell you about Shelby before I explain who these people are. You may just want these outsiders on your farm."

His uncle shot Jeremiah a sideways glance of puzzlement. Very few times over the years had Noah ever wanted an outsider on his land, and he wasn't so sure if he would now either. Giving his nephew the benefit of the doubt, he at least needed to listen to his explanation and the reasoning behind his statement. Noah glanced out the window behind his nephew as Jeremiah began to talk. The first rays of dawn were starting to break through the darkness.

It's going to be a long day, Noah thought to himself as he gave his nephew his full attention.

18

"Emma! Slow down!" Mike exclaimed from behind her. She had gone through an ordeal over the last couple of days, and he was astounded at her energy. The last thing she needed was a setback from overexertion. Besides, Mike had no idea these tunnels were even here! He wanted to check them out, but it looked like that would come later, as Emma was already quite a distance ahead of him.

"Damn it, Emma!" Mike muttered under his breath. Fishing in his pocket, he pulled out a flashlight and shone it ahead of himself before he tripped. Emma was now so far ahead of him that he couldn't use the light from the lantern she had brought with them.

Shining the light up the wall, he quickly ran his hand across the semi-smooth passageway.

Who built these? And when? He didn't remember Emma mentioning construction of any kind. Granted, it had been some time between visits, but he would have noticed the evidence from something this elaborate. Shining the light ahead, he saw a channel taking off to the right. Mentally making a map of the property, that channel had to run somewhere near the house since they'd entered from the ingress by the barn. Continuing, Mike finally saw a faint change to the darkness in the tunnel. *Wonder where this ends up?*

As Mike got closer to the exit, he slowed his pace. Emma was nowhere to be found, and he didn't want to walk into a trap. Coming to the exit, Mike hunkered down to a crouch and slowly crept to the opening.

"Well, I'll be damned," he whispered.

He knew the back of the residence well. He had spent quite a bit of time here sneaking in and out of the house undetected. Memories came flooding back as Mike's eyes slowly traced over the scene before him. Last time he was here, he was just a smart-ass, disrespectful, horny kid.

Chuckling, he realized not much had changed.

Walking out of the tunnel, Mike caught sight of his sister as she disappeared into the house. Damnit. What the hell was so important that she took off like a bat out of hell?

Looking around, Mike didn't see any vehicle in the drive. *Wonder who lives here now?* he thought.

Whoever it was, Emma knew them well to just walk into the house without knocking.

Coming to the door, Mike reached his hand up to enter a little more cordially than Emma had. Knocking, Mike waited. No answer and no sound from within. Mike reached down and, grabbing the door handle, gave it a turn.

Well, it's not locked, he thought.

Scouting the area, he decided to follow after his sister.

Opening the door slowly, Mike paused when the door creaked.

Damn it, he wanted the element of surprise if he needed it.

Once more, he pushed the door until there was enough space for him to squeeze in.

Inside, he found himself in a long hallway. Quietly he crept along the wall, noticing rooms off each side of the corridor. Peering inside each room as he passed by, he slowly made his way to the end of the hallway. Turning the knob on the last door, he gradually opened it far enough to slip inside.

He heard their voices coming from around the corner, Emma laughing, talking to what he could make out as another female. Perplexed, Mike entered the room and stopped dead in his tracks. The look on his face must have been quite comical as Emma turned to look at him. "Mike! What took you so long?" she sang out with a grin on her face.

Standing in the middle of the room was his sister. A glow emanated from her of pure happiness. Mike cocked his head as he recognized the furry white beast with his paws on her shoulders and his tongue licking Emma's cheek.

How the hell? Mike thought.

19

He felt a faint tickle on his face. Trying to open his eyes, he could barely make out the distant haze of light from the morning sun. Something was biting his cheek. Automatically trying to raise his arm to swat whatever it was, he realized his appendage was stuck under his own body. His shoulder briefly flinched as the muscle tried to dislodge it. Crying out in pain, he heard his own mumbled attempt at sound. His lips swollen still, he tried to lick their dryness to no avail. His tongue was just as parched.

Her image flashed before him.

God, just let me die.

He didn't want to see her. Smell her. Hear her. Feel her.

His cheek hurt. He could feel the pain radiating down the side of his face to his ear. Squeezing his eye shut, he tried to scare off whatever was biting him. Over and over he tried to pucker his cheek to disengage the now searing pain that the insect was causing. A tear teased out the corner of his eye. All hope fled his spirit as his thoughts focused on the throbbing on his face. He couldn't move. Every piece of his flesh was afire with a throbbing ache. Concentrating, he discovered he could move his foot back and forth, but the pain in his lower back made him stop.

Again, she manifested in his mind.

"Kill me! Just take me now! Why the fuck do you need to torture me first?" he screamed to no one. Or to God.

Or to anyone who cared. But there wasn't a soul, just the demons teasing his mind.

He felt the cold on his nose as a snowflake landed and quickly melted. The trace amount of water quickly ran down the side of his nostril and taunted his swollen parched lips.

Turning his head slightly, he drifted out of consciousness as the earth beneath him stirred. Organisms crawled over and into the clothing of the man, finding warmth from the coming cold against the man's skin.

From dirt we are formed and to dust we will return. Some will meet their fate in a peaceful setting surrounded by family and friends. Others will not be so lucky.

20

Kneeling onto one knee, Mike braced himself for the impact. The big white dog launched at him with the force of a thousand tanks, almost knocking him onto his back.

"Dixon!" Emma yelled to deaf ears.

"Dixon!" Mike exclaimed as he caught the dog around the neck.

Looking at Emma with a quizzical look on his face, he moved Dixon back to scratch the one place he knew that made the canine moan. His ears.

Arrrrr, the noise that escaped Dixon's throat gave Mike a chuckle. "Easy, boy, there's more where that came from."

"I thought," Mike stammered. "How did—? What is going on?"

"So did I," Emma replied. "In the kitchen. I know," she began as tears started to fill her eyes.

Jane, Dr. Scott's assistant, looked from Mike to Emma and then back to Mike again, completely lost in the whole minimalistic conversation exchange between the two. Turning back to Emma, she finished the instructions she had been conveying to Emma before Mike interrupted.

"The knife barely missed doing any major damage. Any closer and it would definitely have hit a lung. He will have a nice bald spot for a while, but he should fully recover with a nice scar to show off to the ladies," Jane said with a grin. "BTW, he's a bit of a brute. Try to keep him down and quiet for a while if you can."

"Jane, this is my brother Mike. Mike, Scott's assistant Jane," Emma explained. The two gave a quick nod to each other as Emma continued looking at her sibling. "I'll explain on the way home, but right now we need to help Jane with a couple of things and then get home before everyone starts waking up. Dearest little brother of mine, I do have one more favor."

"Which is what?"

"Dixon still needs rest after being patched up and shouldn't even be up and around for a day. We need to get him home, but he shouldn't be walking that far."

"That's a long way to haul one hundred forty pounds over my shoulder!"

"I know, but I have a plan."

"A plan, aye? You do know your plans always give me cause for alarm?"

"Whatever," Emma said, rolling her eyes.

Settling Dixon back down on his makeshift bed, the three quickly got busy making sure that Jane had enough supplies inside the house for a few weeks. Then a security check around the property and closing off some advantage points put Emma's mind at ease for Jane staying at the house by herself while Scott was away.

Scott... Emma thought. How would he feel about Mike being home, let alone in his house? *I'll need to head that off at the pass when Scott returns. Hopefully he does return...*

Walking into a storage room, Emma found what she was looking for. Pulling the heavy metal from inside the containment bag, Emma walked back to the room Dixon was resting in. Laying the frame on the floor, she opened it all the way up.

"Awesome, an old military cot!" Mike exclaimed as he walked back into the room.

"Yeah, thought it might make the job of lugging the mutt home easier."

Dixon's high-pitched whine gave them all a giggle. Reaching over, Emma cupped the dog's lower jaw with her hand. "Oh, you know I love you, you crazy mutt."

"Okay, let's think this through though. I'm worried about this thing fitting through the tunnel. If we don't engage it all the way out and just wrap it around Dixon, we should be able to get in width-wise, but there are the turns. This thing is long, so we may need to shorten it a bit." Emma, lost in thought, didn't notice that she had inadvertently divulged information that she had wanted to keep quiet.

"Um, tunnels?" Jane asked.

Emma gave a quick glance from Jane then to Mike before returning her eyes to Jane's now curious face.

As the wheels turned in Jane's head, several things became clear. "That's how you got here with Dixon, isn't it? I was wondering how you wheeled him over here down all the roads, but that makes much more sense! Let's see these tunnels!" Jane cried out.

There was no stopping this now, Emma realized.

"Listen, Jane, no one knows about these tunnels, not even Scott. So please, you must keep this a secret.

Actually, it might be a good thing that you know. I've been feeling uneasy about you staying here by yourself, but now you can pop over without being seen and come visit and check on Dixon. But, honey," she said as she grabbed Jane by the hand, "listen to me, you cannot risk being seen and someone finding out about this. You must take the utmost care when you do this. Okay?"

"Of course," Jane replied with a look of concern.

"I'm going to go out and scout around before we take off," Mike said as he headed out the door.

"Sounds good. Emma, let's get Dixon ready for travel while he's gone," Jane said. "I want my patient to be as comfortable as possible," she said as she left the room.

Dixon was alone now with his human. Kneeling beside him, Emma buried her head in his fur. "Oh, baby," she whispered, "I am so very sorry this happened to you." More memories flooded back to Emma about that night. Over and over the scene played in her mind until her body started to shake. Dixon, sensitive to her emotions, tried to get up. "No, no. Stay right where you are, big guy," Emma said sternly, looking into Dixon's eyes. Dark, piercing eyes that reflected

Emma's soul right back to her. "I am so sorry," she cried, gently stroking his face. Dixon had no need for these human frailties, licking up with his big wet, coarse tongue, he caught Emma right under her nose. "AH, DIXON," she shrieked, "that's just gross." She giggled as she hugged him tightly around his neck. "I love you so very much!"

21

Megan watched her children sleeping. Such peaceful sweet faces. Her stomach twisted itself into knots as her thoughts turned dark. How was she going to protect them from this harsh world? She wanted to give them a fighting chance! Doubting her own strength haunted her.

"Damn you, Robert," she cursed under her breath.

Her husband. The man she had betrothed herself to and whom she wanted nothing more than to start a family with was gone. It was lonely not having a spouse. Sure, she had her mother and the children, but it wasn't the same as having a partner, someone whom she knew had her back and was there to be a sounding board, was there to carry half the burdens. Now it was just her.

Life had changed so much in the last couple of years that sometimes it left her head spinning. Robert dying in the horrific car accident—she had nightmares about the pain he had to be in before he finally died. The details haunted her for months after the news had broadcast how his car had caught on fire and no one would help him. Later she found out that he had been drinking. It did nothing to relieve her anguish knowing that he might not have felt much due to the severity of his intoxication, but finding out that he had company with him cut her to her soul. According to the reports, the woman was a local prostitute who specialized in high-profile clients. How could he betray not only his marriage but risk destroying his family? He would never know how Megan had tried the best she could to pick up the pieces of their lives.

Within the last seven days, she had allowed two strangers to take her and what was left of her family across the country in an RV to a farm in Ohio. What was she thinking? She felt the knot in her stomach squeeze even tighter to the point of nausea. Taking a gulp of air, she swallowed deeply. Chloe and Mike had been nothing but nice to her and her family, but did she once again act out of haste? She didn't have a good track record for decision making, she felt. Was this a mistake too, like her marriage, like what happened to her son? Closing her eyes, she fought back the need to vomit.

Was this farm in Ohio the answer to a lot of late night prayers? She needed help, not only with dealing with Robbie, but she needed help fighting whatever was dissolving the last bits of saneness she had stored up within herself. She had tried to explain her feelings to her mother, but she felt she couldn't reveal her true emotions without alarming her parent.

Looking at little Robbie, his dark long lashes like his father's, she felt a tug on her heart. *So many obstacles are in his way*, she thought. How could she ever forgive herself for what she'd allowed to happen to him? Autism was tough enough, but giving your son autism because you allowed yourself to be manipulated into believing that all the vaccinations were necessary was inexcusable. If only she had done the damn research. She had brushed off the warnings posted on

Facebook and some of her mom clubs without giving them a second thought. Now, there was no turning back time, or she would have done it already. How was this child going to grow up in this new world? Could she care for his needs properly without the networking afforded by the internet? What if he got worse, then what?

In an instant, the thought pierced her psyche so profoundly that she caught her breath. Taking a step back and turning, her eyes were wide in horror at the thought that now taunted her. Darting left and right, her eyes looked for an unseen answer. Anything to lead her out of the unfathomable evil that had quickly habituated her thoughts.

Could she? She couldn't even speak. Could she kill her own child if she needed to? To save him from the terrors that were knocking on his future? Would she be able to find the strength to stop the pain that beckoned to his small frail soul like a long-lost lover?

Shaking her head wildly, she screamed internally for what felt like hours. Feelings of betrayal for even allowing the thoughts to manifest themselves left tears in her eyes. No, her child would be given a fighting chance. Somehow. Someway.

Startled by Robbie stirring, Megan turned to find him sitting up on the bed, staring at her. Guilt drove deep into her soul. He knew. She just knew that he'd picked up on her thoughts.

"This is crazy," Megan whispered to herself.

Walking over to the bed, she tucked a hand beneath his head and grasped his feet, laying him back and at the same time pulling him towards her at the edge of the bed. "Good morning, my sweet prince," she cooed.

Robbie popped a chubby fist into his mouth and used the other hand to grab playfully at his mother's hair hanging down now that she was bent over him. Zipping down his sleeper, Megan popped his plump little legs out of the pajamas and slid the plastic diaper cover down and off his legs. Unclipping the pins on each side of his diaper, she lifted his little bottom and slid the soft, white cloth from beneath his buttocks. Quickly sliding another in its place, she repeated the same steps in reverse until she was sliding the zipper on the pajamas up towards his chin. Reaching down and grasping him beneath his arms, Megan picked the toddler up and held him in her arms. Gently hugging him close to her, she silently asked for forgiveness for the iniquitous thoughts she had allowed access to her mind.

I've got to get stronger.

Lord help me, I've got to get stronger.

22

Dixon sniffed at the bundle that was lying on the back porch and then let out a whimper.

"Ya, baby, I know. He saved your life by giving his own." Emma said as she ran her hand over Dixon's head. "Can we take him out later and give him a proper burial?" she asked, looking at her brother.

"Sure thing." He replied. "I was positive that was your mutt."

Dixon barked in response to what Mike said.

"Don't even try, you big hairy overgrown snowflake!" Mike laughed, looking down at the dog. "Think there's any more of these things out there?" he asked looking down at the bundle on the floor.

"The wolf? Oh goodness yes. I took a female over to Doc's not that long ago who he said had pups somewhere in these hills. I'm not sure if this is the father, but I guarantee you this isn't the last we see of these guys." Emma said turning to walk around the house.

"Great, that's just great." Mike mumbled, following after her.

"Where the hell have you both been?" Johnisse asked as Emma and Mike walked through the front door. Just as she was about to give another scolding, Dixon brushed past their legs and rambled into the living room. Climbing into the chair that Emma had spent the night in, he sat there with his tongue hanging out like the lord of the manor.

The look on Johnisse's face was without question one of utter astonishment.

"How?" she stammered, lifting to point a finger from Dixon to the kitchen and back to the saintly canine now dripping drool from the corner of his snout.

"Let me get him settled; then I want to see this package you have. Mike said you all left it on the back porch all rolled up. I have a feeling I know what's inside," Emma said. "But right now, this big guy needs a rest." She fussed at her friend as she scratched the dog's ears, making him moan.

"I would expect some hungry guests for breakfast," Mike said, looking at Johnisse.

Lifting her hands quickly into the air, her fingers spread in a desperate sign of helplessness, Johnisse let out a feeble cry. "Someone needs to light that damn stove of yours first."

Giving a chuckle, Mike motioned for her to precede him into the kitchen while Emma went about getting Dixon settled down for a nap. *A good fire in the fireplace should do the trick*, she thought as she pulled her knife and ferro rod from her pocket. Grabbing it tightly, she glanced at the pictures on the mantel. "Where are you, Tommy?"

"What the hell just happened?" Johnisse asked Mike once they were out of earshot of Emma.

"I'm not a hundred percent sure myself, but Emma seems to think she knows," Mike explained.

"If that's Dixon in there with her, what the hell was hanging in the kitchen here?" she asked.

"Your guess is as good as mine. I saw it just the same as you, and I think we both were thinking the same thing. Where's Chloe and Tiff?" he asked, looking around.

"I think Tiffany is still primping upstairs, but I have yet to see Chloe this morning," she replied. "You might want to go round 'em both up so we can try to put some grub on."

Mike sniggered. "You been here, what, a week and already talkin' like you were born here."

"Whatever," she gruffed back. "Go find the girls," she said with a wink.

Mike took off towards the stairs, passing Tiffany halfway up. "Miss Tiffany," he said, giving a slight tilt to his dusty blond head.

"Mr. Mike," Tiffany responded with a grin.

"Johnisse is waiting for you in the kitchen. You seen Chloe?" he asked.

"Nope, sure haven't, but you might want to give a knock on her door," she replied. "I'm just gonna head on down to the kitchen," she sang out loudly as Mike hurried on his way. "You know, downstairs where everyone else is." She continued with a glint in her eyes, "Mmm-huh, yes, downstairs I go."

Mike gave a light rap on Chloe's door, expecting a reply, but heard nothing. Leaning in, he tried to get as close to the door as he could without actually touching it. He knocked a little louder this time, which, again, was met with silence. Was she already downstairs somewhere? No, Johnisse said she hadn't seen her. Maybe she had gone outside? Mike rapped harder.

Grabbing the door handle, he gave a quick turn to feel for resistance. Nothing, the door wasn't locked. Couldn't hurt to take a quick peek to see if she was even in there, could it? The answer hadn't even formulated in his head when he caught himself glancing around the edge of the door.

The room was still dark, as the curtains were closed. Squinting, he took a step around the door. Listening as his eyes adjusted to the dimness, Mike could hear a faint whistling noise. Cocking his head, he stopped breathing long enough to try to hear better. It was definitely a whistle, he thought. Reaching back, he slowly opened the door wider to allow a little more light into the room.

He noticed her calf first, snowy white and smooth as silk. His eyes lowered to where her foot was sticking out of the blanket, revealing bright red polish on her toenails. Traveling upward, he took in the contrast between her pale thigh and the deep green sheet, covering her leg only at the last inch. Quickly skimming over the rest of the sheet covering her body, his eyes fell on the softness of her neck where it met her shoulder, secretly encouraging him to discover its pleasures. Shuddering, he knew he could devour her right then and there.

Slowly backing out of the room, he closed the door, trying not to disturb her. Resting his head against the door, he trained his mind on the least sexy, most morbid thought he could to try to reduce the swelling starting in his crotch. Taking a deep breath, he headed back down to the kitchen, leaving Chloe to sleep for a while yet.

Walking into the room, all eyes were on him. "What?" he asked sharply.

"Oh, nothing," Tiffany responded, exchanging glances and a smirk with Johnisse.

"You want to light this damn thing?" Johnisse grinned at Mike. "Unless you got something better to do."

Mike, try as he might to avoid it, met the edge of the kitchen table with his thigh trying to get to the woodstove. *If that doesn't take my urge away, I don't know what else will*, he thought as he rubbed his leg, not even bothering to look at the two women watching him.

23

It was dark in the room. The strong scent of rubbing alcohol danced with the sour aroma of urine from the bedpan on the chair next to where she was propped up. Shelby was so damn uncomfortable she could scream. After talking with Ridley, she had little hope. She was an experiment. The only thing she could hold onto was that she knew Ridley would do her best, but Shelby still had little faith in what was coming. Without the proper instruments, how was this young, very young girl going to get her up and walking again.

Torture couldn't have been any sweeter than having to lie in bed listening to the sounds of life going on without you. The big blue ball just doesn't stop, doesn't even slow down long enough to be able to catch your breath to jump off. These sounds came from her family and they still pissed her off. The women in her house using her things like they belonged to them clawed at her inner resolve. These items were hard earned or given personally to her, not to them. They had no right, and damnit if she could remember anyone coming in and asking permission to use her cast iron. Would they even know how to take care of them? Would they even care? They could be ruining them this very minute and then just leave and go home! She would have no idea since she couldn't get off this godforsaken bed!

Her face feeling flush, Shelby took a deep breath. "Girl, you are losing it," she mumbled to herself. Reaching over, she could barely grasp the water pitcher and glass that Ridley had placed on the nightstand. Trying not to turn or twist her leg, she braced one hand on her hip as she tried to bend a bit backwards and reach out. Feeling the rough edge of the tumbler with her fingers, she slowly arched her fingertips to try to slide the glass towards her. "Come on, girly girl, just a bit more," she whispered.

The sound of breaking glass made her shoulders bow up to try to cover her ears. "Damnit!" she yelled out louder than she intended, not realizing the shattering itself was enough to summon her Mountain Man.

Opening the door, a trail of light lit the part of the room where the shards were spread out on the wooden floor. "Wait!" Shelby yelled.

The silhouette in the doorway halted briefly upon command and then slowly persisted on opening the door farther.

"Shelby? You okay?" came his thundering voice.

She caught the trepidation in his tone. *He must be tired of dealing with this*, Shelby thought to herself. *I'm not worth anything anymore, just lying on this bed. I can't cook his meals, clean his clothes, or take care of the house he built. How much longer before he decides to get another better woman?* The thoughts entered her mind and pushed her usual dominant thoughts right out her ears. "Where did that come from?"

"Shelby?" His voice broke through the darkness.

"Yeah, I'm fine. Just knocked the glass off the table. I'm sorry." She whimpered.

"It's okay, my love. I'll get another and get this cleaned up. Be right back."

He was gone before she could respond, the room dark again. Staring at the darkness, the thoughts teased her, poking at her resolve. What would happen if she wasn't able to walk again even after Ridley's "miracle" surgery? How was she going to take care of the children? She would never be a burden on anyone! The faces of her babies flashed before her. One by one the thought of someone else taking care of them slapped her heart hard. These were her babies, no one else's. It was her responsibility to raise them as kind caring people, to teach them about life.

"Life," she murmured. Tears streamed down her hot cheeks, cutting through the soft flesh like molten lava.

Flinging the door open, Mountain Man's giant figure advanced into the room with a thud. "Sorry," he said.

Shelby hurriedly flipped the coverlet up over her face and dried the tears before her husband could see them.

Crunching glass as he walked to the side of the bed, he set the glass down and filled it with water. "Here ya go," he said as he handed it to her. "You getting hungry yet?"

"A little, but don't make nothing special. I can eat when everyone else eats," she replied.

"Oh, well, we all ate about an hour after I got home from Uncle Noah's home. It was a while ago when you were sleeping. Didn't want to wake you."

His words cut through her. She was already becoming a burden. Everyone was going on with life without her. She was being forgotten. What happened next? What else would change?

"You want me to bring you a plate?" Mountain Man asked.

Why no, I'll just either get it myself or lie here and starve. Her mind twisted the words around until they lit a fire under her normally calm resolved. Catching her breath at the thoughts that came spilling out, her eyes darted to the glass on the floor. A deeper crimson crept up her neck, nestling against her hairline.

"Jeremiah, you're doing so much already." Her lip quivered as she spoke.

"You're my wife. It's my duty to attend to you until you're better."

Duty was a very foul dirty word at times. He did it because he was obligated? Not because he loved her anymore? Was there another? Already? He couldn't wait? How long had she been an invalid?

"Here," he said as he handed her a small pill. "Ridley said to take another one tonight so you rest better."

Taking it, she popped it into her mouth and swallowed. *Ridley*, she thought.

"I'll get you a plate now. You need food with the meds you're on. Don't go breaking anything else until I get back," Jeremiah directed.

Shelby gave him a faint smile and remained silent as he left the room. She really had no choice at this point.

24

Looking out the kitchen window, Emma stiffened. Somewhere out there was her husband. Was he hurt? Was he with someone? Was he coming home? If only she could remember something.

The kids would be heading over soon. They were going to discuss the next steps to take... except, she hadn't figured out what the next steps were yet. As the matriarch, wasn't that her responsibility? She was the one with all the training, the one everyone else relied upon. Closing her eyes, she took a deep breath. There didn't always have to be an action.

If the path is unclear, pause.

Her eyelashes fluttered open as the words raced across her heart.

Be still.

Turning slowly, the scenes flashed before her like an old flicker film from the '40s. Before her, Tom was on the floor, beaten, his face swelling from the blows being dealt by the other fiend's fist. Over and over he smashed into Tommy's face, blood spewing from each contact. The sound of bones breaking overpowered the sound of flesh smashing into flesh.

Why couldn't she see their faces?

The woman was on the floor, two men holding her by the upper arms so she had to watch Tom being beaten. Anguish disguised her own face before her.

Emma shivered as the images dissolved into a thick mist and finally dissipated. Tom was out there somewhere and needed her. Bruised and broken, Emma had no qualms that he was in trouble. Closing her eyes tight, Emma tried to will the scene back before her but got nothing.

Dixon, who had been lying in the corner of the kitchen, watched as she walked into her office. She sat down on a bar stool that was hidden under the large table in the middle of the room, and Dixon followed. Reaching down in the cubby that served as a leg to hold the table up, Emma pulled out a long roll of paper. Sliding the band down and over one end, Emma gave a flick and extended the parchment out before her.

"Come on, boy, where is he?" she said as she rubbed the dog behind the ear, his head above the top of the table as he watched what his owner was doing with interest.

Her land. The land she had worked her ass off to buy. The land that she had sacrificed so much of her children's early years for to give them a future. There was no way to go back and give them the memories of her attending school functions or church recitals like all the other parents, but she could now give their children a safe haven for their future. It wasn't about the money but about the hours she'd spent away from her family working for something she now realized wasn't promised. Hope? Did she give them hope?

Her land encompassed roughly three hundred acres. The diversity of the plot allowed for a regeneration of natural commodities if needed. She had plenty of acres that were established with old wood, so she had a renewable source for fuel. Just as many acres had lain barren when she purchased it that she had planted with perennial fruits, vegetables and medicinal herbs over the years. Re-creating a natural permanent culture of growth, the plots were well calculated out for food production and were well hidden from the normal eye. She even had kiwi growing on her farm. Something that a lot of people didn't realize was that certain tropical fruits and vegetables could be manipulated for cold-tolerant growth. These kiwi were not like their warm-blooded cousins but had a rather smooth skin, but the taste and the nutrients were still there, and that was important to Emma.

Following the lines on the map, Emma ran her finger out from the house in multiple directions. What made sense? Tom hadn't been gone long, so he couldn't have made it too far in the condition he was in. But what if someone took him by vehicle? There wasn't much Emma could do about that currently, but if they did take him, they didn't intend to kill him. That thought alone made Emma feel a little better.

The nasty little ghost crept in quickly to Emma's thoughts, making her brows draw together. If someone hadn't taken him, he was out there and in horrible shape. That made finding him even more crucial.

"Dix, we have to find him." She spoke to the dog with every expectation that he understood her words, that at any moment he would speak back with wisdom on Tom's whereabouts.

Looking at the clock on the wall, she had very little time before the kids arrived. They would have a fit if they found out she went out alone considering all that had happened, but she wasn't going to wait.

"Come on, Dix, let's go! I can't just sit here any longer. We need to find Tommy!" she said as she gave the dog a rough rub on both ears.

Picking up her Sig P938, she stashed her flashlight and knife in her pocket, grabbed a jacket and walked silently from the house.

Taking a sharp left out the back door, she decided to head down along the creek. The farm itself had an interesting layout, not only because it was involved in the Underground Railroad but because of all the natural resources it contained. For water alone, the land had not only a spring-fed pond, but a creek from the nearest lake not five miles away. Add to that the water-catchment systems on the house and outbuildings and it would take a severe drought or act of destruction by man not to be able to drink a fresh cup of natural water.

The driveway wound back from the main road almost a mile before it reached the main house, crossing the creek and a set of train tracks. If you were going to dump a body, that would be the easiest and quickest place to do so.

Emma picked up her pace as she skirted the edge of the driveway, looking for any signs of Tommy. Her breathing increased from adrenaline as she noticed tire tracks off the side in the soft dirt. Bending down, her fingers touched the indentation from the tread. Not her truck tires, she thought. Bigger. Not a pattern she recognized.

"What do you think?" she asked her dog as he stuck his nose into the ground where her fingers had touched.

Glancing up, her eyes scanned the fields' edges, looking for anything out of the ordinary. Nothing. Checking the ground closer to where she was, she found no broken blades of grass and no indentations.

Standing, she looked around in all directions before taking off. She slowed her pace as she started up the slight incline the drive took over the railroad tracks. "Damnit," she muttered, still not seeing anything out of the ordinary.

"Come on, Dixon," she commanded as she started off down the driveway.

Up and over the tracks she went, coming down the other side to the bend in the driveway that ran alongside the creek. The murky water was violent and brisk this time of year as the lake managers opened the dams to lower the water levels in anticipation of the spring thaw. Glancing around at the ground between the driveway and the rush of water, she saw no tracks of any kind. Realizing she was holding her breath, she released the now spent air and gave a quick thanks that there were no signs that someone had either driven or walked anywhere near the water's edge to dump a body.

Walking back to the drive, she decided to check the other side coming down from the tracks. The road took a sharp right that left a natural ditch between the drive and the railroad tracks. Young trees now grew in the void, having been planted there by the wind or squirrels. Overgrowth filled the space beneath the trees, protecting their young roots from the summer sun and hungry scavengers. Emma had thought about planting berries here at one time, but it was so far away from the house that if she would have, they would have been reserved for wild animal food and not human consumption. The railroad also used to spray along the tracks, so not knowing what was in the chemicals, she'd chosen to find a better location to grow her fruit.

Glancing around, she noticed a recess in the dirt right at the edge of the drive like someone had driven off the roadway. Laying her hand down into the shallow groove, she noted the direction the indentation made and looked off in that direction.

"Dixon, come look at this," she said as the dog stuck his nose down in the dirt. Sniffing, he started walking back through the grass. Emma stood up and followed behind him, scanning the area for any indications of her husband.

Traveling farther back along the railway ditch, the sharp blue caught her eye first. Nothing in nature could account for the hue that seemed so out of place. Stopping, the woman and her dog came to what would amount to a tree line once the saplings spent a few more years growing. Dixon looked up at Emma and started to pace the edge of the field, a high-pitched whimper now alerting his owner that something had his attention. Emma looked for a way to get past the underbrush as Dixon twisted himself back through the trees with little effort. Her pulse quickened as she realized someone or something had already been there. Broken twigs, some trampled to the ground, were attempting to bounce back to their natural position before they had been violated.

She heard a low moan, her eyes now a rapid movement back and forth.

"Please God," she pleaded as she watched Dixon's white coat all but disappear into the overgrowth.

Lifting her arms up and covering any exposed skin below her eyes, she waded into the brambles, going in the direction of the now audible groaning. Thorns from the brambles tearing at her clothing, she pushed in with determination. The eerie sounds now matching in intensity with her pulse, Emma's fears pounded in her ears. Whatever she was hearing was in obvious torturous pain.

The dog's bark tore her attention from the ghostly intonations emanating from the unknown before her.

"Dixon!" she yelled.

Her pulse quickened as she paused long enough to get her bearings; turning towards the sound, she continued on.

Coming out on the other side, Emma stopped. There before her lay her husband, Tomás, with Dixon on alert beside him. The sides of the ditch cradled him while he lay on his back, not allowing him to roll in one direction or the other. His left leg bent back over the edge of the ditch at an unnatural angle, revealing an obvious break. Emma walked over to him and knelt, her soul shaking. Reaching out, her hand trembled as she hovered her fingers over his swollen eye and cheek. Inching herself sideways down his body, her eyes accessed every inch of him. He was thrown into the ditch in such a way his arms disappeared beneath his body. His swollen lips could not contain the expansion of his tongue from dehydration. Looking around, she realized she had no choice. Taking off her own jacket, she laid it over his torso and said a prayer of protection over him.

"Dixon, stay!" she commanded the dog. Jumping up, she didn't look back as she disappeared into the madness of thorns before her.

25

Ben kicked back in his chair, running his hand through his hair.

This is just ridiculous, he thought. *Why am I wasting my time here when I have better things to do?*

"Sir, you are wanted in the communications room as soon as possible. Some call from Washington," the deputy said, disturbing Ben's thoughts.

Turning around, Ben looked at the man like he didn't understand what he was saying.

"Er, yes. I'll be right there," Ben replied.

Some days he forgot that all hell had broken loose and they were still missing parts of their old life. Phones were still considered a luxury in this new world. Lucky for him that he had happened to magically show up at Emma's when the military was there.

"Gullible bastards," he muttered with a smirk.

Lieutenant General Sean Kissler followed orders, but something knocked in Ben's gut that he might not be as naïve as Ben thought. He would need to handle the guy with some caution. Nina wasn't around anymore, but Kissler could give him access to areas of the government he wouldn't have otherwise.

"Sheriff Olan here," Ben said over the mic.

"Sheriff, Kissler here. How are things up your way?"

"As good as can be. Again, thanks for hooking us up with all these radios. It helps in a big way keeping us in contact with others and relaying up-to-date information. We had no idea this was so widespread," Ben replied.

"Yes, well… I'm not sure if it's all over yet."

"Really? We should still expect another threat?" Ben asked.

"Always," Sean replied. "Hey, did you track down that dog that we were looking for?"

"Yes, sir. Same night. It's all wrapped up and put to bed." Ben spoke the words into the handset, quickly looking around to see if anyone was listening.

"Outstanding! We will be having some type of services maybe next week. We will need you to get Nina's kids down here by then," the general said.

"Alrighty," Ben stammered, still not sure how he was going to make that happen, but it was an easy trade for the Jeep those boys had left at his disposal. At least now he didn't have to ride that damn bike around town.

"We appreciate all your help. Let us know if we can be of further assistance," Sean said.

Yes, why yes, you will be of future assistance, Ben thought. "Ten-four. Over and out."

Ben clipped the mic back onto the front of the radio, feeling foolish that he didn't know how to speak on one of these things. Bloody hell! They were probably laughing their asses off at him right now! Walking out of the room, Ben yelled for his assistant. He needed to get his hands on information on how to run the radios so this didn't happen in the future. He had plans, and there wasn't anyone or anything that was going to stand in his way.

26

Tom could feel himself floating, being lifted high into the air, like on a cloud, soaring.

Is this it? he thought. *This is what going to heaven is like?*

Jolted back to reality, Tom let out a prodigious cry from his bones being shifted. Trying to open his eyes, he could only distinguish shadows looming above. *Sweet Mother Mary, I am going to die! Please, please, no! Don't let me go this way! I have things I want to do before I go. Please, someone hear me. Stop this.*

Tom emitted a cacophony from his throat like that of a dying lamb.

The sounds coming from the silhouettes continued to trouble him as his thoughts drifted to various animals that he knew walked these woods. A white flash caught his attention.

That damn wolf!

His whimpering increased, causing the silhouettes to pause with concern.

They lifted his body, leaving his arm hanging like a limp worm. The pain in his shoulder was excruciating. White bolts of light lit the insides of his eyelids. Tears fought to reveal his weakness as his breathing quickened. He could feel his heart beating in his ears.

Please don't let me be eaten alive! his mind screamed. Trying to wiggle any part of his body he could to scare off whatever was trying to have him for dinner, Tom passed out from the intense amount of pain that he was causing himself.

Emma looked down at his face as the group lifted his lifeless body. So many memories were etched in the fine lines around his eyes, in each of the gray strands of hair that now resided above his ear. Her heart beamed from finding him alive, but her gut wrestled with the pain she knew he was in. Judging from what she had observed so far, Emma knew that several bones were broken, starting at his face and working all the way down to his legs. Mentally calculating the items she would need, she had already sent Mike and Chloe out in the RV to get the sheriff and a physician if they could find one. He needed to know what happened out here, if only the small amounts she could remember. And with the mess that town was in, she wasn't sure if the local doctor was even alive after the hospital got hit.

Clutching the handle of the same cot they had used to bring Dixon home earlier, she straightened her back, preparing for the walk ahead. They had to be as gentle as possible for she wasn't sure if he had internal injuries or not.

Staring ahead, with each step she took, she said a silent prayer to God. Each footstep reminded her of the story about how God carried you even when you thought you were all alone and couldn't take another step. Footprints... in the dirt, she thought as she kept pace with her three helpers. She didn't dare look at them, as she would break down in tears. This wasn't the time for that. Right now her main objective was to get Tom into the house and as comfortable as possible.

Best she could guess, he had been out here since the night he disappeared. She had picked a few leeches from his neck and ears that had followed the trail of blood. He had been left in stagnant water alongside the railroad tracks, and she was surprised that there weren't more ingesting his dead flesh. As they rolled him gently onto the stretcher, she noted that his entire backside was covered in, best she could tell, oil that was alongside the tracks. The railroad sprayed every summer. She wished now she had paid attention to what chemicals they used. The wounds on Tom's back were flooded with whatever the substance was.

The hardest part was getting Tom carried out of the briars beneath the young trees. The rest of the way was easier footing, as they would simply travel up the driveway. Once they reached the house, Emma had her assistants help carry him into the downstairs bedroom. She had Lauren, her daughter, set up the massage table in the room so that she could use it as an examination table. She was glad she had set this space up as a temporary infirmary if needed. It was close to her office and the supplies she would need to try to help him. It had a small private bathroom and several large windows that could be opened for fresh air if needed. The windows were large enough that in an emergency they could be used as a door to the outside if the room had to be quarantined.

Help him! her soul screamed. Help him... why did she have the nagging feeling that she had caused this? Burying the thought, she set out to make her husband as comfortable as possible. Looking up, she noticed her helpers staring back at her, the room silent. Smiling, Emma looked from face to face. The oldest, Kevin, was still so young and naive. Needing a father to guide him still even though he himself had his own family. Jonathan, their middle son. His facial piercings a sign of his spirited nature, he needed a father figure who had a soft heart instead of harsh words. And Connor, their youngest son, the strongest of the three in spirit. He needed a father through the most formative years coming up. A man to teach him how to tame the forces that were at war within his soul.

These three men were silent as they watched the woman tend to the damaged body barely recognizable as their father. Each was deep in thought on how life was changing rapidly as hour by hour the clock dusted the past from its hands. What happened if they lost him? If he wasn't strong enough to survive? Who would take his place? Was their mother wondering the same? Their eyes darted back and forth between the two figures who had spent their life protecting them. Now who would protect these two?

"Mom?" Kevin asked. "You need us right now?"

"No, hun," she said, looking around at her children. "Why don't you all go get a drink and relax. I will need help when I start cleaning his backside, but right now I just want to do an assessment on what I can see. I'll come and get you when it's time. Oh hey, can you take Dixon with you and get him something to eat?" she said as she knelt down and gave the big dog a deep hug.

Giving their mom silent nods of agreement, the three boys walked from the room, coaxing the hesitant canine with them before they gently shut the door.

Emma, finally alone with her husband, couldn't keep the tears pent up any longer. As they streamed down her face, she didn't bother wiping them away. Bending over, she kissed him gently on his forehead. *"Mon amour,"* she whispered.

Emma gently unbuttoned what was left of the shirt he wore, revealing bruising, but she noticed no signs of an entry or exit wound from a bullet. Lightly prodding his rib cage, she noticed that he had an indentation. His right chest area was not its normal shape. Guessing a flail chest, she wondered how many ribs could be broken under there. Noting to roll him away from this direction later, she needed to stabilize it after she bathed him.

Taking a pair of scissors, she tenderly cut the rest of his clothes off to expose his naked body. Years ago she had wandered each curve and dip that he offered her with fascination. The years had brought a comforting carnal knowledge, a secret wonderment that only the two of them shared. This information would serve her well now as she examined his body, looking for anything out of the ordinary.

Walking into the bathroom, she turned the faucet on. Waiting for the water to reach a tepid point, she gathered a basin, washcloths and soap. Walking back into the room, she left everything on the side table she had pulled over beside Tommy. Walking back into the bathroom, she reached under the sink and grabbed a pitcher. Placing it under the flow of water, she caught a glance of her face in the mirror. Gasping, her fingers touched the scratches across her face, like war paint readying her for battle. She could feel the tiny stickers still in her skin as the tips of her fingers touched the torn flesh. *Damn brambles*, she thought, *serves me right.*

27

"I'll drive," Mike said as Chloe sat in the driver's seat.

Giving a high-pitched huff, Chloe moved without arguing and slid over to ride shotgun.

Inserting the key into the ignition, Mike started the RV. Finally turning over, black smoke puffed from the exhaust until the engine finally idled down.

"Remind me to have a look at her later," Mike said, giving the RV a tap on the dashboard.

"You're one of those guys who names your vehicles after women, aren't you?" Chloe asked.

"What if I were?"

"Figures," Chloe said, raising her chin and looking out the side window away from Mike.

"You one of those self-righteous bitches who thinks they're better than everyone else?" Mike asked.

The bluntness of Mike's question caught Chloe by surprise. "I-I..." Chloe began to stammer.

"No! Please tell me you aren't one of those types," Mike begged.

Chloe was quiet. So quiet, in fact, that Mike began to wonder who the hell this woman really was. She didn't seem to think she was better than everyone else, so why the offense to his question?

Chloe was still looking out the window, her past knocking at the window in front of her face. She thought she had left it behind, but here it was begging to rent space in her head.

"What's the plan?" she quickly asked.

Distracted by the mission at hand, Mike bit hard on the interruption. "Emma wants the sheriff and any kind of doctor we can find. She said the hospital was hit by a plane, so we may need to do some digging. I'm hoping this cop knows where to find one and fast. Listen, I haven't been into town, but it sounds like they got hit hard. I'm not sure if anyone has seen any kind of moving vehicle since this all went down, so I want you to stay in the RV. Don't let anyone in unless I tell you otherwise."

"You want me to protect this... this... thing?" she exclaimed, motioning her hand around like Vanna White.

"Well, yeah," he said, nodding his head in agreement. "You see anyone else in here with us? There are still a lot of supplies in here, and we can't afford not to have a moving motor vehicle, no matter what it is."

"Point taken, but how do I protect this thing if I need to? If some big dude has a gun, I don't stand a chance."

Mike reached his hand around to his back under his shirt and pulled out a Colt Python.

Chloe, her eyes huge, reached out to touch the firearm. "That's beautiful!" she exclaimed.

"It is. The guy this brand of gun is named after, Sam Colt, referred to them as the great equalizer. Consider yourself equivalent to any 'dude,'" he said with inflection, mimicking Chloe.

"This wheel gun," he continued, "is a .357 Magnum. My sister has a dog named after a favorite character she liked on a television show. She got me hooked and I wanted the revolver one of the other guys had. He was the sheriff before a zombie apocalypse happened. Kind of ironic now, considering."

Taking the firearm in her hands, Chloe turned it over, examining every inch of it.

"You know how to shoot that?" Mike asked.

Flipping the firearm over in her hand, Chloe pushed forward on the thumb piece. While pressing the thumb piece forward, she used her opposing hand to cradle the revolver and pressed the cylinder out from the right side of the firearm toward the left side. When she did this, the cylinder rotated out of the frame and came to a stop. Looking at Mike, she grinned.

"Alright, what are the four rules of firearm safety?"

"Number one, all firearms are considered loaded, no matter what you may think," she said, flipping over the revolver and dumping the cartridges out of the cylinder. "Number two, never point it at anything you wouldn't want to destroy. Number three," she continued, "number three is keep your finger off the trigger until your sights are on the target, and," she said, taking a deep breath, "make sure you know what's behind your target."

"I'm impressed!" Mike exclaimed. "There's a story here."

"Emma," Chloe said nonchalantly.

"Emma?" Mike asked.

"Some other time. Right now, we need to come up with a plan in case things don't go down as planned," Chloe said.

"Emma." Mike satisfied his need to have answers with the simplicity of his sister's name. Emma definitely had some influence over this girl riding beside him. "This might be easier than I thought," Mike mumbled to himself.

The silence in the new world left few options for sneaking into town in an old RV. Their arrival preceded them by about three miles. Some people came out of their homes to witness the noise maker; others watched from afar. No matter where they were, everyone heard Mike and Chloe coming even if they didn't see them. Including Sheriff Olan.

Chloe fidgeted a bit at all the stares they were getting, but Mike was seemingly oblivious to the attention. Calmly he pulled the large beast of a vehicle effortlessly down the empty street until he was almost in front of the police station. Pulling off to the side, he put the vehicle in park and motioned to Chloe to move to the driver's seat. Stepping up and out of the driver's pit, Mike opened the door and stepped out of the vehicle.

Not having to wait long, Mike squinted his eyes at the man walking towards him. About the same height, this guy had about thirty pounds on Mike. No real muscle tone—Mike assessed that the most this guy worked out was walking across the street to the local pub. Glancing at the man's waist, Mike wasn't surprised to see the Glock 17 nestled in the holster. *Typical*, he thought.

"Hey, aren't you..." Ben drifted off.

"Yeah, we had dinner the other night. Emma's brother."

"Yeah, I thought you looked familiar. Sorry, take no offense, but there was a little more estrogen than I could handle in that room. You could have been Brad Pitt and I wouldn't have cared."

"No offense taken," Mike replied to the odd statement. *Brad Pitt? Really?* he thought. "Listen, there's been an accident out at Emma's farm. She requested I come see if you can get out there. Oh, and where's the nearest doctor?"

"Doctor?" Ben was obviously shaken by the question, Mike noticed.

"Yeah, doctor. You have one around here?" Mike asked, watching Ben's face.

"Uh, yeah. What happened out there?" Ben asked, finally getting his wits about him.

"Not quite sure, but Emma thinks you need to come on out. She wants to talk to you."

"Okay. Well, why don't you head on back, and I'll grab the doctor and be right behind you," Ben said.

Knowing his sister, Mike wasn't about to show up back out at the farm without a doctor with him, nor the sheriff. "How about I just wait here, and we can all drive out together," Mike replied. "Where's the doctor?"

Ben pointed at the bar down the road. "Most days you can find him in there."

"Lovely." Mike grimaced. "Just fricken lovely."

"I'll be right back," Ben said as he walked away, calling over his shoulder. He disappeared into the square block building

Mike turned and walked back and into the RV, figuring he could wait for the two men inside. No sense standing outside. Besides, he wanted to see if Chloe was behaving inside. She seemed to know her way around the revolver; he was curious what else she was experienced with.

"I'm not sure I like that guy," Chloe said before Mike could even say anything.

"Oh really. How so?" Mike asked, taking his seat back behind the steering wheel.

"Gut's telling me not to trust him," she said, moving in front of him, her scent filling his nostrils. Mike felt the familiar stirring from earlier this morning. *Not now*, he willed to himself.

"Your gut ever been wrong before?" he asked, trying to distract his loins from their overzealousness for the blonde now beside him in her seat.

"Nope," Chloe replied.

28

"Are you sure you want to go forward with this? I really need you to be sure," Ridley said, looking from Jeremiah and then back to Shelby. "There is no turning back once I get started."

Jeremiah looked at his wife. She was a strong woman, but this had taken its toll on her. It wasn't the pain she was in but the feeling of helplessness. She was designed to help people, and her being confined in the bed was worse than any physical torture.

"I've nothing better to do, hun," Shelby replied. "Let's get this done," she said as she smoothed out the sheet covering her legs.

"Okay," Ridley replied quietly, her gut secretly excited to allow her hands to do what she felt they were born to do, heal. Her heart, though, that was another story. Something was off, and she just couldn't put her finger on it. Did it always feel like this before a surgery? Would she be able to eventually work herself out of the feeling in her stomach? "One way to find out," she mumbled as she crossed over to the doorway.

"I'll be back in just a little bit," Ridley said to no one in particular as she walked out the door, her mind already a million miles away.

Jeremiah walked over and sat down next to his wife. Grabbing her hand, he lifted it, flipping it over, and placed a single lingering kiss in her palm. Shelby flinched and the reaction startled Jeremiah. Looking up from under his lashes, his gaze made her shudder.

"Jeremiah," she whispered.

"Hey, everything is going to be just fine," he reassured her.

"You can't promise me that."

"Can't I?"

"No."

"You really think I would let that little girl even touch you if I thought she would harm you in any way? She has skills. She also has heart. She cares. She has been nonstop examining every possible outcome of this."

"I may never walk again if she messes this up."

"Not to be mean, but you won't walk again without this. Your leg is a mess. There really aren't any options at this point, or trust me, I would have made it happen. Ridley is right when she says if we don't do something soon, you could lose your entire leg. Her worst fear is not about being able to repair anything but about the huge chance that infection will set in. Then it's no longer just about your leg. I don't want to lose you."

Those last six words really hit Shelby. "I don't want to lose you" played over and over in her head.

Ridley coughed to break the spell between the two on the bed as she walked back into the room. "I need your help, Eminem," she stammered.

"Of course. What do you need me to do?" Jeremiah asked.

"That big long side table in the dining room needs to be cleared off and brought in here. And I need to go back to the barn," she said, looking at Shelby.

The look exchanged between them was shallow. Shelby had already checked out and was a million miles away while Ridley had stepped into the role of surgeon. It was now all business.

"I'll get some help with the table and be back in a bit," Jeremiah said, leaving the room.

Ridley walked over to the bed and uncovered Shelby's leg. Checking the area above the bandage for redness or swelling, Ridley was pleased with what she saw. She would unwrap it once they got Shelby up on the makeshift table she wanted to use for the operation. Grabbing a thermometer, Ridley went about checking Shelby's temp and then continued with her examination. If anything at all gave her cause for concern, she would stop this procedure immediately. She knew her limits, and not being in a sterile environment was distressing enough. Her first fuss was about the comfort of her patient, not only before, but during and after a surgical procedure.

"Blood pressure is a little high," Ridley garbled.

"What?" Shelby asked, not understanding.

"Oh, sorry. Just making a mental note. Your blood pressure is a little high, but quite honestly, it's to be expected. You've been through a shit storm the last few days," Ridley reassured her.

"Yessum. Hasn't been the most fun," Shelby replied.

Laying her hand on Shelby's arm, Ridley could feel the tension. "Listen, it's going to be okay. And it's okay to be concerned about this. Stop trying to be all tough and stuff, it just makes it worse. You have to release your emotions, or they get stored all up within your body, and that's not good!"

The look that Shelby gave Ridley was enough. It distracted her attention for the moment that Ridley needed. "Listen, once this is over"—Ridley swayed her hand over Shelby's leg for emphasis—"I want to work with you on something. I need you to be open to it, but I think it will help with not only the emotional trauma part of your accident but also any past issues."

"Is this new age stuff? I really—" Shelby started.

"No." Ridley stopped her before she could get another thought converted to words. "Okay, it actually is biblically based, and I think you will find it quite intriguing. I know I did, anyway," Ridley said, smiling. "It's called energy healing."

"Energy healing?" Shelby asked, looking puzzled.

"Yeah, think of it like the 'laying on of hands' to pray over someone," Ridley explained.

"Oh!" Shelby exclaimed. "I've done that myself and seen the power of it! You actually use that in your medicine?"

"Yes. Yes, I do." Ridley smiled.

"Fascinating! Yes, I want to learn more," Shelby said, the first look of anything less than stress on the woman's face.

The door opened and Jeremiah walked in. "Your table, ma'am."

"Awesome, let's put it right over here," Ridley said, walking to the side of the bed that Shelby was on.

Jeremiah caught the look on his wife's face as he settled the table near her bed. Puzzled, he knew something had transpired while he was gone, but knew enough to wait to ask. If anything, he was happy to see the slight improvement in her spirit.

"When do you want to go to the barn?" he asked Ridley.

"Let's go now. We can finish anything up in here once we get all the supplies in the room and organized."

Jeremiah winked at his wife as he turned and walked out the door with Ridley following.

Ridley continued trailing the large expanse of a man into the barn, lost in her own thoughts.

Jeremiah stopped too fast and Ridley ran right into the back of his solid form. "Sorry," she said as he reached out and pulled the cord on the light fixture in the middle of the room.

"Some habits are hard to break," he said, realizing he needed a flashlight instead. "Don't worry about it," he said as he turned to face her. "But you can tell me what you said to my wife."

"What are you talking about?" Ridley asked.

"When I left to go get that table you wanted, she was a mess. When I came back, well, it was the first bit of hope I've seen in her eyes since this all started."

"Oh! I understand. We were talking about healing energy and the studies I've been doing. She agreed to be my subject after the surgery," Ridley replied.

"Healing energy?"

"Yeah! I told her it was kinda like the experience you get when you lay hands on someone for healing. We, as doctors, treat the physical, but we neglect the emotional impact of a trauma such as what your wife has gone through. These emotions, a lot of the time, get stored within the body, causing more damage down the road, even years after an incident."

"Fascinating."

"It truly is. Our bodies are remarkable once you start diving into all the intricacies of how they function. Given the right circumstances, diet, exercise, etc., they heal themselves much more efficiently than most people can even imagine. We, as a society, have become so dependent on modern medicine that it's ridiculous. Do you know how much money these pharmaceutical companies make off of keeping us sick?" Realizing what she was doing, Ridley paused for a moment.

"Listen, sorry for that. I have a pretty big soapbox sometimes," she said sheepishly.

"Don't apologize. You need to speak out more. This is another reason I brought my family out here and why we live the way we do. I understand exactly what you're talking about. We raise our own nourishment, whether it come from animal or plant. We know what we put into our bodies. Most people can't say that. "

"Exactly!"

"Ask Shelby about her issue with pop later after she recovers."

"Pop?"

"Soda. Pop. Whatever you call it. When she was much younger, she drank a lot of it. I'm talking several cans for breakfast. Easily going through a twelve-pack in one day herself. She tried multiple times to stop, but it would last for a while and she was right back at it. Horrible back and forth."

"What got her to stop?"

"Moving here. Not having access to it. It really was an eye-opener for us, the amount of control that it had over her. Almost like an addiction," Jeremiah stated.

"You realize, it technically is a real addiction. It controls you. It leads to a person needing a fix and just a vicious cycle. The bad part is, other things set it off without you realizing it. It's more an addiction to sugar than to the actual beverage. When we consume something sweet, the taste will trigger our brains to release chemicals called opioids, which make us crave more of what we found pleasure in. You want to read something that scares you, study what manmade opioids are! Vicodin for one!" Ridley exclaimed.

"It really is all about the money, isn't it?"

"No. There's some good out there… just got to find it. Right now, though, we need to get what I need and get back to the house and set up. Tomorrow morning, I want to get started. After that we will have plenty of time to talk. That being said, I want to know what I'm going to need to improvise with." Pulling a sheet of paper out of her pocket, Ridley handed her list to Jeremiah. "In a perfect world, this is what I need."

Jeremiah grabbed the list and scanned it. Taking a deep breath, he looked at Ridley as he flailed the paper. "I don't think we have half this stuff!" he cried out.

"Hey, I didn't think so, but improvise, adapt and overcome is part of my motto! The other half is drink more beer and have more fun, but that's a whole other story!" she quickly retorted.

The look on his face made her giggle. "Jeremiah," she said, laying her small dainty hand on his holding the list, "it's okay. I got this. This list is made from the other world we knew, but there are alternatives to most everything. I will need your wisdom here, as I am not as skilled as you are on naturopathy. Most of my life has been spent in allopathy, and it wasn't until not so long ago that I woke up from drinking their Kool-Aid."

Giving her a sideways glance, he felt his pulse start to decline back to a normal state.

"Let's get started, then," he said, turning his back on her and walking to the cabinet that held jars of dried herbs.

Ridley looked around the room. This was her future in medicine. Not the stark white room she began her career in, where everything was sterile and in its perfect position. No, here she would have the sky above her and a dirt floor below. Her equipment would not be shiny silver pieces of metal but rudimentary tools that would have to feel the flames of fire.

Slamming her fists into the pockets of her pants, she took a deep breath. Feeling her heart beat faster in her chest, she knew what she was up against. It was going to be a challenge, but one she would not, could not back down from. Besides, if it were easy, they wouldn't need her.

29

He was cold again, his body shivering. *Why can't I stay warm?*

He strained to open his eyes, but they fought back and denied him. He felt his world spinning out of control as the fog enveloped his thinking. *Why can't I fight my way out of this dream?*

Something was on his nose, tickling. He tried to reach his hand up and scare it away. *Is my arm even moving?* His brain said yes, but his nose was still being harassed by something. Scrunching his nose, he was startled when he felt the breath of her voice on his skin.

"Tommy?"

Emma leaned in closer and whispered again in his ear, "Tommy, I'm here."

She had leaned over to kiss his cheek, not realizing her eyelashes were playing havoc on his nose. But it was enough to give her a sign of him waking up. He had been in and out of consciousness since the doctor had attempted to patch him up.

The doctor, what a joke, she thought. She had half a mind to chew her brother out for dragging that man out to her farm.

"Tom, please wake up," she said with a hint of desperation in her voice.

Tom stirred. He felt like he was riding a never-ending roller coaster uphill, waiting for the climax at the top, his stomach being left behind trying to catch up. Shaking his head to try to clear the thick haze, Tom moaned loudly as his brain erupted into lasers of bright colors flashed on the inside of his eyelids.

Damn! That hurts!

"Tomás."

He could barely hear her voice over the noise of pain going off in his head.

"Leave me alone!" he tried to scream.

Emma watched as her husband became restless. *Why can't I comfort him?* she silently cried out to God.

Being careful, she slid into bed beside him. His lung and ribs were still bruised, and she didn't want to risk more damage, but she needed to somehow help him. He had always found solace in her body before, would he now? Spooning against his side, she snuggled her face into the side of his neck. His arm filled the hollow formed against her stomach and chest, and her legs slid up against the side of his. He felt so cold, so hard, and so different, she thought. Breathing in, his scent no longer carried the faint aroma of his aftershave. Gently laying her hand on his chest, she felt his heartbeat. *God, please*, she silently begged, tears beginning to spill down from the corners of her eyes.

He could feel her against him, like a nymph trying to seduce him and steal his soul. The miasma of perfume burned his nostrils, making him want to retch. He needed to escape but couldn't get his body to respond. He was succumbing to her taunting. How did this form have so much control over his own body? Betrayed by his own bag of bones, he could feel a warming in his groin. A bead of perspiration broke out across his forehead, the internal battle taking external form. He had to control this, somehow. Trying to stretch out his legs was useless, as he could barely feel his thighs, let alone anything lower. He tried shifting his trunk, his mind trapped within his carcass. Taking a deep breath, he gave up and drifted into a dreamless sleep.

Emma lifted her face to kiss his cheek and felt the cold pallor of his skin beneath her lips. His fever had broken!

"Thank you." The words left her lips in a whisper.

Quickly backing out of bed, she retucked the blanket around him. Grabbing the washbasin, she refilled it with cool water and a little bit of apple cider vinegar, bringing it back to the table beside his bed. Dipping a washcloth into the tepid mixture, she wrung the excess liquid out and gently wiped the man's sweaty face. His breathing had leveled out and he wasn't laboring so hard to take a breath. She knew the drugs she had given him would take the edge off the pain, but he had to still be in an enormous amount of discomfort. Wiping his closed eye, she became fixated on his lashes. Their youngest son had those same long, gorgeous lashes. Their son needed his father as he was growing up, to teach him and instruct him. He was in his most volatile years for influence, and having a father alongside him would be crucial in his development into adulthood. Emma couldn't imagine Connor without his dad by his side. They were so close, the best of friends. Emma envied their camaraderie but knew the love between herself and her son was also unique.

Wringing out the washcloth again, Emma folded it over onto itself and laid it gently on his forehead. She would leave it for a bit to help keep him cool. Drying her hands on the towel, she looked at her husband lying helpless before her.

His beard was coming in, as he hadn't shaved in a while now. She would look at maybe taking care of that tomorrow depending on how he was reacting to the medications. Last thing she wanted to do was irritate him even further, but she also knew how he would complain about how his beard itched when he tried to let it grow out. A goatee was one thing, but a full-on beard just irritated him.

His hair was also getting a little long, as it was starting to curl just below his earlobe. She wasn't going to touch that, as she preferred his hair a little longer versus the flattop that he usually wore. He could cut that himself when he was better. Taking a deep breath, she fought the thoughts trying to swarm into her present. He would get better. He had to. She would not allow herself to think otherwise. She wasn't about to go into the apocalypse without her love by her side. They had fought so hard for so long to get where they were in life with a better home, a better relationship, and she wasn't about to give that up now.

"Satan be damned," she muttered.

If there was anything about Emma, she was a fighter and a survivor. All of her life had been a struggle. She used to envy those who had a cushy life with no problems until she realized how weak they were. Challenges were now faced with her chin held high and a grin on her face. This was just a bump in the road. Her God was bigger than this, and she felt secure in the fact that He had everything under control, even if sometimes she didn't agree with how He went about it.

30

He had been there in Tunguska on the hundred-year anniversary of the so-called White Night event. His expertise was in geology, and with the high content of iridium deposited in the bogs after the catastrophe, the government thought it best he investigate, completely off the books, of course. Today they romanticize the term and call it black ops, but back then it was just called incognito.

He had seen the devastation that had brought over eighty million trees to the ground, the land still struggling to recover from the devastation even a century later. Two hundred square kilometers had felt the impact of what some scientists speculate was an airburst from a meteor while others thought it was the second coming of Christ himself. Theory has it that if the blast had happened four hours and forty-seven minutes later, due to the rotation of the earth, the blast would have completely taken out Saint Petersburg, Russia, once the capital of Imperial Russia. The blast, bigger than even Hiroshima, had a death toll of zero.

Not one human had died in an area that completely flattened all other structures. The last time such elevated levels of iridium were discovered was during the excavation of the Cretaceous-Paleogene Boundary, when the earth revealed her only extinction-level event.

Now he was looking at the same data levels. The isotopic signatures of stable carbon, hydrogen, and nitrogen isotopes in the layers near Memphis were damn near the same as in Russia, along with the high amount of iridium.

"Damn," he muttered under his breath.

Opening another file, he took a deep breath. While the nitrogen was probably deposited as acid rain during the fallout from the explosion, his eyes kept coming back to the levels of iridium.

Did they succeed? he wondered.

Standing and stretching his back, Sean closed his eyes and rolled his head back and forth until he heard the joints in his neck pop. Bending back over his desk, Sean clicked on a photograph on his computer monitor, zooming in to see if he could detect a blast pattern.

"Bingo," he said as he sat back down in his chair and punched "Operation Blowdown" into the search bar. Scanning the article, he jotted notes down as he read.

"The trees directly below the explosion are stripped as the blast wave moves vertically downward, while trees farther away are knocked over because the blast wave is travelling closer to horizontal when it reaches them."

Glancing back at the picture on his screen, he had to admit, while it looked a lot like the pictures of Tunguska, it had its differences. Not nearly the size of the Russian explosion, Memphis still had the telltale indications of something being detonated from aloft. It still didn't explain the other cities that were hit. Los Angeles and San Diego were in California, and Memphis and St. Louis were together along the Mississippi, so there could be something he was overlooking there, but it still didn't explain how Houston, Colorado Springs, Atlanta and DC fit in. Running his fingers through his hair in frustration, he was missing something glaringly obvious and he knew it.

31

He heard the kids, their melodic melody of laughter causing his headache to intensify. Turning his head away from the noise, he felt the light against his face. Opening his eyes, he was perplexed. The lace of the curtain outlined the window that was allowing the light into the room. His brow furrowed as he wondered why someone hadn't shut the curtain and allowed him to sleep. But then again, what was with all the ruckus outside his room? Kids were supposed to be quiet! A man needed his rest!

He tried to pick his arm up to slide out of bed and silence the commotion outside, but it weighed a ton. Flicking the blanket back, he tried to swing his leg out from under the rest of it and try to sit up. The pain in his chest from the movement released a scream from his throat that quieted the noise from the children outside his room. His door swung open and multiple people rushed into the room.

"Tom!" a young man shouted. "Stop!"

Tom turned his head and looked at the man in puzzlement.

A black woman behind him was already yelling behind her for someone to, "Go get Emma!"

Both of these characters surrounded him and gently shoved him back into his bed.

"Dude, you shouldn't get up yet. You've been through an ordeal, if you haven't noticed," the man said as he helped Tom swing his leg back onto the bed.

"Yes, take it slow," the woman said as she plumped up his pillow. "Emma is on her way."

Emma… the man mouthed the word.

The energy of the two people kept Tom distracted as they resituated him comfortably back into the bed. Tom licked his lips, trying to talk, but the dryness of his tongue made it impossible to speak. Pointing to his mouth and gesturing like he was drinking, both people looked from one to another like he was speaking a foreign language.

"Wait, Tom. You need to wait until Emma gets here. We don't want to do anything to cause any further damage, and I'm not sure if you can handle anything to drink right now," the man said.

Tom laid his head back against the pillow and shut his eyes. *Who the hell do these people think they are? And why are they in my room? And... and... what the hell happened?* The thoughts swirled around in his head, making his stomach want to hurl.

"Tommy?" He heard her voice but kept his eyes closed. That voice. The one that had been haunting his nightmares. *Is she real?* So much anger escalated beneath his skin. He tried to concentrate on his breathing. In through your nose, out through your mouth. He could feel his heart beating against his chest, pushing against his ribs, trying to escape. The pulse from the rhythm of his blood crashed against his senses like a wild ocean storm sending waves against the unprotected shoreline.

"Tom." Her voice interrupted his thoughts again, this time causing him to open his eyes. There before him stood a frightened but hauntingly gorgeous woman. He knew her, somehow. Her eyes drank in his very essence as they stared at each other.

"Tom," she said so gently that he had to shift his eyes to her mouth to see if there was any trace of words left on her lips. Blinking, he looked back into her striking gray eyes, seemingly mesmerized.

"Tommy?" she said again with more clarity.

That voice! his head screamed. The voice from his dreams.

Back and forth his heart wavered between drinking in the quintessential beauty of her eyes against the detestation of emotions that her voice caused. *Who is this person?*

Leaving the side of his bed, Emma walked into the bathroom and poured a glass of water. Walking back to Tom's bed, she lifted the glass to his lips. Again their eyes locked above the rim of the glass. Parting his lips slightly, Emma laid the edge against his mouth and tilted the glass slightly. The cool liquid felt like molten lava as it slid down his throat. Coughing wildly, Tom grasped at his chest as Emma wiped his mouth with a cool washcloth. "Easy," she said.

"You have several broken ribs. You were hurt pretty bad, and it's going to take some time for you to heal, but you are alive. And you're home and safe," Emma explained with a forced smile.

"Home?" Tom questioned, the word stuck on his tongue, not wanting to be spoken.

Emma looked at her husband's puzzled look. She had never thought that he might have amnesia from his injuries, but looking at him now, she needed to face the possibility.

"Do you remember anything that happened to you?" she asked him.

Laying his head back against his pillow, Tom closed his eyes. Trying to replay the last few days over in his head, he couldn't bring any memories to his mind. Nothing except her voice and the feelings it encapsulated.

Emma watched as his eyes darted back and forth behind his eyelids, searching for whatever was lost, her heart breaking as she realized the man before her had no recollection of her.

"Listen, you rest. I'm going to go fix you a light meal so we can get something in your stomach. We need to go slow though, as you haven't had any real food for a while, so a good bone broth is what is needed. I'll be back in a little bit." She lifted the glass again and used the water to lightly wet his lips. Readjusting his pillow, she left the room.

Tom stared after the woman. She was his wife, his sister? Who was she? Why did he have such feelings of dislike towards her, then? Why did he want to drink in her loveliness yet stab her in the chest at the same time?

Emma walked through the door, gently closing it behind her. Leaning her back against it, she lifted her chin towards heaven and closed her eyes as the tears streamed down her face. "God, please," she pleaded once again.

32

It was the quietest she had ever seen her children. Glancing from face to face around the table made her stomach twist into knots. She didn't have the answers to their unspoken questions and that made her feel worthless. She took care of things, everything. It was in her nature to be the caregiver, but to see the spirits of her children so broken damn near destroyed her.

She had to tell them something, but they would not settle for anything less than the truth. Could they handle it? Could they handle her laying everything all out on the table between the baked chicken and the salt and pepper shakers like another entree on tonight's dinner menu?

Oh hey, by the way, it's great that your father is alive, but he may never remember you. How does one dress that up and serve it for dessert? There were no justifications to how all their lives had been turned upside down and no resolutions to how they could get those lives back. They had to find a new way, and it was going to take all of them working together to get there.

"Listen, this is going to be hard to talk about, and it's why I asked for the wee ones not to be here, but we have to throw everything out here and keep communication open. Trust me, I know this is hard, but I have seen all of you step up and help out in your own way. I truly believe we can get through whatever may happen if we stick together. I love you, every part of me wants to take this from you, but I don't know how," Emma began.

"Mom, it's not your fault," Kevin replied.

"I know but I somehow feel responsible. Like I somehow didn't yell loud enough to get your attention."

"You knew how this was all going down exactly?" Jess asked.

"Well, no. But..."

"No buts, there was no way you saw what was coming, but honestly, because of what you had done beforehand, we are so much better off than most people. I for one am sorry that I doubted you," Kevin replied.

Lauren dropped her head and stared at her fingers fidgeting in her lap. She had been the hardest when it came to giving her mom crap about prepping and her tinfoil-hat conspiracies. Lauren had tried to ignore the guilt since it began, but she knew it was time to fess up.

"Mom, I am truly sorry," she began. "I look back and see what an ass I've been, and now wish beyond high heaven that I had paid better attention to what you were trying to get me to realize.

Emma stood and walked around behind the others' chairs to where her daughter was sitting. The tears started to stream down Lauren's face as Emma wrapped an arm around her from behind and gave her a squeeze. "No need to apologize, little one," she said as she gently kissed her daughter on the top of her head. Lauren reached up and clutched onto her mom's arm.

What if I lose her too? Lauren thought. *Then what? Who would help us stay alive?*

"Mom, I..." she stammered, choking on the tears starting to overwhelm her.

"Honey, listen to me," Emma said as she tilted her daughter's face upwards towards her own. "I love you and I will not let anything happen to you!"

"You loved Dad," Lauren whimpered.

The silence was back, but all eyes were screaming at Emma for answers. *How do you respond to that? How do you tell your child that you failed and their father almost died because of it? How do you convince your child that you are not omnipresent nor omnipotent when you led them to believe that all these years you were? How do you convince your child that you are not a god and that they now need to treat you as a human? A human who fails and does not have all the answers. How?*

Emma let go of Lauren and backed away, her heart continuing to break as her world continued to crumble around her.

"Lauren, that was uncalled for." Kevin sternly spoke towards his sister, sliding into an authoritarian role now that his father was not able to oversee his family.

Lauren shot a glance at her brother and dropped her head. The words had slipped out before she realized it, but the words were there taunting at the back of her thoughts.

"No. It's okay. We need to talk about this," Emma replied with a new gentleness in her voice. Her kids were hurting and searching for answers, and now was not a time for a debate or unkind words. More than anything, they needed love and understanding.

"All these years," Emma began, "I have had a feeling, or some would say a calling, to try to figure out the future. I knew deep in my gut that this world we live in would change, and over the years I have seen more and more people with this same feeling being drawn together for whatever reason, to learn, to try to figure out what was possibly going to go down. We weren't concrete on anything... just a gut feeling or the voice of God trying to warn me, you can pick, but prophetically speaking, things are getting interesting and coincidently follow along with God's Word."

"So all this time, your prepping and all this moving to the farm wasn't always about the economy or a slower way of life for the kids?" Maria asked.

"Well, no, I mean yes." Emma sighed. "It's a combination of things. I have always been fascinated with eschatology, and out of this study there are certain things that would unfold. So, yes, to get to a one-world government, you have to have countries set up correctly to be able to have the people accept that. We here in the United States have been blessed for so long and pretty much have had a huge say in the global economy, but if God's Word was to be fulfilled, then we would need to see a decline in our dollar. We would have to see an ability to control the movement of goods and monies. How? Most likely, electronically."

"Is that why you talk about Bitcoin and RFID and chips a lot?" Maria asked.

"Yes. I want people to wake up, but they need to wake up and come to an informed conclusion on their own. I can deliver the information straight into your lap, but if you don't want to dig into it, there isn't a lot I can do to convince you that this is our reality," Emma replied.

Emma glanced over at Lauren, who still had her head down. She was Emma's biggest challenge. Lauren was the second to the youngest and the artist in the family. Her dream was to move to Chicago and create her own comic book series, but there was no way Emma could afford to pay her tuition outright. Lauren had spewed some bitter words towards her mom when Emma told her she would not be using her retirement to pay for her daughter's college, which was not what Lauren had wanted to hear. She expected her mom to do whatever it took to ensure her daughter's liberal arts degree with no guarantee of employment after and little actual work from Lauren. It was all about sharing the wealth, right?

"Listen, for whatever reason I felt led to do what I do, all I know is that you kids are the most important part of my life and the bottom line on why I felt a need to carry all of this through," Emma explained.

"And Dad? How does he fit into all of this?" Jonathan asked.

"Same way he always does. He didn't want to, but I showed him some things and he realized that I may have been right. It didn't help with the situation in Indianapolis getting worse and worse and wanting to keep all you kids safe. While there was no guarantee that you would follow us, we at least wanted to give you a safe place to come home to if you chose to do so. Promising your father a new gun and a range he could go shooting anytime he wanted went a long way in moving him out here to the farm," Emma said with a half chuckle, remembering how Tom was easily swayed with a new firearm.

"Okay, let's say your gut has been right all along and what you think might be unfolding is actually coming true. Now what?   Where do we go from here?" Jonathan asked.

"I think the question should be more about how we can help and get everyone through whatever is coming and out the other side alive!" Maria shot back at her husband. Turning her head to speak directly to Emma, Maria continued, "Unless you don't think we can survive what's coming?"

"I don't know what to say to make this any easier. While I would like to say, yes, we will all survive, I can't give you false hope. I think you need the truth, or the truth as I see it, and I think we need a plan," Emma explained.

"Or two," Kevin quipped.

"Yes, or two, three, whatever it takes," Emma replied.

Lauren finally lifted her head. "I don't know where I fit into all of this, but I am extremely tired. Can you guys figure all this out and catch me up to speed later. I think I need to go lie down for a bit?"

"Sure, honey," Emma said softly.

No one really paid much attention to Lauren leaving the room except Emma. Her eyes followed her daughter as Lauren left the room, catching every movement and burning it into her memory. If there was one child she was concerned about the most, it was Lauren. Emma made a note to talk to Jessica later and see about starting some training classes and having Jess invite her. She figured that she stood a far better chance of getting Lauren to attend with Jess asking than if Emma asked her herself. Lauren had always been a bit defiant if Emma was involved somehow, and this was no time to gamble on the outcome.

Continuing on, the kids took turns asking Emma questions about the uncertain possibilities of what was to come. Giving them as much hope as she could, she made sure that she stressed the importance of having their spiritual life as one of the most important preps that they should be paying attention to. Time would be set aside to come together weekly at the farm to pray together as a family. Since Jess was overseeing the homeschooling of the grandkids, Emma also talked to her about adding additional curriculum concerning the importance of prayer and a few extra first aid classes. They also orchestrated a class on scenario drills to go over with the kids in case they were separated from all adults or ended up in the company of adults that they did not know. The last thing that they discussed was the development of their own family language to be used to communicate without making their plans known to the outside world.

33

Mike watched as Chloe bent over and reached under the hen. She was becoming quite the domesticated goddess, if he said so himself. With Emma being consumed with nursing her husband back to health, Chloe had really stepped up to helping around Emma's homestead.

"Hey, you," Mike chimed out.

"Hey yourself!" Chloe sang back. "How's things going with Tom?"

"Physically, not bad. He will bounce back quite nicely, I think. Mentally though, I've no idea. It's eating Emma alive, I can tell you that," he replied.

"Understandably so. They seemed tight," Chloe said.

"Love of her life. You could never separate the two of them. Their hearts are joined, their souls. My sister will reach him. If not, I've no doubt he will fall in love with her all over again."

"Ah, that's sweet! You love your sister very much, don't you? It shows."

"Yeah, it's just the two of us left. She has my back. "

Handing Mike the egg she had stolen from its owner, she walked over to her next victim. Sliding her hand under the back end of the next hen, she let out a shriek. Her hand reappeared with a very squishy oval object. "What the—?" she started to say.

"It didn't form completely. She might be low in calcium, or she might be new to this whole egg-laying form of employment," Mike explained.

"I've still got a lot to learn, don't I? I've read about it in books, what Emma does, but actually doing it, man! It's a whole other world out here than I'm used to," she said nonchalantly.

"What kinda world are you used to?" Mike asked.

She'd slipped. She'd let her guard down just enough, and he tried to get his foot in the door.

Damn it, Chloe! she scolded herself. *Laugh it off, laugh it off.*

"Oh, just typical working-girl stuff. Being someone's bitch. Do this, do that. Work hard, party hard. Nothing glamorous. Oh, look!" She pulled a blue egg out of the next nest. "How do they change colors? I mean, how do you know what color chickens lay what color eggs?"

"Their ears," Mike replied, amused.

Chloe looked at the chickens quickly, a shocked look on her face. "Ears?" Chloe said, looking back at Mike. "Nuh-uh! Chickens don't have ears!" she said, looking back at the chickens.

"Yes, actually they do. Here," he said, pointing at the small flap on the side of the hen's head. "See this white earlobe, probably white eggs," he said as he reached his hand under the hen, pulling out a white egg. "Red earlobes are going to probably be brownish-colored eggs."

"That's cool!" Chloe exclaimed. "Wait, how did I get a blue egg?"

"Those are Easter Eggers. They lay all kinds of shades between green and blue even though they don't have those colored earlobes. Silkies," he said, pointing at the fluffy white chicken, "actually do have blue earlobes but lay a really light brown or almost white eggs. I guess it all comes down to knowing your flock."

Chloe laughed. "Why do I find this all so fascinating? A chicken with blue ears! Who would have thought it?"

"You're gorgeous when you laugh," Mike said without thinking.

Chloe could feel the color rise up through her cheeks. Here she was, a high-priced prostitute who was used to men telling her such things, and now this one guy had the power to make her blush.

"Thank you," she said quietly.

"I want to know everything about you," Mike said.

Panic now reached its way into Chloe's heart, stealing away the moment of innocence. Chloe looked at the man standing before her. She studied his face, the chiseled cheekbones beneath the steel blue eyes.

Damn it! her heart screamed. He could never find out.

Lifting a finger up to stroke the side of her face, Mike watched for any sign that would help him read her expression. "What's wrong?"

"Nothing. Well, it's just weird, you putting the moves on me here in a chicken coop."

"Oh really?" he asked as he moved in closer to her.

"Yeah, really," she said, her panic starting to subside.

Pushing her back against the wall, Mike placed both of his hands on her hips and pulled her up against him. Chloe dropped the basket full of eggs that she had collected, spilling the bounty onto the straw-laden floor.

Mike devoured Chloe's bottom lip as he slid his hands around to her back. His tongue slid between her teeth and a tango ensued between the two of them. Gasping for air, Chloe slid her hands around his neck and entangled her fingers in his hair above the collar of his shirt. Over and over their tongues danced back and forth, their arms pulling them together tightly until there was no distance between them.

"Er-a-Er-a-Errr!"

Chloe shrieked as she tore her lips from Mike, nearly climbing onto his shoulders from fright!

"WHAT THE FUCK?" she yelled.

Mike doubled over in laughter. "Oh my god, it's just a rooster!"

"Why are you laughing? What is going on?" she said, still terrified.

Mike set her down on the floor, gasping for air as he tried to contain his amusement.

"It's a rooster crowing. Probably because he thought we were a threat to his ladies!" Mike chuckled.

"A rooster?" Chloe said, clutching her chest. "A fricking rooster."

"Yeah, they do that occasionally."

"I thought they only did that when the sun was coming up?"

"No, actually there are a multitude of reasons why. Sometimes a bright light makes them crow. Sometimes if they feel threatened. Kinda like a pimp warning his hos!" Mike explained.

The comment struck Chloe right in the heart. She felt the blood drain from her face as the reality of her life caught up to her standing in a chicken house.

"Hey, you okay?" Mike asked, concerned.

"I think I need to go in. I'm feeling kinda dizzy," Chloe responded.

"Here, let me help you," Mike said, extending an elbow.

Chloe was out the door and headed towards the house before Mike had a chance to see the tears welling up in her eyes. Mike followed after her; the basket of eggs now lay forgotten on the floor of the coop.

34

Ridley watched the two out in the yard with fascination as she drank her tea. Rubbing her stomach, she thought of how fickle love was. Here she was, carrying a small life within her, watching a couple with envy at their blossoming relationship. It was like they were all part of one equation.

"Ah, baby, maybe one day we will find that kind of love," she said softly.

The tiny flutter in her stomach caught her by surprise. Was that her child answering her in agreement? A ball of overwhelming love caught her in the heart. This was her baby, her creation. Smiling, Ridley set her cup down in the sink. She needed to go check on her patient, but she wanted to etch this moment into her memory forever.

Walking into Shelby's room, she glanced over at Jeremiah still asleep in the chair. Such an awkward position, she knew he was bound to have a kink in his neck when he woke up, but for now she would let him sleep. Turning her head, she caught Shelby looking at her. "Hey! How long have you been awake?" Ridley asked.

"Not long. The snoring got to me," Shelby said, thrusting her chin out in Jeremiah's direction.

"Oh goodness! If I had known it would disturb you, I would have kicked him out!"

"No, it's actually comforting. It means he's near and watching over me behind his eyelids," Shelby responded, giving Ridley a wink.

Ridley walked over to the table and grabbed a stethoscope and thermometer. Walking over to Shelby she placed the stethoscope on Shelby's chest and listened. "How do you feel?"

"Not too bad," Shelby replied. "What did you find once you got in there? How's my leg going to be?"

Sticking the thermometer into Shelby's mouth, Ridley took a deep breath and exhaled. "Well, you are going to experience some long-term nerve damage. Your muscle had separated itself from your bone, probably where the hoof came down. On the bright side, your bone is actually not broken, but you have a severe amount of blood pooled in there. I inserted a tube to try to drain the hematoma to relieve some of the pressure. I also want to monitor your kidneys to make sure there is no damage there. Once we get some of the swelling down, we will adjust the diagnoses accordingly. In the meantime, since we are without modern medicine as we know it, along with the drain, you have a nice comfrey compress added to try to speed along the heeling. All in all, I think things went well."

"I thought for sure she had shattered my leg when her hoof came down. Bella got spooked and I shouldn't have been in the pen with her."

"Well, as much pressure as the clotted blood was putting on your tissue, I can imagine. They are very painful, but once the swelling goes down as it drains, the pain will decrease. We are just going to keep you as quiet as possible for at least a week to help this along, so no fancy dancing, lady!" Ridley said with a wink.

"I can probably deal with a week considering I thought I was going to lose my leg."

"In all seriousness, infection is your enemy. Any signs and it could still happen," Ridley said with no sign of emotion.

Shelby blinked at the bluntness the young girl spoke with. "I'm not trying to scare you," Ridley explained, "but you need to follow orders."

"Okay," Shelby said, nodding her head slightly in agreement.

"Should we wake the beast and let him know the good news?" Ridley asked with a flip of her head towards Jeremiah.

"No. Not yet," Shelby said. "Before we do, tell me a little more about this energy touch you were talking about earlier."

"Ah yes, energy healing. Well, in a nutshell, humans are made up of small balls of energy. All life is. Well, these balls of energy travel through the body along micro-thin pathways called meridians. This energy is said to flow through the body and requires harmony and balance in order to facilitate health and long life. Our bodies seem to store all of our emotions over the years in files. Think of when you smell something that reminds you of a time in your past. When you smell that, a file is activated and the memory associated with that smell is replayed. These can be both good and bad memories. Bad memories have a tendency to clog the pathways, and illness, etc., can occur. What I have been working on is identifying where the body is storing the emotional charge and activate that site while thinking about that specific emotion."

"Interesting, but it seems kinda new agey to me," Shelby said.

"I understand that. We can talk about that more as we go along. But right now, I think we need to alleviate your husband from the painful situation he's in. That chair looks like it needs to be rescued before it collapses and dumps him onto the floor." Ridley chuckled.

"Oh, alright!" Shelby chuckled.

"It's good to hear you laugh again," Ridley said.

"Yes, yes, it is." Shelby sighed. "Now wake my husband up!"

35

He must have counted the tiles on the ceiling a million times. Over and over, back and forth, around the edge working towards the middle. It didn't matter where he started or where he ended, the number always came out the same. Rolling over onto his side, he traced the window trim with his eyes.

There needs to be a damn curtain on the window, he thought to himself.

He was tired of the morning sun intruding into the room and disrupting his sleep.

Why the hell aren't there curtains on this window?

Rolling back over, his eyes drifted back to the ceiling. Closing them tight, he blew out his breath in a forced vent. He could feel the pressure increasing in his body and he needed to release the tension somehow.

Damn her! his mind screamed. Heaven forbid if he tried to leave the room, she'd have her bloodthirsty posse all over him.

A prisoner, that was all he was. A prisoner among fricken lunatics.

Well, he could play this as long as he needed to so he could get out of here. Fuck her and the rest of these idiots. Once his health was back, he would take what he needed and leave. It was all her fault he was like this, and she could deal with the consequences of her actions. It was her fault, at least as far as he could remember.

But he couldn't remember. He had tried to remember. He wanted to remember, maybe, but there was something inching its way into his forethoughts that maybe not remembering wasn't so bad either. Not remembering gave him a freedom that he was starting to enjoy. He could speak his mind and no one could hold it against him. A few times now he had made some pretty harsh comments and probably should have apologized, but something stopped him. Some invisible force was pushing him away from this place, away from what he couldn't remember and away from finding out what his past held captive over him. Was that a bad thing? What if he was truly miserable? What if he was contemplating leaving before the accident? Maybe his mind was just making the unconscious decisions that he himself had been putting into action before everything blew up in his face.

Running his fingers through his hair, he gripped his hand into a fist and pounded it upon his forehead a few times. Why couldn't he remember? Anything? There were bits and pieces of very few memories, but even those memories were so distorted, so mixed with images that made no sense, he didn't even trust his own mind for the truth. So why blame her if he wasn't sure?

"Good question." The words snuck out before he could capture them between his lips.

He needed some fresh air, something. He needed to get out of this room somehow. Just get out and feel the sun on his face. He had no idea how long he had been locked up in the room, but he had had enough. He needed to figure this whole mess out and give himself some peace over the situation, good or bad.

36

Sean sat down at the small table and pushed the chair across from him out with his boot. A stout man, he needed some room to kick out his legs.

"What can I get ya, sugah?" the waitress asked.

"Bourbon. What kind do you have?" he asked.

"Wild Turkey or some kind of mark," she replied.

"Maker's Mark?" he questioned.

"Yeah, that's it, sugah!"

Looking at her face, Sean was surprised the woman saw the light of day. Pale with deep crevices in her face, she obviously spent a lot of time in this dive. "Maker's Mark it is, then, double, neat."

"You want ice cubes?"

"No! Who does that? Neat means dry, no ice. Whiskey is meant to be warmed with your hands not chilled with ice!"

Intrigued, the woman could tell the man knew a thing or two about his whiskey. "Sure thing, sugah," she replied with a wink.

Sean watched the woman walk away. Her frail figure matched her face, petite with no muscle tone, slightly hunched at the shoulders.

She probably cuts her own hair in the bathroom, Sean thought to himself.

Putting his forearms on the table, he mindlessly played with the salt shaker. Twirling it between his fingers allowed him to drown out his surroundings. He needed to think. He needed a plan, and one that would ensure a positive outcome on his part. Collateral damage was expected, but he needed a good payout. Without Nina around, he now needed to tread carefully and make new alliances without setting off alarms.

Damn her for being careless!

The distaste for females that lay on his tongue made him look around for the waitress and his bourbon.

Seeing her standing at the bar, holding a tray with drinks in one hand while she tried to dump some nuts into a bowl made him like them even less. This one here was definitely not the brightest of the species.

Getting up, Sean walked over to the bar and grabbed his bourbon off the tray, almost spilling the rest of the contents. Lifting the cheap glass to his lips, he tilted his head back and swallowed the amber liquid in two gulps. Putting the glass back down, he took a twenty out of his wallet and tossed it on her tray.

"Thank you, sugar," he shot back at her, deliberately enunciating the last word.

Outside the door, Sean looked around, both up the street and down. Flipping the hood up on his jacket, he decided a walk might help clear his mind. Heading east, he walked towards the capital itself. He had lived here all of his life, being raised in a military family. His father had been involved in the underworld that very few knew about in Washington, DC, the gray government, if you will. Most people thought the president of the United States ran the country, when in fact, it was a select group of masterminds who had been in position for fifty or more years. This cluster of souls determined the ebb and flow of the success and failure of this once great country. Lately, the failure rate had far exceeded her success, and the buzz around town was the eventual collapse of this life they were used to.

Sean knew that the partial collapse that had just happened was a planned event. He had been warned to stay out of the areas affected and warned not to open his mouth. Collateral damage was something that had been beat into him since an early age. People were horrified by the Islamic extremists raising "bomb babies" while not realizing the government they paid taxes to was raising its own sheep for slaughter. Agree with it or not, it was a fact of life that many did not want to admit to. It would change the paradigm of their normalcy bias. Soccer moms would be carrying AK-47s if they truly understood what world their seven-year-olds were being groomed for.

He could feel the bourbon warm the inside of his belly as he made his way across the empty street. The walk was doing him no good trying to work out the kinks in his plan, all it did was keep his mind replaying a history he would like to forget instead. His old man was one of the coldest human beings he had ever met. His mom, he barely remembered before she was killed off. Someone had wanted his dad to behave and work the agenda, and one of the easiest ways to do that was to remove a piece of someone's heart and soul. It had a tendency to really grab your attention when that happened. It also made it harder to get close to another human. You were always wondering when they were next. Hell of a way to live let alone raise kids.

Walking slowly now, he kept an eye on his six. He had been to this side of town a few times in the last year. It always helped to relieve the tension he was feeling by the time he left. It was a sick and twisted way to spend a few hours, but then again, there were worse ways. This great city was harboring such nasty secrets beneath its crooked exterior, and it always gave him a bulge in his pants knowing he was one of the privileged to reap its benefits.

Disappearing down an alley, Sean made his way to a wooden door amongst many others. Knocking, he waited until he heard the knock in return. Glancing around, Sean tugged his shirt collar back, revealing a tattoo on his collarbone. He could hear movement from the other side of the door as someone unlocked the door. Quickly Sean slid inside the dimly lit foyer.

"Nine," was all Sean said.

The old man who opened the door escorted him down the hallway past multiple rooms. Finally the man paused and motioned Sean into a room. Closing the door behind him, the old man locked the door from the outside. Sean glanced around the very Baroque-inspired room.

This will be different! he thought.

Walking to the huge 1600 French secretary cabinet, Sean opened the doors to the contents provided. Sifting through the half masks provided, he chose a black disguise with silver trim. Sean grinned as he slid it over his head and glanced in the mirror provided in the wardrobe. Perfect. Closing the doors, Sean tossed his jacket onto the settee in front of the bed and walked over to the side table holding the decanters of alcohol. Lifting a crystal carafe, he pulled the topper and took a whiff. Pouring the amber liquid into a snifter, he lifted it to his lips and let it transfer to his tongue.

"Hmmm, Yamazaki," he murmured.

Taking the glass with him, he made his way to the lone chair in the room. He would wait here, the excitement already arousing him. He gently massaged his crotch as he sipped the whiskey, delighting in every swallow. His dad would be proud. Sitting here, now a part of the "in crowd" of Washington, DC, the fruit of his loins about to partake of some of the world's finest.

"Damn, I wish you were still alive," Sean muttered.

Taking another sip, Sean was startled as he heard the door being unlocked. His excitement level increased as the door slowly opened, allowing the light from the hall to trespass inside. Sean's eyes stayed locked on the girl entering the room. Her long dark hair hung to her waist, swaying back and forth as she walked forward. Her costume betrayed her body's denial of puberty. The young child approached Sean and paused in front of him, her eyes downcast behind her mask. Sean smiled. Yes, it definitely would be an interesting night.

37

Emma heard the commotion before she saw what was going on. A man shouted, "Shut up!" with such anger in his voice. Emma cocked her head. *Is that Tom?* she thought to herself with puzzlement.

Standing up, Emma started in the direction of the noise, her basket of eggs long forgotten. Her stride quickened as she made her way towards the house. With each step, the shouting intensified. She could start to make out hostile words, such profanity she was slightly taken aback. Her temper started to rise as she approached her home, the thought that such hostility was happening on her soil. Sure, Emma swore. Occasionally. It was a bad habit she had picked up over the years working with mostly male peers, a habit she had spent some considerable energy on trying to curb. Now, words filled with hatred were erupting from around the side of the house, words that confused her yet drew her towards them like a moth to a flame.

Deciding it best not to rush full into whatever was going on, Emma slowed her pace and slid in behind the plantings that lined the side of her house towards the corner. Inching forward, she lowered herself until she was at knee height to anyone standing. Listening above her breath, Emma was shocked to hear what sounded like her husband berating someone. The language was a mix of Spanish and English, but Emma could still make out that the conversation was not about peace and cookies.

Peeking around the corner, Emma saw two small children standing at attention, their faces filled with fear. Tears had fallen down their cheeks and mingled with the dust that had collected on their sweaty skin from playing outside in the yard. She couldn't see her husband, but judging from the direction of the children's eyes, Emma guessed he was on the landing of the porch.

Backing up slowly so as not to be noticed, Emma paused to listen.

"Why are you even here?" the man shouted. "Just shut the hell up! I need to rest and you bunch of no-good, unappreciative brats are making that fucking impossible. Too bad your mom died, or you wouldn't even be here right now."

Emma gasped as the words hit her heart. Quickly untangling herself from the bushes, she rounded the corner with such intensity that she almost ran over the children as she tried to get between them and the man screaming at them.

"Tom, please stop now!" she shouted at the man.

Turning, she knelt and placed a hand on both of the children's chests. "Please, take your sister inside and go upstairs to my bedroom. I want you to get washed up for some lunch. Stay there until I come up and get you, okay?" She nodded at both children. "You can get the coloring books and markers out until I get up there if you get done early! Okay?" she said, nodding again. Emma's eyes looked into the tear-filled eyes of the two small children standing before her. Her heart was breaking, as she knew how much the words Tom had spat at them had hurt. They had been through so much already, and this truly was intolerable.

The little boy took his sister by the hand and started toward the door, then stopped. Looking at Emma, then back at the man, Emma knew what was going through the little boy's mind. He didn't want to go near this person who was so harsh to them. Emma stood and walked to the child, grabbing his other hand, and led them both to the porch. Glaring at Tom, he understood that any further verbal exchange would now involve her. Opening the door to the house, Emma ushered the children in past Tom and motioned for them to go on. Watching as they made their way towards the stairs, Emma closed the door and turned towards her victim.

"What is going on here?" she asked.

"Don't chastise me."

"Chastise you? What do you think you were doing to those poor children?" she asked.

"Those little bastards shouldn't even be here still," he spat out.

"What? Who the hell are you?" she retorted with stunned disbelief.

"What do you mean, who am I? I'm your fricken husband, I guess, from what everyone says. Not that you can tell by how I'm treated around here in your majesty's castle!" he shouted at her.

Emma looked at the man standing before her. This was not her Tommy, this was not the man she had fallen in love with. She wasn't sure who he was. Taking a deep breath, Emma calmed her voice.

"Yes, Tom. You are my husband, and yes, this is my farm. But that gives you no reason to scream at two small children like you did. They have been through enough." Her voice was low and steady.

"They? What about me? Haven't I been through enough too?" he whined.

Emma saw where this conversation was going and knew it would not end well if she voiced her thoughts. A grown man acting like this would not be resolved in one conversation. First, she needed to diffuse this situation and let him calm down.

"Why don't you tell me what happened?" she asked quietly.

"I was fucking trying to sleep! I've been hurt, if you haven't noticed, and it's damn near impossible to sleep in this hellhole!" he spat out.

"I'm sorry, Tom. Yes, you need your rest. Let me help you back into the house, and I'll make sure no one bothers you anymore today. I'm so sorry," she replied barely above a whisper. Turning, she opened the door and allowed him to enter before her.

"Would you like some lunch?" she asked from behind him.

"Yes, that would be nice," he replied, his voice already quieting down.

"Would you like me to bring it to your room?" she asked.

"Yeah, that's fine. Just keep the noise down around here," he said as he disappeared off towards the room he was sleeping in.

Emma watched him walk away as a piece of her heart ripped out of her chest with each step he took. Tears filled her eyes as she tilted her head back. "Where's my Tommy?" she whispered to heaven.

38

The black woman smiled as Sean entered the room.

"How was your visit, Sean?" she asked with a smile.

"Superb as always, Miss Duval," he replied with an equal amount of pleasantry.

"Excellent. I always like to know you are taken care of properly. What year did you partake of this time?"

"I believe that would be 2008?" Sean replied.

"Ah yes, young, fertile and eager to please with a hint of innocence. Excellent choice, my friend," Kate Duval quipped.

"I will be bringing you a gift soon. Probably next week. They are being delivered from out of state. I would be careful, though, where you train and utilize their skills, as they were associated with the elite here at one time. It might be best to ship them overseas."

"Understood. Who's the connection?" she asked.

"Varga."

"Really? Well, okay, then." She trailed off in thought.

"Don't play with this one. They will need to disappear fast."

"Yes, I can see that. Don't worry."

"I'm not worried, but I will expect to see an addition to my account."

"Of course. Were you pleased today?" Kate asked.

"Very much so."

"Excellent. Your hand, sir," Kate instructed as she held up a small wand.

Sean lifted his left palm as Kate quickly passed the rod over it. A green light blinked as the transaction was completed.

"Pleasure doing business with you," Kate said as she lowered her lashes and bowed her head.

"Pleasure was all mine, I assure you," he replied as he grazed her cheek with his hand.

"Joseph! Please see the gentleman out!" she instructed the man quietly hiding in the background.

Sean was astonished that he did not see the man until he was summoned. Kate winked at him to reassure him that there would always be secrets even he could not stay ahead of in life. Following the man to the door, Sean quickly put his hood up and disappeared into the night. Walking back into the room where the woman was, Joseph waited for further instruction.

"Joseph, we need to make plans for a trip," Kate said. "Saddle up the horses!"

39

Emma walked into her bedroom, not sure what she was expecting to find. What she did find melted her heart. There on her bed, snuggled up with her blankets around their sweet faces, were these two children who had stolen her heart.

Walking over, she turned the light overhead off. The only glow in the room now was from her nightstand light as it cast a warm blush over the room. Standing beside her bed, Emma looked down at the cherub faces nestled on her pillow. Peace, even after all that they had been through, was evident on their sleeping countenances. They felt safe here.

Emma knelt down beside the bed, laying her hands on the blankets over the children.

"Father," was all she could say. Her heart cried out, but the words just would not come. There was an unspoken language that passed between Emma and heaven that night. Her heart was begging for so many things, protection for the children, for her husband to be healed, for her life to return to normal.

Emma rested her forehead on the edge of the bed, closing her eyes. So much had happened. She missed her life, the way it had been. The doting husband. Her homestead. The comforts of having electricity and the internet. She missed talking with her friends on Prepper Chicks. She wondered how everyone else was surviving the catastrophe that had happened. She had dear friends across the country that she hoped she would talk to again. What would Jimmy tell her to do now? He never hesitated to tell her straight up what was what. She valued his friendship greatly. How about Michelle? Michelle, who owned the Princess with a Gun company. Emma's memory flashed back to their first meeting in a hotel in Utah. They had become fast friends and Emma valued her insight greatly. God, she wished she could pick up the phone and call her cousin Michael. He always made her laugh. "Father," she cried out again. Sliding down, Emma curled up on the rug beside the bed. She remembered lying here one other night not long ago. That time too she remembered begging God for guidance for what was coming ahead.

Turning over onto her back, Emma stared up at the ceiling in her bedroom. She could hear the children's breathing as they slept, the faint whistling of breath as they dreamed their dreams. These sweet babies didn't deserve this. No one did. Someone out there had caused all of this chaos, probably to make a buck. So many lives had been changed, including hers. These children had now lost their mother. No matter the issues she had with Nina, the woman was still their mother. Who knows, maybe she wouldn't have ended up being like she was if none of this had happened. Stress changed people and not for the better normally. Her thoughts turned to her husband and how he had changed since this all happened. She always thought she would have him there to lean on, to pray with, and to hold at night. He was nothing more than a stranger at this point. How could you live with someone for so long and feel like you didn't even know them? Maybe it was the trauma, the strain from everything on his mind, but there was no way Emma was going to be comfortable with the direction her family was going to have to take when it came to putting him as the head of the household.

Emma jumped when she heard the pounding. "What the—?" she muttered under her breath.

Stretching, Emma realized she must have dozed off while she was praying. Sitting up and glancing over, Emma saw both children still asleep in her bed.

Maybe I was dreaming, she thought.

BAM.

"Nope, not dreaming, but I know where that came from," she said in exasperation.

Getting up, Emma silently exited the room and made her way downstairs to the room her husband was staying in.

Knocking lightly, she called out, "Tom?"

"Where the hell have you been? I could have starved!" he was saying as she opened the door and peeked in.

Sitting on the edge of his bed, Tom was looking at the door when she peered around the edge of it. Emma locked eyes with him just for an instant, the coldness holding her in his gaze.

"I'm sorry. I went to check on the kids, and I guess I fell asleep. I'll get you lunch now," she said, waiting for a response.

"Those fucking kids again? Really? Haven't they screwed up our lives enough already?"

Emma didn't want to hear anymore. She had had enough of his hostility since his accident to last her a lifetime. "I'll be back shortly," she stammered as she backed out of the room.

"Yeah, see if you can stay awake this time," he chimed out, loud enough to make sure she heard.

Emma let the words drift past her and down the hallway. They hurt, but she didn't need to accept the pain they could cause. Instead she asked God for an extra portion of grace to cover her heart and protect it. Walking down the hall to the kitchen, Emma paused as she remembered that night. It caught her every time she walked in here. Taking a deep breath, she walked over to the kitchen sink, grasping the edge with her hands and squeezing tight. "Father," she said.

Sometimes, especially lately, it was all she could say, her soul so twisted up inside her that she couldn't release the words she needed to find. But she knew he understood. Her God had been there with her whatever it was she was going through, guiding her, protecting her and sometimes just listening. Right now, she just needed a hug, and right now, He was all she had.

Lifting her head, she straightened her back. Feeling the strength supplied to her, Emma walked over to the refrigerator and began to pull items out and place them on the butcher block. Some good old BLT sandwiches made with homemade bread baked that morning, tomatoes grown in her own garden, bacon from her own pigs that had been smoked out back, and lettuce from the garden. The only think she needed was some mayo. Walking over, she pulled the oil from the pantry and returned to place it on the counter. Looking around, she realized she had left the eggs from this morning in the barn before all the commotion started. Making a mental note to grab them later, she walked over to the door leading to the fruit cellar in the basement. Placing her hand on the doorknob, she hesitated.

Why?

Taking a deep breath, she opened the door and went downstairs. Her gut was telling her something that she couldn't quite make out, but man, there was something definitely wrong here. Something waiting, watching, making the hair on the back of her neck stand on edge. Gathering some eggs and a couple of lemons, Emma quickly went back upstairs. Closing the door, she shuddered. Something, whether supernatural or not, was down there. Her spirit recognized it as not belonging. Where did it come from, and why was it here?

Emma walked over and grabbed a glass bowl. Her nerves still on edge, she busted a couple of eggshells into the bowl before her hands steadied themselves. Two egg yolks now smiled at her from the dish. The deep orange color made her thankful for her own chickens. Grabbing a whisk, she beat the yolks to get them blended. Taking the lemons to the sink, she gave them a quick roll across the counter as she pressed them downward to break up the insides a bit. Rinsing them under the cool tap, she gathered them into her apron. Turning back toward the table, she dried the lemons as she walked, not noticing until she was almost upon her work area that the rest of the eggs now lay on the floor, busted open.

"What in the world?" she murmured.

Again, that feeling of being watched overwhelmed her. Standing still, Emma took a deep breath and waited. "Lord, protect me," screamed in her head. Waiting, her senses attuned to every vibration of energy in the room.

"Emma!"

Breaking the silence, Tom's voice nearly caused Emma to faint. Grasping the back of the chair, Emma steadied herself.

"I'll be right there!" she yelled back with more emotion than she intended.

Slicing the lemon in half, she ended up cutting her finger a bit. The bright red blood mingled with the lemon juice, causing her to wince in pain. Tears filled her eyes. What would she give to make all of this chaos disappear? The thought bounced through her brain as images of happier times teased her relentlessly. Pausing, she straightened her back and took a deep breath. "I'm not for sale," she said out loud. Three teaspoons of lemon juice chased by two teaspoons of white wine vinegar made their way into the bowl of beaten egg yolks. Picking up the mason jar of homemade mustard, Emma removed the ring and lid with little effort with her new determination. One half a teaspoon later and she was putting a beating on the ingredients that would make Julia Child proud. Picking up the spoon, Emma began drizzling a quarter cup of the oil into the yolk mixture as she continued beating. Four minutes later she was ready for the rest of the oil. Gradually adding another half a cup of oil in a very slow stream, she continued whisking until the mayonnaise turned thick. Another eight minutes had gone by, and she felt her nerves returning to normal. Dipping her pinkie finger into the foamy concoction, she gave it a quick taste.

Salt, it needed salt.

Giving it a sprinkle, she whisked the homemade mayo lightly one last time.

Taking a plate, she slathered a thick slice of fresh bread with the mayo and laid it down. Several leaves of lettuce, a couple of slices of fresh, ripe tomato and a crisscross of bacon, she spread another slice of bread with mayo and laid it on top of the pile. Laying her hand on top of the sandwich, she gently stabilized the tower as she cut it in half. Grabbing a handful of homemade potato chips, she piled them between the two halves of the sandwich and moved the entire plate to the carrying tray. A napkin and glass of cold tea added, and Emma was off to deliver her bounty to the awaiting beast in the other room.

40

Nothing in the world smelled as bad as rotting flesh to Ridley. She had a strong gag reflex and had seen a lot of gruesome bodies in various forms of dismemberment, being a pre-med student, but rotting flesh always got to her. Unwrapping the bandage, the smell intensified with each section being removed. Her eyes started to mist up and her mouth started to salivate. Ridley was fighting not to vomit all over her patient.

How the hell am I supposed to be a doctor like this? she thought to herself.

"I'm so sorry! Can we open a window in here or something?" Ridley blurted out.

"Rid, you okay there, girl?" Shelby asked, looking at the paleness in Ridley's face. The worried look got Jeremiah's attention too, and he came around behind Ridley just in time as the girl passed out cold. Jeremiah was close enough to catch her under her arms and make for a smoother transition to the hard floor than Ridley just falling on her own.

"Did that just really happen?" Shelby asked with a giggle.

"Stop laughing. It's not funny," Jeremiah said, looking at his wife. The quick glance was enough to crack a smile on his face and send his wife into full-out giggles.

"Tell me that did not just happen?" Shelby begged.

Jeremiah looked down at Ridley lying at his feet. "Yep, 'fraid so."

"Okay, well, get the smelling salts out of her bag after you open the window, please!" Shelby chuckled.

Jeremiah walked over and propped the window open, letting clean cool air into the room. "Thank goodness there's a nice breeze going, or I would have to drag her outside!" Jeremiah said, now getting caught up in the hilarity of the situation. Walking over, he dug into the medicine chest and grabbed a small white cylinder. Stooping beside Ridley, he broke it in half and stuck it beneath the girl's nose.

"Ah, man, that smells!" the big burly man squelched.

"Suck it up, buttercup," Shelby said with laughter. "We gotta save the doctor!"

Jeremiah lost it. The huge brute of a man began to giggle in a high-pitched squeal. Before long Jeremiah and Shelby both were grabbing their midsections in pain as tears cascaded down their cheeks.

"Wha... What happened?" Ridley mouthed as she slowly started to come around. Fluttering her eyes open, she was a little taken aback that Jeremiah was kneeling over her with tears all over his face. As she propped herself up on her elbows, Jeremiah pushed her back a little.

"Slow down a bit. You took a bit of a fall." He snickered, causing Shelby to burst out laughing again.

"What is wrong with you both?" Ridley demanded.

"Honey, it's okay! You just passed out is all," Shelby said.

"Oh god, not again!" Ridley cried out.

"What do you mean, again?" Shelby asked.

Ridley sat up fully now and crossed her legs, resting her head in the palms of her hands and her elbows on her knees. "Oh my gawd, this is so embarrassing."

"Honey, it's okay! As long as you don't do it in the middle of surgery." Shelby tried to use a soothing voice, but it was upset by the hiccups she had now from laughing.

Ridley stood up slowly, walking over to stand in front of the open window. "They told me to visit the morgue. They said to put Vicks VapoRub under my nose so the smell wouldn't bother me, but I never did either. I know I have to acclimate myself to the smells of medicine, but I kinda skipped that part," Ridley explained timidly.

"Oh hell, I can fix that right quick!" Jeremiah chimed. "You can hang out with me down at the barn for a couple of days. Won't matter if you throw up all you want. Plus, if you pass out, you'll be falling into cow dung, so it won't hurt much."

Shelby bust out laughing. There was just no way to hold it in any longer. Trying to breathe, she ended up hyperventilating and lost her breath.

"Shelby, slow your breathing. Look at me." Ridley talked low and slow to get Shelby calmed. "Take your finger and close one nostril. Good, now breathe in your belly, not your lungs. Fill up your belly."

Shelby put a finger on her nose, closing one nostril, and concentrated on filling her belly with air. She calmed down enough to regain control. Returning her breathing to normal, Shelby held her arms out to hug the young woman sitting on the bed beside her.

"Oh, honey, I'm so glad you're here!" Shelby cooed. "Please don't think any different. You are a part of our family now."

Ridley sank into the woman's hug, feeling the pull of emotions redefining their relationship. Ridley wrapped her arms around Shelby and squeezed her back, returning the flow of energy.

"All right, girls, let's get a move on so my wife can get out of bed and make me a sandwich!" Jeremiah joked.

"Oh! No way you just said that!" Ridley squealed, turning around to slap Jeremiah on the arm.

The atmosphere in the room was joyous as Ridley begged Jeremiah to finish unwrapping his wife's leg and give it a quick wipe down while she waited outside the room. Back and forth the trio teased each other until Ridley finally walked back in the room from the hallway and ambled over to the bed. Shelby watched her face for any signs of concern while Ridley examined her leg.

"You doing okay, kiddo? You're being kinda quiet," Jeremiah asked.

"Yeah, yeah. Just thinking," Ridley replied.

"What's the verdict, Doc?" Shelby inquired.

"You have a long road ahead of you. Don't expect to heal overnight," Ridley explained.

"So I'm not going to lose my leg? Ridley, come on. I need to know what's going on here!"

"Oh, I never thought you were going to lose your leg, and you aren't, but you're not going to walk the same again either. You have extensive nerve damage, and the longer your leg stays swollen, well, the more of a chance for a blood clot or more damage. You really need to behave for a while, I mean it could take a good year until you're back up on your feet completely."

"A year?" Jeremiah repeated.

"Yes, a year."

Shelby felt the demon taunt her again. A year. Three hundred and sixty-five days of feeling useless? That was a long time to have to depend on someone else for the most basic of needs.

Shelby looked down at her hands lying in her lap. How was she going to be patient enough? How was she going to be worth something without taking care of all the others? What if they found someone to replace her with? This was her house. What if they brought someone else in to cook the meals for her family and to do their laundry while she just lay here in this bed?

Over and over the thoughts accumulated in her head, wearing on her heart. She had her leg, but to what capacity?

"Hey, you're going to be alright, okay?" Ridley cooed. "Relax!"

"I know, it's just... I guess I'll figure it out," Shelby replied.

"We will," Jeremiah chimed in.

Shelby looked at her husband, not quite meeting his eyes in agreement. Yes, they were a team, but a team takes two players, and Shelby felt like she was letting her half down.

41

Emma watched the sight from the kitchen window. It was hard to believe that the scene playing out before her harbored any effects of the last few months. Here were mommas sitting around a picnic table chatting while their small ones played in the yard around them. A sweet, rosy-cheeked baby boy was cooing beside his momma in a windup swing. Contentment was drifting along the swirls of wind that encircled and ensnared the tendrils of hair on the young babes running and chasing each other. Autumn was almost gone. They wouldn't have many more days outside to play this year.

Emma's stomach clinched at the thought of winter approaching. Autumn had always been her favorite time of year, but now it was like the grim reaper was knocking on the door, announcing that doom had arrived.

How many out there will not survive until spring? she thought as her eyes cascaded to the trees that ran along the edge of the far field, their leaves already showing a hint of transformation into the coldness of winter. There was no stopping mother nature.

Turning from the window, Emma grabbed the kettle from her woodstove and began filling it with water, her eyes once again falling on the ones she loved outside. She would fight for them with every breath she had. They were her loves, her reason for being. She had spent so much time giving them everything she could when they were babies, everything except her time. Dixon walked over to her, sensing her distress. Giving him a quick scratch behind his ear, she lifted his chin to look into his brown eyes. "We got this, boy," she whispered to him, a secret once again shared with her best friend.

"Damn," she swore as the water overflowed the kettle. While water was not in short supply, she knew every drop was valuable. And then there were the demons that had crept in to remind her of what she had sacrificed. What she had made her kids sacrifice growing up. How she wished she could go back and change things. To not miss the winter concerts because she had to be in a meeting. To be there when a heart was hurting and just hug them but couldn't because she was "the boss" and her time was required elsewhere. The fights between her and Tommy because, well, because he wanted something to be bought and it would mean more time away from their kids. The resentment because he wasn't stepping into his role.

Her eyes drifted to where her daughter, Lauren, was sitting. Her mind flashed back to when Lauren was three years old, sitting at Emma's desk at work, crying because all she wanted to do was go home. Emma felt her heart break at the memory. She wanted to go back and fix so many things, but she couldn't. All she had was the future and the ability to love them. Was it enough?

Emma set the kettle on the woodstove and took a deep breath. Her past was coming back to haunt her. She was under attack and recognized that all too familiar adversary. Taking a step back to the sink, she looked out the window at her family. "God, protect them."

A flood of love washed over her as her eyes fell on Lauren once more, sitting at the table, paper and pencil in hand, drawing. Her Lauren. Her mind drifted to the day when she was three once again. She remembered walking into her office to comfort her and giving her sheets of paper and pens and sitting for a moment and drawing with her. Was that the start of Lauren's obsession? Emma could not remember a time when the child was not drawing. She had saved quite a few of the scribbles on paper and would look at them from time to time. She'd had some of them bound and had given the book to Lauren when she graduated from high school. They had sat together, turning the pages in the book and laughing at the improvements she had made year after year. Emma knew she hurt though. But like her momma, she had taken the pain and put it to work to build her own little empire. She was one of the top graphic artists in the country with her own comic book line, well, until the grid went down. How would that play out now? How was that affecting Lauren, knowing that without the internet, her business was severely damaged? All of her life's work revolved around being able to connect with others.

Emma smiled as the thought started to evolve. She would have to make sure it was Lauren's idea, as her strong-willed child did not like to be told what to do, especially by her bossy mom, but Emma had an idea that might help Lauren continue to fuel her obsession but add a new leg to her business.

Hearing the rumble in her stomach, Emma decided that lunch outside was the way to go today. What better way to spend the day than surrounded by laughter from those you love!

"Emma!"

She heard his voice and instantly felt the guilt over her own happiness disappear.

"Be right there!" she replied as she began fixing Tomás a snack. The man needed his coffee and was less than pleasant until he got it, but Emma was not going to allow him to destroy the mood she had fought so hard already this morning to be in. Love was waiting for her outside, even if it did not live in her husband's heart anymore.

42

Ben knocked on the door and waited. He was risking a lot coming out here, but he needed to get this ball rolling and put the plan in play. Knocking again, he listened for any kind of movement in the house. Nothing. Jumping down off the front porch, he strode around the house to the back door and knocked louder. Peeking in the window on the door, he thought he saw someone coming towards him, so he knocked again.

"Hold on a minute!" he heard a man yell from inside the house.

Backing up a few steps, Ben slammed his fists into the front pockets of his jacket and waited for what seemed an eternity. The old wooden door creaked open slowly, teasing Ben inch by inch with a view inside the house.

Ben's face lost all color as the man standing before him remained quiet. Ben couldn't speak, stunned by what apparition revealed himself behind the door. Not even blinking, Ben was in a state of shock.

Finally breaking the silence, the man asked if he could help Ben.

"Uh, Tom?" the sheriff asked.

"Yeah, so I've been told. What do you want?" he grumbled.

"I was told your wife wanted to talk to me. Any idea where she is?" Ben asked.

"I think she took those damn kids over the hill to visit someone. I don't remember. I'm sure she'll be back later if you want to come back later," Tom said, nearly closing the door in Ben's face.

Perplexed, Ben stuck his arm up to keep the door from closing. "Tom? You don't know who I am?"

"Should I?"

"Well, I'm the local sheriff, Ben Olan. Maybe I should come in, and you can tell me what's been going on out here for you not to remember who I am. Emma asked for the doctor and it looks like he made it out here okay, for all the good he could do. Sorry it took me so long to get here but there's a lot going on in town. But, seriously, what the hell happened?"

Tom stared at the man, mentally turning over the options that lay before him. He could just tell the man to shut up and slam the door in his face, but since he said he was the local law, that probably wasn't the best choice. He could tell him that he needed to go back to bed and guilt the man into leaving, but Tom was sensing it would be good to have this man as an ally and not an enemy. Hell, he might be able to help Tom figure out exactly what did happen. Besides, he could use a beer and some company other than Emma.

Tom swung the door back open a bit and invited the man in. "You want a beer?" he asked the lawman, motioning him to get a seat at the kitchen table.

"Ugh, sure. I guess times have changed, so drinking a beer when the world's going to shit won't hurt much, aye?" Ben quipped as he looked around the kitchen.

Damn, Emma thought of everything, he thought as he looked at the tie-in to what obviously led to a battery bank somewhere downstairs.

Tom walked over to the refrigerator and pulled two beers out of the cold box. Putting them both on the table, he walked over and was trying to find the opener when Ben just popped the top with his hand. "Want me to take yours off?" Ben asked Tom.

Tom felt the warmth of embarrassment drifting up his neck as he stuttered back at Ben. "No. No, I, um... Sometimes these bottles break if you're not careful. Emma bought a different brand the last time she brewed a batch, but..." His mind drifted off as he realized he was remembering something from his past.

"Here, let me help you out, bub. You seem to have been going through a tough time here. What the hell happened to you anyways?" Ben asked nonchalantly, trying to fish as much information out of the man as he could. He needed to see what he remembered but not push him so hard it forces his memories to return.

"I don't know," Tom said, wrapping an arm around his rib cage.

"What do you mean you don't know? Weren't you there? You seem to be in a lot of pain."

"I mean I just don't know. I don't remember. All I know is my ribs hurt like hell."

"Damn, that must suck! No idea at all? No memory whatsoever?"

"Nothing."

"How far back can you remember anything?" Ben asked, intrigued.

"Well, I can tell you I don't remember my wife at all."

"Woah."

"Yeah. It's not been fun trying to live here with people who tell you they're your family, but you can't remember a damn thing about them."

"I bet," Ben replied, wanting to laugh a bit in relief. This was too perfect. "Anything I can do to help?"

"Yeah, get me out of here. These people are driving me crazy. And these little brats that Emma has staying here are driving me up a fucking wall."

Ben was taken aback by the comment. Here was a man who had treated Ben like a sworn enemy for years now begging him to relieve him of his pain and agony of living with his wife. Ben was trying to savor every bit of the conversation of a lifetime.

"You do know that the government has requested those kids be transported back to Washington, right?" Ben watched for Tom's reaction to his statement.

Nothing, no sign of recognition to anything that triggered a memory. "Take them," Tom replied.

"I seriously doubt if your wife would just let me take those kids out of here. We've never really seen things eye to eye," Ben said.

"I don't know why. You seem like a nice enough guy to me. Besides, aren't you the law? Shouldn't they be with their own family?" Tom asked.

"Yes, but your wife is tough to handle most days. You must really want those kids out of here if you're willing to risk pissing off Emma!" Ben exclaimed.

"Hell, take me out of here too. I'm about fed up with all of this. I'm not allowed to do a damn thing around here. I don't even remember these people."

"Are you serious? I'm getting paid to get those kids back home. We could always split that if you want to take a trip and blow some steam off for a bit. Probably save me a lot of hassle," Ben said.

"You'd pay me to take those kids home? How much?" Tom asked.

Judging from the expression on Tom's face, Ben knew this man had no clue what he was walking into. Chuckling to himself, Ben felt like he had just hit the lottery. "Well, probably a couple of thousand."

Tom's face lit up. This could be what he was looking for to escape this godforsaken place. "Let me think about this. You say you're the sheriff in town? How about I come in to see you in the next couple of days. Is that okay?"

"Sure. I'll be in my office, usually."

"How are we going to transport these kids to Washington? I can't exactly walk," Tom asked.

"I have a couple of military Jeeps that were gifted to me, being the law and all. I have to be able to get around. I'll be using one of those, or you will be if you decide to go."

"Sounds like a plan. Say, we don't need to tell anyone about this, right? I mean, if Emma is dead set against those kids leaving, she would probably be upset about our conversation. We should probably keep it between us boys, right?" The desperation in Tom's voice was apparent.

Ben stood to leave, slapping Tom on the back. "Sure, bub, sounds good. I'll see you in a few days, then?"

"Sure thing. Thanks for stopping by, Sheriff. Let me see you out before anyone gets back."

Tom watched the sheriff sputter down the driveway. A smile lit Tom's face as the wheels were spinning on escaping his own home. As Ben drove away, a smile illumined his face as he realized he had to be the luckiest son of a bitch on the planet right about now.

43

"Let's go to the back field so we won't bother anyone," Emma said as she started packing up all the equipment.

"You mean so we don't bother Testy Tom!" Tiffany shot back quicker than she expected to.

Emma gave her a sideways glance of disapproval.

"Sorry," Tiff whispered to everyone. "It's just, he's so uptight, and all we do is walk around on eggshells. I mean, what gives with his cranky-ass self?"

"Tiffany Louise!" Johnisse yelled at her girlfriend. "I mean, the man has been through hell and back. Give him a break! How would you be if you couldn't remember anyone after you had been left out in the rain and had all kinds of creepy, crawly, eight-legged, bug-eyed, hairy creatures crawling all over and into who knows what!" Johnisse had moved over and was standing behind Tiffany, leaf in hand as she reached up and teased the skin on the other woman's neck.

"Jay!" Tiff screamed. "That is not funny in the least little bit!"

"Ladies!" Emma used as much authority in her voice as she could muster to get their attention. She was not in the mood for fun and games. This was serious business and their lives could depend on it, and if they wanted to act like kids, then Emma wanted no part in it.

"Yes, ma'am," Tiffany said as she looked at Emma like she had just been called to the principal's office.

A snicker crossed Jay's face as she watched her old boss get control of the group.

Just like old times, she thought. Jay had never once seen Emma step over that line of dictatorship, that wasn't Emma's style. Instead, Emma won your loyalty by respect, a trait few bosses had these days. The woman didn't make you do anything she wouldn't do herself, including cleaning the public restroom to show her expectation of clean. She would show you once but then expected it to be kept that way, and the pride showed in her business, as they always scored high on cleanliness when under an inspection.

"Let's just get this stuff packed up and get the rest of the group and get out back so we can get started. I want to at least get through a few rounds before the sun starts to go down, and we need to get back here and get chores done. You ladies about ready?" Emma asked as she looked at the mess that Tiffany and Johnisse had made of the ammunition that was supposed to have been neatly packed in the wooden crate.

"I almost have all the clips ready to go," Tiffany replied without looking up.

Jay looked at her boss over the top of Tiffany's head and rolled her eyes. "Noobs!" she mouthed at Emma, who was about to open her mouth before she caught the twinkle in Jay's eye.

"Make sure you count all those clips, Tiffany. There will be a test question later," Jay added.

"Test?   No one said anything about a test!" Tiffany exclaimed as she continued to load her equipment into the box.

"Yes, there is a test." Emma chuckled. "First question is what is the difference between a clip and a magazine?"

It was a gorgeous day to be outside and having fun while learning something at the same time. Emma had a sneaky way of making that happen, learning while having fun. She used it to her advantage over the years not only on her kids but her employees in the corporate world also. She wasn't a "Here, do it this way because I said that's the way we do it" kinda teacher. Her skills were more involved for lifetime learning, as she wanted the student to understand the whys, the foundation of why you were expected to do something in a particular way. She found that, especially with female students, it was necessary to teach the building blocks so that they understood how all the moving parts played a part, and this was just as important when building a pizza or learning how to shoot a firearm. Today was no different. She had spent time sitting and reviewing each part of the tool they were about to shoot before they even laid hands on the firearm itself so that way, when they were ready, they could identify specific terms and match them to the action but also for the respect of the firearm itself. A lot of instructors liked to dive head-on into teaching someone how to shoot and neglected the fundamentals of learning.

Taking a step back, Emma observed the basic form each of her students had relaxed into during practice. She could then tweak their stance, head position or hands until their alignment with the target improved.

"Tiffany, are you ready? It's your turn!" Emma said as she looked around for her next student. Everyone looked around when there was no reply.

"Where's Tiff?" Jay asked to no one in particular.

"No idea. She was just here a bit ago," Jess replied.

"Hmmm. Jessica, watch the troops. I'm gonna go check the house and be back in a minute. Keep 'em busy," Emma said to her daughter-in-law as she took a gun case and emptied the contents and started repacking it with what she thought she might need shortly.

Emma started off back to the house, having a feeling she would find her student checking on something fictitious that absolutely needed her immediate undying attention. She saw the reservation in Tiffany's actions when it came to firearms. Something was there, hiding behind the curtains in the dark, that was hindering the woman's ability to relax and enjoy the teaching, and Emma was on a mission to find the demon.

Emma walked up over a small knoll that was situated right before the entrance to the chicken coop. As she ascended, she caught a glimpse of the woman's blouse going inside the enclosure. Slowing down, Emma circled back around and decided to try to head her off on the opposite side before she could exit the other side by the house. Damn if she wasn't feeling her age! She needed to get her troops up and out running the hills behind her house, if not for their benefit, for her own. With all the commotion lately going on, physical exercise was not a high priority on anyone's list, let alone hers, but now that things had started to calm down, it was time to get back out and get active. She didn't need a fancy gym out here, she had nature at its finest. There was nothing better than running straight uphill and conquering the fictitious enemy at the top, even if that enemy happened to be your own self and the lack of willingness to do it.

Emma made it around to the opposite side and was leaning against the fence, a little winded but waiting nonetheless for the woman to exit the pen.

"Tiff," Emma said in a low almost growl.

Completely caught off guard, the woman swirled around, dropping all of the objects she had so tentatively gathered from under her unwilling victims.

"DAMN IT, EMMA," Tiffany screamed as she tried to catch any eggs that she could before they splattered all over the ground between the two women.

"You want to explain to me what you're doing over here to begin with instead of out with all the others? You're supposed to be learning how to defend yourself!"

"I, um, remembered that we needed to get Mr. Tom's dinner started before he started doing all that yelling at you again," Tiffany tried to explain, using her best innocent look, fallen lashes and all.

"You let me worry about Mr. Tom's attitude, and you, my dear, better start worrying about pissing me off! Now, let's get back out with the girls. It's your turn to shoot," Emma said sternly.

"Emma, listen. I just..." Tiff started as she lost the words to explain what was going on in her head.

"I know. It's why I came after you."

"You know? Then why are you making me do this?" Tiffany asked.

"Because I know you, and I believe in you to overcome this fear you have. Listen, I don't know what happened to cause this, but I do know, without a doubt, that you can overcome this if you put your mind to it and if you trust me," Emma said gently.

"I don't know, I just don't know how," Tiffany said as she started to walk around Emma back towards the house.

Emma grabbed her arm to slow her down and swing her around to look at her face. "Listen, honey. I refuse to let you fail on this. I know it's hard, but I want to help. Seriously, Tiff," Emma said as she tilted Tiffany's face with the tips of her fingers. "Tiff, let me try."

"Yes, Miss Emma. Okay."

"Okay? Okay, let's do this. And we don't have to do it with all the others. Let's go off down by the pond. We can use some one-on-one time until you feel more comfortable, okay?"

Tiffany pinched one of her cheeks up to give a halfhearted approval of Emma's plan, but she went with it. She knew she wasn't going to get out of this. Once Emma latched on, it was all in.

Emma sashayed her hand out to show Tiffany in which direction she expected the woman to walk. Quietly they walked around and down the hill to the pond that the cows used when penned closer to the barn.

Setting the silver case down that she had been carrying, Emma unclasped the top and opened the two panels that kept the contents secure. Reaching inside, she pulled out the foam that was protecting the cargo that Emma had been lugging around.

"So tell me, Tiffany. Have you shot before?"

"Yes. Jay took me to a range a couple of times."

"And?"

"And what? I just didn't like it."

"Why? What didn't you like about it?"

"Everything."

"Listen, we can do this the easy way, or I can sit here and ask you every little question until I get the answers that I need. Spill it. What is everything? You didn't like the gun you used? The place smelled bad? You didn't like the decor? What is everything?" Emma asked.

"Well," Tiffany started as she began to relive the experience, "it was bad from the get-go. The men who were running the place acted like we didn't know what we were doing, so Jay kinda got a little ruffled and wasn't in the best of moods."

"I'm sure that didn't make for a fun experience for you."

"No. It was miserable after that. She was more worried about what those guys were saying about us than actually teaching me anything."

"What was she having you shoot?"

"Same thing she had. Her gun."

"That forty-five?! Are you kidding me? Well, that explains a lot!" Emma exclaimed. "Alright, girly girl. Take a deep breath. You have my undivided attention. No one here to see us, and I bet the place is a lot cleaner even though we are in the middle of a cow field."

At that, Tiffany busted out laughing. "You know us too well, girl. The bathroom in that place was absolutely disgusting! I know it's mostly guys, but come on now!"

Emma chuckled. "I had a feeling," she said, looking at her friend.

"Okay, let's do this, my girly girl!" Tiffany said, more relaxed now and much more confident. They took the next few minutes reviewing the components of the twenty-two that Emma was going to start her out on. Seven feet from the target and Tiff hit it dead-on.

"WOW! That's like shooting butter! I couldn't even feel it kick!" Tiff squealed in excitement.

"That's called muzzle flip, and if you have proper control of your firearm, it reduces that effect. Let's take a few steps back, and you are still going to aim for the same spot on the target. Now remember, part of this is to build muscle memory for when you can't think straight. So it's important that you practice the fundamentals each time."

Taking a couple giant steps back, Tiffany turned and gave Emma the biggest, happiest grin. Emma sighed. It was what this was all about. She was teaching firearms training, but she was also teaching confidence, and when it clicked in the student, there was no better high for Emma. They continued practicing until Tiffany was hitting dead on the target at twenty feet. Emma then walked Tiffany up the calibers, giving her the time to feel comfortable until she was as proficient with each until Emma reached in her case and pulled out the last one.

"This is it, girly girl. Last one," Emma said.

"That's a forty-five like Johnisse's?"

"Yes. Different brand, but this is a forty-five."

Emma handed the firearm to Tiffany and watched as the woman looked it over.

"Well, hello there," Tiffany said as she held the gun in her hand. "We are going to be good friends," she said as she turned the firearm over and looked her up and down, learning her curves. Tiffany ran her thumb over the engraved letters at the bottom of the grip. "X-O-M?"

"X-D-m," Emma corrected. "This is a Springfield XDm. The company that manufactured it is Springfield. The XD stands for X-Treme Duty, the M is for the match-grade barrel and match-grade trigger. Polymer frame with a striker fire, it's pretty lightweight at about thirty-one ounces without the magazine. It's one sweet little firearm. Here," Emma said as she handed Tiffany a magazine with one cartridge in it. "Same drill, okay? Keep your thumbs up, and I don't want you to use your sights. Feel this baby. Feel it all the way to the target."

"Yes ma'am," Tiffany replied as she lined herself up. Taking a deep breath in, she slowly started to release it as she pointed her thumbs at the target, and just as she was ready, she held her breath and pressed the trigger straight back with the pad of her index finger.

The blast from the firearm ricocheted up and into Tiffany's wrist; then her arm and shoulder absorbed the blast just as it should. There was very little muzzle flip as the projectile left the barrel, hitting its target dead-on. The smile that crept across the woman's face showed the success.

"Y'all may wanna start action right, posthaste. I just shot a forty-five and hit the fricken target!" she squealed. "Again, correctly and, like, textbook beautiful! To be clear, call your momma and get right with Jesus. Give me a couple more of those cartridges, and don't say I didn't warn you! Your badass has arrived."

44

Both the curtains and the blinds were closed against the brightness of the sun. Tomás lay on the bed with his arm haphazardly thrown across his eyes. His head was throbbing. He was damned if he could get any rest around this place, but he had to stay on his plan. Once the right time hit, he would be gone along with a few things that would help him get set up in his new life. He had been lifting supplies quietly for a few days now and stashing them in one of the cabins while he was out on his daily walk. Even if someone visited the cabin, he had hidden the items well. So far he had handheld radios, medication and a water filtration system. He still needed some firepower and ammo, but Emma would notice something missing if he collected those items too soon. He would need to wait until right before his escape before he took the guns.

Gold. He still needed to get the gold. He knew it was here somewhere, if he could just remember where! Emma always talked about how currency would change after a collapse, or so she thought it would. Tomás had often wondered if she had an ulterior motive but couldn't figure out what it could be. Was it control over him? He could still take it and spend it and easier now that it fit into his pocket as opposed to another of her damn solar panels. So far they hadn't needed to make any purchases with the amount of forethought that had gone into setting up the farm, so there was still quite a bit in the vault. The vault! The damn vault!

About fricken time you start remembering!

The problem was a small one but still posed an issue nonetheless. The vault was hidden behind a closet in Emma's bedroom. He needed to get access back in there without sending up red flags, and with him sleeping downstairs, that was a small issue. Could he stomach making Emma believe he was ready to move back into the bedroom he supposedly shared with his wife prior to all this shit going down? Probably, as she was gullible as hell when it came to her feelings towards him. He watched her even now, walking on glass every time she was around him, her heart dripping out of her chest.

Oh, poor me. Poor little Emma who has a husband who can't remember her awesomeness. What is she to do, the poor helpless excuse for a human. The Queen Bee of her kingdom is going to crash and burn if I have anything to do with it.

Hell, he didn't even see it as half his anymore. Emma owned everything. It was all hers. All the hard work was hers also. He just rode her coattails, just along for the ride.

She owed him for all the years that he'd kept his mouth shut. All the years that she made him feel less than a man, less than a human. Emma this and Emma that.

Fury flung his arm from his eyes and onto the pillows beside his head. Over and over he picked up his arm and beat the bed beside him, trying to release the frustration building up inside. It was becoming uncontrollable. He felt the anger creep over his face and down his neck, heat turning his skin red beneath his otherwise olive-hued casing.

Jumping up off the bed, Tomás walked around to the bathroom. Leaving the door open, he turned the cool water on that flowed into the sink. He watched it swirl into the drain for a few moments. Captivating his attention, he didn't hear a soft knock at the door. Reaching his hands down into the cool water, he cupped his hands and gathered as much liquid as he could before splashing it on his burning skin. Over and over he covered his face and neck until he could feel the nerve endings returning to normal. His eyes closed, he reached out and grasped for the hand towel that he knew would be there. The agitation returned as the demons in his mind taunted him on who made sure the hand towels were perfectly placed. Emma.

Slamming his towel-clad hands against his face, he tried to stop the thoughts of her.

Damn her.

Throwing the towel on the floor, he walked abruptly back into the bedroom.

"What the hell!" he shouted.

"I knocked. You didn't answer, so I thought you were out. I came in to clean up a bit," Emma said, her eyes drifting to the towel he had just thrown down.

The fury in his face startled Emma. Walking past him, she was going to straighten the bed a bit before she tried to talk with him about the next few days. She needed to leave for a few days and go check on some family scattered around the county. Two days max was all she needed, and Tomás could take care of himself now fairly well, but she had things taken care of to make her time away easier for him.

Something made Emma pause in front of Tomás and turn towards him, face-to-face. His pupils, clouding over, made her blink.

Did she just imagine that?

She blinked again.

"Tommy?"

"What?"

"I, um, I'm leaving for a few days. Will you need anything before I go?" she stammered.

"Where the hell do you think you're going?"

"I, um... I just wanted to go check on—"

"What the hell, Emma! Other people are more important than taking care of your own husband?" He was screaming at her now.

Emma took a step back. "I just thought—"

"That's your problem, you been thinking again. I need clean towels. My sheets need washing." He started his list of demands, his arms and hands flailing with each command.

"Now wait a minute, Tom, I'm not here to be your slave! I will gladly take care of you, but don't demand from me what I'm currently giving willingly!"

"Are you sassing me?"

Perplexed, Emma bent down to remove the dust cover from the bed.

"Emma, I asked you a question, and I demand an answer!" he screamed.

"I'm not quite sure who you think you're talking—" Her voice cut off as the palm of Tom's hand made contact with her cheek.

Out of habit, Emma brought both forearms up to protect herself. Backing away, she braced herself for more violence from the man she loved.

Emma swallowed the lump in her throat. She wasn't about to let him see her cry. They stood staring at each other for what seemed like eternity.

"You need to leave," Tom seethed from between his teeth.

Emma backed to the door, not taking her eyes off the person before her. Reaching her hand around her back, she opened the door without turning around. Backing out, she closed the door quietly in front of her, releasing the handle like it was ablaze. She couldn't bring herself to turn her back on the door. Reaching up, she laid her palm on the wooden crossbeam as the tears started to flow. Closing her eyes briefly, she exhaled and backed down the hallway.

A line had been crossed that could no longer be denied. Boundaries were broken, but could they be repaired? Trust was destroyed in the blink of an eye. People change whether intentional or not. Denial of someone's true nature does not change them, it changes you. The rules change after a traumatic event. Play the game or get played. How far will you bend in the wind to save someone you love? Will you allow it to destroy you? When do you sever the ties that bind? Vows made and love promised will not keep evil at bay. Demons stalk our innermost playground, waiting for the chance to jump on in and tell us lies. Some souls cannot break free from their taunting. Some souls begin to sing the same song...

45

"What's all this?" Scott said as he walked around the table, looking at the scraps of metal and plastic that had obviously met an unfriendly end.

"Well, I wasn't sure when to bring this up, considering Shelby's surgery and all, but I would like your thoughts on some things."

"Okay, well, I'll give you whatever thoughts I have, but I don't need to tell you that this Tinkertoy was blown apart," Scott replied.

Pulling up a chair, Jeremiah motioned for Scott to take a seat. "Here ya go. Let me bring you up to speed on this."

"Sure! I seem to have all the time in the world lately," Scott replied with a partial grin.

"As you know, I wanted some answers to what exactly happened out there," he said, pointing with a flip of his thumb towards the outside. "So I had Ridley and Angie keep Shelby busy for a bit and headed down towards Memphis. Seems to me that was ground zero for the blast I saw."

"I agree. When Ang and I were trying to get back to Ohio from Memphis, that blast was somewhere at our back. We didn't see it straight up, but we certainly felt the repercussions!" Scott explained.

"You all were damn lucky," Jeremiah said to the man sitting across from him.

"You don't think I think about that? One more day, hell, twelve more hours and neither of us would be here right now. I saw nothing unusual when we were cleaning out her apartment, so I have no idea what the hell happened," Scott added.

"My uncle Noah lives about thirty-five miles outside Memphis. He said that rumor is the city was destroyed. I think 'flattened' was the term he used," Jeremiah said, using air quotes.

"Jesus..." Scott replied, trailing off.

"Yes, well, like I said. You were lucky."

"What's that got to do with this heap of crap?" Scott asked, motioning to the fragments on the table.

"My uncle found this on his farm," Jeremiah stated.

"Yeah, well," Scott said as he started to pick the pieces up and examine them. One in particular caught his attention. Long and black like a spider's leg, Scott flipped it over, looking at the wiring hanging from its sheared end. "Could it have been one of those drones they use to look for marijuana in the outlying fields?"

"Could have been, but I don't think so."

"Why not? They use them all the time out in places like this."

"Well, because three have now been found after the blast, all pretty much blown apart."

"Yeah, so? Maybe they got caught in the blast like everything else around there?"

"Uncle Noah said that a blue light like a spotlight was seen prior to the blast, all within the same general areas that these things came down."

"These things were looking for something? I'm not following," Scott asked.

"Here, look at this," Jeremiah said as he pulled a shard from under the blanket the pieces were lying on.

Scott reached out and grabbed the fragment from Jeremiah. Turning it over, he ran his thumb over the etching on the side. "Have I seen this before?" Scott asked himself, perplexed, as the emblem looked familiar.

"Flip that over, Scott. What do you think that means?" Jeremiah asked Scott.

"What, these letters? U-A-V," Scott read out loud as he felt the letters under his thumb. "That's easy enough. My guess is it's just a UAV, an unmanned aerial vehicle. Just a fancy name for a drone. Our government likes to tack on fancy names when they're trying to cover up the obvious. You ain't figured that out by now? That's not surprising looking at all these pieces and parts. My question is what was it doing, and what does DEW stand for?"

"I've been wondering that myself," Jeremiah said with a sigh.

"Hey, boys, whatcha doin?" Ridley asked as she walked into the room. Startled, both guys looked like they had been caught doing something their mother wouldn't approve of.

"Nothin, kiddo," Scott said as Ridley walked around the table, eyeing all the remnants of the machine.

"Kiddo? I just performed miracle surgery and you want to still call me kiddo? Besides, this is fascinating! Where did you find this, and why is something from Lockheed Martin all over your dining room table?" Ridley asked.

Jeremiah looked at Scott, who was already looking at Jeremiah. Unspoken words passed between the two men. How in the world this little girl saved Shelby's leg already left them with much respect for her, whether they wanted to give her the affirmation or not, but to be able to help unlock a piece of a puzzle that had left both men with a million questions was difficult for their testosterone levels to handle.

"Uh, Rid, you want to sit down for a bit and tell us how you know this is from Lockheed Martin, one of the largest defense contractors our government has?" Scott demanded.

"Am I in trouble somehow?" Ridley asked, confused.

"No, not at all!" Jeremiah was quick to explain. "Goodness no, but how do you know where this is from? I thought you were in medical school?"

"Oh! Yes, but Lock does more than just design military stuff. We use a lot of their equipment in the medical field, especially where lasers are involved," Ridley explained.

Scott took a deep breath in as he raised his hands above his head, locking his fingers and resting them on top of his skull. "Lasers, aye?"

"Any idea what DEW stands for?" Jeremiah asked Ridley.

"I can tell you what DEI stands for. Our equipment had the same emblem, here." She pointed at the half blue star on the side of the piece Scott had in front of him now. "Our equipment with that star all was manufactured by Lockheed. Our DEI stood for directed energy instrument, but I have no idea what DEW would be... directed energy... I just don't know."

"Weapon?" Scott shot back at her. Silence hung in the air like the fog on the first cold October morning. Looking at the mess on the table, Ridley threw the fragment with the emblem back on the table and started to gather the blanket at each end.

"What are you doing?" Scott asked.

"We need to get this out of here. There could be residual diffractions coming off this thing!"

"What the hell does that mean?" Scott, now shouting at Ridley, started to help her gather the blanket.

"The instruments we used had the ability to manipulate the energy, to divaricate it for a prolonged treatment within the body. If this thing is in any way a bigger version of that, a weapon like you said, there could be fallout even a month or more outside of its normal operation."

46

Tom glanced around town like he had never been there before. He needed to find the supplies on his list and find the sheriff, but he had not the first clue where to start looking. As he guided the mare down the main road, he caught sight of a dive of a bar that looked familiar. Tying the nag onto a small bush outside, Tom entered the dimly lit room. The only light came from the filthy windows, and Tom squinted as he tried to make out if anyone he knew was inside.

"*Anciano!* Why are you here?" A female voice broke the stale fermentation of air.

"*Hola*," Tom replied. "I'm looking for some supplies. Could you help?"

"*Qué es esta lista?*" she asked.

"Just some things I need back at my farm. Is there anyone here who could help me?"

"*Loco*, go find sheriff. He will help you." She laughed as she turned away from him and sauntered back across the floor. "*Vete*."

Tom glanced into the back room where she entered. Several grungy-looking men were standing around a pool table, laughing. The woman walked over to one of them and tossed her head back towards Tom. The man glanced back over his shoulder in the direction she indicated, the smile quickly disappearing from his face. Laying the cue down on the table, he walked towards Tom.

Tom's eyes tightened as something within him recognized the man approaching. Realizing he was holding his breath, Tom stammered a bit to try to conceal his nervousness.

"I understand you're looking for supplies?" Ben asked, giving Tom a wink.

"Yes, so you're the sheriff, then? Here?" Tom said, looking around the shit hole of a bar.

Ben cocked his head with a twist. *Am I the sheriff? What game is he playing?*

Ben decided to humor the man and play along. "Why yes, I am the sheriff in these parts. I know everyone and everything that goes on around here. Even what goes on out at your farm," Ben said, extending his hand.

"I guess you were serious the other day, then," Tomás replied with a grin.

"Well, come on in, then, have a drink! Let's see what's on your list," Ben quipped. "You like some homemade beer that ole Jim back here has shared with us?"

"Um, sure," Tom responded as he was shoved into the back room. Tom looked around at the room he had just entered. A pool table took up most of the room. Several bar stools lined two walls, with a couple of tall tables thrown haphazardly between them. Half-empty bottles and overflowing ashtrays littered the tabletops.

Tom gasped when he saw the two girls in the corner. Not much more than fourteen or fifteen, the girls were chained to the base of one of the tables.

"See anything you *NEED*?" Ben sneered.

"I, uh, I think I came to the wrong place," Tom stuttered as he turned to leave the room. One of the men lurking in the shadows had anticipated Tom's hasty exit and quickly blocked his path. Tom took a couple of steps back, staring at the guy.

"No. Actually, you came to the exact damn place you wanted to, now didn't you, Tom?"

Tom whipped his head around as a flash of memory came back. Ben understood the recognition on Tom's face.

"Damn, you do remember me after all. My feelings were about to be hurt, but I can see you're starting to recall our times of yore!" Putting an arm around Tom's shoulder, Ben turned Tom around to face the girls.

"Everyone, this is my good friend Tomás Montalvo. Tomás, meet your next of kin. Here, Tom, pull up a chair, we have a lot to talk about."

"What's the price?"

"Two thousand for the girl. Five hundred for the boy."

"Wow, that's a big difference!" Tom exclaimed.

"Their uses vary greatly. The girl will be sold, probably to a certain gentleman with particular tastes. She will be moved overseas. The boy, aye. If he survives, he will probably end up joining the revolution. There is not much need for him other than to carry a gun and fight. The girl, on the other hand," he replied with hand gestures emulating a sexual act.

What did Tom care what happened to them after they left? These kids had screwed up his life enough. They were of no use to him other than mouths to feed. He could use the cash, though, and add it to what he had stashed away. It would help greatly in his getting the hell away from Emma. A little bit more and he would be able to leave without looking back.

"Let me think about it. The prices seem low," Tom said as he scuffed his boot on the dirt floor.

"I assure you, *amigo*, I pay you the top price with no strings. Quiet and simple and I disappear."

Tom nodded his head quickly up and down. "Yeah, okay," he muttered.

"We have a deal?" the man asked, excitedly grasping for Tom's hand.

"Yeah, yeah. We have a deal. Just give me some time to work out the details," Tom replied.

Tom walked out of the seedy little bar, his eyes squinting as the sun hit his pupils full on. Lifting his hand, he shielded his eyes. Glancing around to see if anyone saw him, he quickly walked up the street towards the sheriff's office.

A bead of perspiration broke out across Tom's brow. Shrugging off his jacket, he swung it up over his shoulder as he walked.

He could do this. How hard could it really be? These kids weren't his. All they did was remind him of, well... he wasn't sure what they reminded him of, it was more of a feeling they gave him when they looked at him. Like they were blaming him for something. Something he couldn't put his finger on.

Stepping off the curb, Tom automatically looked for traffic. Chuckling to himself, he figured it would be years before things got back to normal around here. A couple of years before anyone would come looking for him, as he saw it. He anticipated his wife would search for him at least, which was why it was important for him to get a head start. He figured he could make it to Florida before anyone would really realize what had happened, and by then it would be too late.

47

Picking up the clothes that had been tossed on the floor, Emma dumped them into the middle of the bed. Grabbing the closest corner of the fitted sheet, she tugged it loose from its captivity and walked to the next corner until there was a mass of soiled clothes, blankets and sheets piled into its own cocoon. Lifting the bundle, she deposited it near the door. Gathering the neatly folded ensemble of freshly washed bedclothes off the chair, she walked back to the bed and flipped the contents out of the pillowcase as she fondly remembered where she had learned how to fold sheets like an expert.

Karen had lived across from the farm that Emma had grown up on. Roughly the same age, with Karen being only a year older, they had spent many summer days at each other's houses, hanging out and doing chores together. Emma's way of folding sheets prior to watching Karen was just wadding it up into a ball and stuffing it in a drawer. After Karen, all that had changed. Neatly folded, each set of laundered bed ware would get tucked into its own pillowcase, making it so simple to find pieces and parts when it was time to change the bedding.

Fitting the corner of the sheet over the mattress, Emma walked back around to the other side. How much longer would she be making this bed for her husband to sleep in? When would he come back to their bed instead of sleeping here in this room by himself? Deep in thought, Emma wrapped each corner and tucked it under the mattress. Swiping her hand across the top of the sheet to smooth it out, she reached out and grabbed the flat sheet and shot it free from its folds over the top of the bed. Watching as it fluttered down almost perfectly into place, Emma decided maybe it was time to move her husband back upstairs. He was getting around just fine, including taking off on several adventures to who knows where, leaving Emma slightly apprehensive, but she knew she had to relax. He was a grown man, and even though she was worried about his health after his accident, she knew he needed some space. She was actually hoping it might chill him out.

So many mixed emotions were making Emma sick to her stomach. Tom had changed since the accident. He wasn't the Tommy that she had been married to for the last thirty years. While she could see hints of his old personality, there was an essence about him that she didn't particularly care for. Hitting her across the face was something new that she still needed to deal with. Her Tommy had never raised a hand against her. This new personality, this Tomás was someone she had not met yet. It seemed to be the easiest way for her mind to wrap itself around what was happening between them. Tommy was her husband. Tomás was this new intrusion into their lives. The question being, who exactly was he, and how long was he going to stay?

Sitting down on the edge of the bed, Emma looked down at her hands now resting in her lap. Tears taunted her as she felt helpless to understand what to do next. She wanted nothing more than her husband back, but she knew that was near impossible. She needed to grieve. She wanted to run as far and as fast as she could and forget that any of this happened, but she knew running wouldn't change reality. It would just put off the inevitable for a bit.

Giving a halfhearted chuckle, Emma thought how different life would be if the catastrophe hadn't happened. If they were still living back in Indianapolis, Emma would just jump in her Jeep and go for a long drive. She would have sought the advice of people she trusted, and she would probably have gone onto the internet and done tons of research on Tommy's condition. Now though, with very limited resources, she was at a loss. Hell, it felt like the walls were closing in on her on some days. How much longer would she be able to tolerate her husband's behavior? How much worse would he get? Then what? Throw him out? Make him leave? Then he would be out there, and she would have no idea where he was or what he was up to. That old saying crept through her mind like a slimy snake: Keep your friends close but keep your enemies closer. Was that what Tommy was becoming, her enemy? Chills ran through her at the thought of losing him again. She needed to get out of here, and fast.

48

Picking up her head, Emma looked back at the house that was now quite a distance across the dead field. She couldn't wait for spring with the rebirth of everything around her. Would her life return to normal? Slowly closing her eyes, she breathed in the still-chilled air. If only she could forget the past few months. If only there were some way she could click her heels and make everything rewind. Breathing forcefully outward, she knew the truth. Looking down, she kicked the hard dirt beneath her boot. No way in hell would life ever be the same.

"I need a plan, God," she muttered into the faint breeze. "I've no idea what to do, where to go, or how to get all these people there safely. All I know is I need some direction."

Lifting her face towards the heavens, she waited for an answer. The sun teased faint warmth against her skin, fleeing as a still chill in the air chased it away. A faint smile curled at the corner of her mouth as she turned, half expecting God to shout down His instructions to her. What a relationship they had built over the years. It was a connection that she relied heavily upon to keep her sane. He listened when she screamed, He held her tears when she cried, and He laughed when she laughed. What better friend to have was there? She could almost sense at times a face palm or two going on, but all in all, she knew she was loved.

Walking the rest of the way over to where the field ended, she turned left and headed to the back corner of the field. She needed some alone time, just to think and breathe, and there was no better place to accomplish that than deep in her woods. She had seen a lot of these trees grow into adulthood over the years, some etched with her initials now distanced in their bark way above her head. She had skipped school a few times here, hidden amongst the outstretched branches like arms enveloping a child, offering protection. She had cried here, baring her soul to the moss covering the rocks and to the mayapples standing in attendance, offering an ear. She had grown to love all the families that roamed these hills, hidden among the forest's surreptitious milieu. There was a feisty bunch of chatty squirrels who resided in the big oak tree that stood by the big rock halfway up the main hill. An army of bullfrogs, green and bumpy, serenaded her if she were out there at dusk, singing songs of long-lost love and such, and resided down at the edge of the creek that ran through her property. Emma had few that she included in her tribe, but here, deep within the folds of her land, she was home. The trees, the animals all spoke to her better than humans could most of the time.

Today she walked with a purpose. She needed peace. No chaos or noise, but a gentle whispering of tranquility to her soul. She had almost made it out of sight of the house when she caught the white ball of fur bounding across the countryside in her direction.

How could I leave him behind? She chuckled to herself.

Waiting as her devoted accomplice caught up to her, she watched as he tore through the wind like a white sail on the waters with a hurricane chasing it. A beast of a dog, she'd had the pleasure of having him in her life since he was a pup. Her mind lapsed back to the day she'd arrived at the farm to purchase two goats. She had just gotten out of her truck to walk up to the house when she was accosted by a horde of dogs, big and small. What resembled a family unit was now swirling around her with much excitement as their owners, catching wind of the commotion, were walking up from the barn to meet their visitor.

"Looks like you have a friend there," the woman said, looking down at Emma's feet. Sitting there beside Emma's leg was a cherub of a pup, all white and fluffy like cotton balls stuck on a whelp.

Emma glanced down and met the clearest brown eyes she had ever seen. "Oh my!" she exclaimed as her heart melted.

Raising her head quickly, she looked at her host, her eyes large with determination. "I just came after a couple of goats!"

Laughing, the man of the farm turned to walk back down to the barn. "Come on then, let's just see if you can take two goats home."

As Emma walked, the little glob of fluffiness stayed with her, stride for stride. Arriving at the barn, Emma paused inside the door to let her eyes adjust, and the pup sat down and waited right beside her. The man of the farm watched the two move in unison. "Just two goats, aye?" he said.

Emma let out a sigh. "Yes, two goats," she replied as she stepped forward, the pup following. Stooping down, Emma couldn't ignore him any longer. Scooping him up, she raised him to her chest and was overwhelmed with laughter as his little whippet of a tongue began to ravage her face.

"These goats will need a protector," the man of the farm started to explain, watching the bonding between woman and canine. "So will you."

"Yes, yes!" Emma shrilled, not paying attention to the words of the man. All she knew was that there was no way she could leave without this little guy.

Finally getting her attention, the man of the farm explained to Emma that the price of the goats had gone up a bit. Emma tilted her head in confusion. "I just talked to you this morning before I headed out here. How could you raise the price on the way?" She now sounded annoyed.

"Don't worry, we'll throw in a free puppy of your choice, of course." The man chuckled.

Emma laughed. "Oh, I see what you did right there. Okay, you've got a deal."

His tongue now dangling from the side of his mouth, Dixon had almost made it to her when Emma turned to continue her journey across the field. Today would just be about decompressing all the excitement over the last few months, and with Dixon by her side, she knew she was in good hands.

The two companions disappeared into the darkness of the woodland as the man let the curtain fall back into place. He had watched the hideous display of affection between woman and beast as his lip snarled around the emotions that made his stomach uneasy. He had work to do before they returned, and he needed to shake off any further doubt on his objective.

49

Emma took the path around her property backwards on this trip. She would end up at the cabins last, but for now she wanted to check out the bottom and wind her way up to check on Big Bertha, her eighty-foot-high antennae that Emma had built in a grove of trees on the highest hill she owned. The tower was well secluded and not currently in use, so she sat barren. Down over the hill and along the creek that ran the length of the property was a cave that Emma had painfully dug out with her family to stash a lot of the electrical components.

Secure underground, Emma thought it best in case of any type of EMP episode, whether manmade or from a natural phenomenon. At this point, it was hard to know which would come first. While she knew they were approaching a solar minimum thanks to her friend Annette, she had also been aware of how the North Koreans were making the rest of the world nervous with their childish behavior. Throw in an election that was supposed to happen this year here in the United States, and it all seemed like a recipe for disaster.

Walking up the narrow path to the top of the hill, Emma paused to watch a covey of grouse as they scurried along looking for something to eat. It was so peaceful up here away from the rest of the world. The short ticklegrasses swayed against the breeze and made feasting easier for the ruffled chorus. Watching the medium-sized birds make their way across the path, Emma held Dixon on command so as not to disturb the group. They were native here and would be a valuable asset in rebuilding what man was about to destroy. If her hunches were right, what the world below her was fast becoming was not a pretty sight. Right now though, she wanted to protect as much as she could of her own piece of it.

Walking farther up the path, Emma bent and picked up one of the white tail feathers from her meandering friends. Tucking it into a quick braid in her hair, Emma felt the pull of her Apache heritage becoming stronger. This was her true home, out here among the trees and where she felt the most at peace.

Mattie Bear, or more commonly known as Harriet after she came east, was Emma's great-great-grandmother. An Apache squaw, she was removed from her home in Arizona and brought across the Mississippi, settling in the Ohio valley. As the family lore was told, she was bought as part of a trade, for what exactly was never known, but she gave root to some very strong women who walked the same lands she had as a young woman. Today, her great-great-granddaughter stood on top of the same hills, her long hair being caught in the wisps of wind as the white feather danced along to the drumbeats of nature.

The sun was sinking below a far hill as the gray pallor of dusk began to settle on her land. Emma found a half-exposed rock and sat, patiently awaiting the finale of the day. Her two favorite times of the day were when the sun made her grand appearance and when she curtsied for the final curtain call of the day. She stroked the white wiry hair of her chaperon as they shared the quiet of dusk.

Once the yellow orb was engulfed behind the far ridge, Emma stood and stretched her legs.

"Dix, let's get to the cabin and get a fire lit. It's getting a bit chilly for these bones," Emma said as she slowly surveyed the hills before her. Turning slightly to the right, she caught a glimpse of light. Something that she had not seen for a while. With the grid in the area down, it was an anomaly that made Emma's stomach twist. She even made sure her family did not power the generators after dark and made sure the curtains were pulled, as she did not want any unwelcome visitors to the farm. But this light was different. Dropping her pack, she removed her monocle from the front flap and peered through the device.

FIRE!

It wasn't a manmade light but a fire. Looking around, she realized the flames were coming from the chimney of her son's house. Bending, she unclipped the handheld radio from her pack and scrolled her thumb up to turn it on. Selecting the channel her family used for emergencies, she was going to try against everything to get through.

He must have a chimney fire and probably doesn't even realize it yet, Emma thought.

"DIXON!" she yelled as she started to run towards her son's part of the farm. "Come," she said as she dropped her pack again, taking a small notepad and marker out of the pocket. Writing on the note as fast as she could, she tucked it into Dixon's carry bag. Standing, Emma pointed to Kevin's house and firmly commanded the dog, "Dixon, go to Kevin."

Then she prayed against everything she had that he was at the house as she took off running.

Halfway down the hill, Emma's foot twisted sideways, causing her ankle to jackknife inside her boot. Pain shot up her leg, causing her to stumble headfirst down the rocky decline. Rolling herself over while grasping her knee, Emma braced for the inevitable.

I can't break my ankle now!

The searing agony burned up her leg and made her roll to her side and eject the contents of her dinner onto the dusty earth. Wiping her mouth on the back of her hand, Emma was losing time. Horrible visions danced through her mind of her son and his family caught in the burning house, unable to leave. She could hear her grandkids' laughter from last Christmas as the twins, Jack and Jamie, ripped open their gifts, their little cheeks as red as cherries from all the excitement of the day.

Rolling back over, Emma sat up, grasping her ankle in her hands. She had to get down the hill. The darkness, now not her friend, made the trip damn near impossible. She kept praying that Dixon found Kevin in time.

The pain starting to subside, Emma knew taking her boot off was out of the question, but she needed to see if she had broken it. Wiggling her toes first, Emma felt the pain increase but was relieved to be able to feel movement. Slowly, she tested the ankle itself. It moved! A bad sprain she could work with right now. A bone protruding out of the skin of her ankle would cause an entirely new set of issues. Grabbing the bandana she was wearing, she wrapped it as tight as she could around the outside of her boot. Skootching backwards, she backed up against a small tree. Using it for balance, she pulled herself to a standing position. Tears now streaming down her face, she gingerly set the foot on the ground and pushed a small bit. Spasms tore into her calf and shin, but she waited. The pain subsided enough that she put more weight on it. Slowly, she hopped to the next tree, then the next.

It took Emma nearly two hours to get down the hill and to her son's house, which was normally a twenty-minute brisk walk. She could smell the smoke halfway down the hill and knew it wasn't a good sign. Clearing the edge of the forest, she stood in awe at the sight before her, the heat from the fire lapping at her face, Kevin's house now all but ashes. Beams that he had hand milled on the farm were now crisscrossed within the debris, having fallen from their original positions holding the roof up. Flames whipped around like dancehall girls in various hot spots amid the now blackened rubble that once sheltered her son's family.

Emma was afraid to look any longer, afraid of what she might see.

"Kevin!" she shouted. *God, please let him answer!*

Nothing.

"Jessica! Where are you?" she shouted again, the fervor of her pitch increasing. "Jack! Jamie! Where are you?" she wailed as she collapsed, tears quenching the hot skin as they sparkled against the swirling flames. There was no sound other than the crackle against the darkness.

Oh my god, Dixon! Where is he? He should have been here by now!

She sat there in silence, afraid to move. Afraid to disturb the quiet that had possibly consumed her loved ones.

Please, God, no... She whimpered, her eyes shielded from the sight. If they were in there, there was no way anyone survived. Looking around, she needed to get back to her own home. There was nothing left to do here but mourn, and she needed to get the others. Standing, she felt the rush of blood into her foot. Stepping down, her leg gave way since the adrenaline rush was over.

How am I going to get back home?

She stood off in the distance, her white hair shining in the moonlight. She had been in the family for quite a few years, now a pet that the family had respectfully put out to pasture. Right now she was Emma's only hope.

"Bossy girl!" Emma yelled across the field as she hobbled towards the fence dividing the two. "Here, girly girl! Here, Bossy!" she cooed.

Climbing up the wooden fence, Emma gingerly swung both legs across the top and waited for the friendly bovine. Once she was close enough, Emma started to scratch her face and made her way back over her ears, all the while the cow moving her body farther along to benefit. Once she was parallel to Emma, the woman swung her leg up over the cow and hung on around her neck, not sure if the cow would act like a wild stallion corralled in a pen and meeting its breaker for the first ride.

She did nothing. Maybe it was her age or the trust the cow had for Emma, but she let Emma guide her along the fence to the gate. Emma leaned over the cow's neck and unlatched the fence, shoving it as hard as she could to let the duo through. Finding the point right behind the cow's legs, Emma sank her knees gently in and tapped her on the rump. Bossy moved through the gate and headed off down the drive.

Emma reached down and gave her a quick scratch on the neck as she kept nudging the heifer along.

Lauren rubbed her eyes at the sight coming towards the house. She thought she was hallucinating. Was that her mom? Riding a cow?

"Mom?" she yelled.

"Oh, thank god! Lauren, Kevin's house. We need to get back over there immediately!" Emma screamed back at her daughter.

"Mom, Kevin left to go find you up on the hill." Lauren's tone grew quieter as her mom got closer.

The cow, seeing more humans and the possibility of food, decided she needed to pick up speed even with the frantic woman trying to stay upon her back.

"Mom!" Lauren screamed as the cow was now at as fast a pace as she could muster.

Emma's eyes were wide with fright as she approached her daughter at a rapid speed, and just as the cow decided to pull a full stop, Emma decided it best to try to dismount. Lauren watched in horror as her mom fell from the cow, straight down onto her back on the pile of leaves that the kids had all been playing in the day before, knocking all the air from her lungs.

"Mom!" Lauren screamed as the others from within the house started coming outside to see what all the commotion was about.

"What the—" Tiffany began as Johnisse nudged her in the side.

"The kids," Jay whispered, pointing to the small quad of little ears standing next to the leaves.

Emma pointed up at the twins, Jack and Jamie, and started to bawl, no intelligent words leaving her lips. The twins looked at each other, wondering what trouble they had gotten into now.

"Mom, try to calm yourself" Jessica said as she stepped before her mother-in-law. The puzzled look on Emma's face was enough to explain what words could not escape her mouth.

"Dixon came to the house, but it was too late. We all ran outside, but the roof had already caught from the embers coming out of the stovepipe. We brought the kids over here to get out of the cold since there was nothing we could do but watch it burn. We didn't particularly want to do that. We had no idea where you were, so Kevin and Mike took a couple of horses and headed back up over the hill to try to find you," she explained.

"Dix..." Emma tried to breathe out.

"Oh, there was no way anyone was stopping that dog from coming to find you. All Kevin said was Emma and he tore off like a bullet."

Emma laid her head back into the mess of leaves supporting her. She was afraid to move as the rush of excitement started to wane. Looking up from her position, Emma looked into the faces of the ones she had prayed were not lost in the fire... and a cow. Uncontrollable laughter filled the night air as the group gently picked up the woman and helped her inside, well, all but the cow, who'd found a forgotten patch in the garden and already had a mouthful of beet tops.

Inside, the group deposited Emma in the living room as Lauren went and fetched a basin of warm water. Jessica was already trying to remove Emma's boot so they could see what was going on beneath the worn leather. Tom walked into the room after hearing all the commotion, giving his wife the once-over.

"What happened?" he asked.

Jessica gave her father-in-law a brief synopsis of the evening's events as Emma searched his face for any kind of emotion after their son's home had burned to the ground and his wife was hurt in the process.

"Oh," he replied. "Then who's making dinner tonight?" he asked as he walked towards the kitchen.

Emma's heart sank at the raw coldness of the man who'd just left the room. Jess looked at Emma's ashen face with astonishment. Reaching out, Emma patted her hand. "It's okay, really. He hasn't been himself since the accident," Emma tried to explain.

"No, it's not alright!" Jessica nearly shouted. "Accident or not, the man is not right! Tommy would never have treated you or anyone in the family the way this... this..." She trailed off, searching for the most accurate word to describe the man without hurting Emma any more than she had been hurt already. "Listen, this is hard on everyone. Heck, I just lost my own home, but because of what you have taught us over the years about being in situations like this—" she pointed around at nothing in particular "—it made it easier. The house can be replaced. My husband, your son and your grandkids, they cannot. You showed us all that, and tonight it was cemented into all our brains. I can't just sit here and let that man treat you like a slave anymore. He needs to start contributing or nothing," she continued as she haphazardly reached over and pulled a leaf out of Emma's hair.

"Jess, listen. I'll handle Tom. Right now we need to get this boot off and get you and the kids settled. Deal?" Emma asked with her lips in a big pout, trying to gain her daughter-in-law's sympathy.

Jess rolled her eyes and pulled a footstool over to sit in front of Emma's chair. Lifting Emma's foot as easily as she could, Jess rested it on her own knee as she untied the bandana that Emma had wrapped around it earlier. "You might feel the blood start to pump back into your foot now that you're off it and this thing is off," she said, throwing the piece of rolled-up cloth aside. "It's probably going to really start to thump once I get your boot off, so brace yourself."

Tiffany walked in with a glass of water and some ibuprofen just as Jess was going to pull off Emma's boot.

"Mercy sakes, what in tarnation has gotten into Mr. Tom?" she said, slightly exasperated.

"He's just hungry, Tiff." Emma began to make excuses.

Tiff looked from Emma and then to Jess, their eyes locking as she handed the water and pills to Emma. "Here, take this. I'm about to go make the man a sammich!" Tiff said as she turned to head back into the kitchen.

"Shit!" Emma haphazardly said before she caught herself.

"Mom!"

"I know! I know... I'm sorry!"

"You were doing so well with your cussing, too. Looks like that man is bringing out the best in you," Jess said with a hint of sarcasm.

Emma popped the pills into her mouth and swallowed a gulp of water, laying her head back on the recliner.

"Just pull the damn boot off," she said, a little more agitated than she intended.

50

Mike watched the big white dog make his way through the underbrush and disappear into the woods. He made it look easier than it was going to be on horseback, that was for sure.

"Hold up," Mike commanded as he pulled the reins back. "Dixon?"

The dog came back and circled around the two men on horseback as Kevin inched in closer to Mike.

"What's wrong, Unk?" Mike asked.

"Not sure, but something is off. Let's just take our time. Keep your eyes peeled. I'm sure Dixon will lead us to Emma, but something else I can't explain has my Spidey senses activated," Mike said to his nephew.

The two men reined the horses towards the opening and entered the forest. It was dark enough outside under the stars, let alone add an umbrella of trees to block out the moon's glow. Following the trail, the men went past cabin after cabin, making note that each were empty.

"Where the hell is your mom?" Mike asked Kevin, now visibly agitated.

"Maybe you should ask the dog," Kevin said, shooting Mike a look.

Swinging around, Mike looked at Dixon, who was sitting watching the two men.

Grumbling something unintelligible under his breath, Mike yelled at the dog, "Emma? Where the hell is Emma?"

Dixon immediately was on his feet and taking off down the trail.

"Don't stop him this time!" Kevin said, barely missing a tree branch hitting his head.

Mike hunched down closer to the horse's neck and followed the dog as best he could while still keeping the walking trail in sight. Dixon took them up the hill in the back of the property and stopped at the rock that Emma had sat on earlier in the night.

Mike and Kevin dismounted the horses to get a better look around.

"She was here alright," Mike said, giving the area a quick glance.

"How do you know that?" Kevin asked.

"Look here," he said, squatting onto his haunches. "See these blades of grass bent like this. If you want someone to know which way you went, you break them in the direction opposite so that the head points the way."

"How did Mom know someone would be up here looking for her though? She hadn't planned on being back for two days."

"Habit maybe. I don't know."

"So where is she now?" Kevin asked. "Or which way did she take off?"

"My guess is that way," he said, looking at the ground and not looking where he was pointing.

"Damn. That's towards my house! Do you think she saw the fire?" Kevin asked.

"If she did, that means we went entirely the wrong way around the trail. That means we have quite a bit to go before we may find her."

Jumping back up, Kevin took off towards his house without waiting for his uncle. The path now was an old oil well road and, other than the steep incline, was easy to see.

Mike mounted and paused, again getting the feeling that something was just not right.

"Dixon, let's go find Emma," he commanded the dog.

Laying straight back on the horse, with his head almost resting on the animal's hindquarters because of the steep decline in the trail, Kevin did not see the backpack along the pathway until he was right up on it.

"Hold up!' he said as he reined his horse in.

"What's wrong?" Mike shouted from behind.

"That's Mom's pack!" Kevin yelled back, pointing to the black clump just off to the side of the trail.

51

Dropping his hat onto the pile of papers on his desk, Ben ran his fingers through what was quickly becoming a lost cause for a professional image. Walking over to the mirror on the wall, he grimaced at what stared back. He needed a shave, which was apparent. But if you looked deeper, you could see the emptiness lurking behind his eyes. When was the last time he had any fun? When was the last time he got all cleaned up and went out with the boys and blew off some steam, when he didn't worry so much about work? Times had changed, but damn if the need to sow some oats and drink some beer wasn't still needed now and again. Grabbing his jaw between his fingers, he gave himself the once-over.

"Damn, Benjamin, even now you are one fine-looking man!"

Startled by a noise behind him, Ben turned to see Emma standing there with a grin on her face.

"Ben."

"Emma, when did you get here?"

"Oh, long enough ago to see you gushing all over yourself. I see some things never change."

"What brings you here into town? Not often you leave your farm and that husband of yours," he chided.

Ignoring the obvious dig, Emma hobbled over to his desk and sat down in one of the two chairs set out for visitors.

"What happened to you?" he asked, looking down at her leg.

Ignoring his question, Emma pulled the other chair around and propped her ankle up on it. "Lots going on in the outskirts of town. Wanted to see if you knew anything about it. My aunt and uncle were broken into about a week ago, and they said you haven't even been by to take a formal statement."

"Emma, I am but one man in the apocalypse. I'm sure that there have been more important things to take care of. If you are that concerned, why don't you cart them off to your farm so you can keep an eye on them?"

"Because they have a perfectly good home and because they know who did this"—Ben started to reply, but Emma kept talking—"and if you did your job, you could get these people off the streets before more people lose their belongings. I'm going to be here for a few more days, and I will expect to see you over at their house before I leave."

"Honey, the jail is already full of thugs way worse than someone stealing junk. I got no more room. You of all people should understand the dynamics of this after a blowup like we just had."

"Oh, I do! Which is why I'm here giving you the benefit of taking care of it first," Emma replied.

Ben looked at her sideways. "What do you mean, first?"

"I mean if you choose to ignore this, then I have no choice but to take matters into my own hands."

Opening the pencil drawer at his waist, Ben reached out and threw the contents at her. "Here. Welcome to the club."

Laying on the desk between them was a dull gold-colored star with the letters DEPUTY inscribed across the top. "Have at it," Ben moaned.

"Don't mind if I do," Emma replied as she reached down and picked it up. "Someone's gotta do your job."

Emma slid the trinket into her pocket and limped out of his office, leaving Ben nothing to do but stare in disbelief at the insanity of the woman he so secretly admired.

A couple of days, aye? Maybe it's time to get ole Tommy out of the house for the night. With Emma away from the farm, what better opportunity was there?

"I think I'll even shave for this!" Ben said out loud for no one to hear. Popping his head out the door to where his secretary sat, Bens only words were, "Find me Johnny," before he disappeared down the hallway.

52

Tom heard the knock on the door and had forgotten the only one home to answer it was himself. Whether he admitted it or not, he was becoming accustomed to being waited on and taken care of. Sliding his legs off the bed, he made his way to the back door in the kitchen.

Must be one of the neighbors if they're coming to the back door, he thought.

"Hang on," he yelled as the frustration began to set in. He still wasn't up to his old self physically, and whoever was beating on the door wasn't stopping anytime soon. He could only go so fast!

Swinging the door open without even checking to see who it was caught Tom off guard. He was completely surprised to see Ben standing there and even more surprised when it took him a minute to recognize the sheriff.

"Ben, what brings you out to these parts this time of night? I hope everything is okay?" Tom asked.

"Of course, just thought I'd stop by and see how you were doing. Boys and I were heading out to blow off some steam, thought you might be interested."

"Oh, well, I'm not really—"

Ben interrupted him. "Ah, come on, man! You need to get out, and me and the boys have more than enough room for you! Come on! I won't let you down!" Ben said, wrapping an arm around Tom's shoulders.

"I'm not even dressed, and by the looks of you, your plans might be above my pay scale," Tom said.

A wicked stream of laughter erupted from Ben's throat. "Above your pay scale! That has to be one of the funniest things I've heard you say. Hell, sounds like something Emma would say!"

That was enough to hit a nerve with Tom. "Give me a few and I'll get changed. Jeans and boots are the attire of the night?"

"Yessum, sir, it is. Be comfortable," Ben replied.

Left alone in the kitchen, Emma's kitchen, Ben helped himself to a class of cold milk out of the fridge. Walking around, he ran his fingers across the pan rack hanging from the ceiling, impressed with the amount of weight it could hold. Pulling a chair out from the table, he sat down facing the basement door as he finished his glass of milk. That door. It pulled his attention.

"You about ready there, Tom?" he yelled out.

No response.

Ben got up and headed over to the hallway leading to the room Tom was recovering in. Hearing the shower, he knew it would be a while before Tom was ready. Retracing his footsteps back into the kitchen, he walked over and placed his hand on the doorknob to the basement. It was eerily quiet in the house when no one was home. Like the house was breathing. Like the house was watching his every move. Gently turning the handle, he waited before tugging the door open.

"Damn it," he muttered under his breath.

The door stuck and made way more noise than Ben had anticipated trying to get it to open. Almost like it intentionally wanted the noise, Ben thought, spooking himself.

"Stop it, you idiot," Ben swore to himself.

Peering inside, Ben flipped the light switch and watched as it slightly illumined the steps going down.

How the hell does someone not kill themselves with this mess? Ben thought.

Peeking his head back up and around the corner, he could still hear the shower. Taking a step in, Ben slowly went down the stairs. One thing that always scared him as a boy was stairs with no backs on them. Emma's stairs opened up into a dark room behind the stairwell that was hidden by the lack of lighting. Ben had to convince himself he was an adult and no longer believed in the boogeyman, but it was hard. Every hair on his body was at attention!

"Damnit, man, you were just down here not that long ago!" Ben said to himself.

It was like the house whispered back to him, "But you weren't all alone then."

Ben had enough. This was just too much even for him. Turning, he started back up the stairs as he broke into a cold sweat.

One at a time, he kept telling himself, but peering into the darkness behind the treads brought back too many nightmares as a kid. Night after night he would dream about hands coming out and grabbing his legs, pulling him behind the stringers.

Jesus, he needed to get out of here fast!

Hitting the top step, he catapulted himself out of the stairwell and back into the kitchen just as Tom came around the corner.

"*Dios*, you look like you've seen a ghost!" Tom exclaimed.

"I, eh, I heard something," Ben started, pointing towards the steps.

"It's okay, man. It's scary down there and I live here," Tom replied.

"Yeah, I need a beer," Ben gasped.

"Let me lock up and let's head out."

"Lock up?" Ben chuckled. "From what? Come on, break a rule! Hell, leave the back door wide open! Be a rebel!"

Tom looked at the man and chalked his odd behavior up to whatever had happened in the basement but grabbed his keys and a jacket just in case. Ushering Ben out the door first, Tom twisted the lock and pulled the door shut behind him after he quickly scribbled on some paper on the board by the door. Hopping into the Jeep that Ben was driving, Tom tossed his jacket in the back and buckled himself in.

Ben just shook his head. "Man, you got to loosen up." Reaching into the cooler in the backseat, he tossed a Miller High Life into Tom's lap. "Don't open that this direction. Point it out that way," Ben said, shoving a finger past Tom's face. Ben grabbed two more, opened the first and downed it in what seemed like one long gulp to Tom. Tossing the can into Tom's yard, he popped open the second can and took a swig before he started the Jeep.

Settling back, Tom opened the can and drank the cold beverage. He had to take several large gulps just to get the beer far enough down in the can that every time Ben hit a hole, it didn't come sloshing back out. After a while he opened another and handed one off to Ben. It wasn't like they had to worry about traffic, as the Jeep that Ben had gotten from his military friends was about the only working vehicle in the collective six counties.

Before he realized it, Tom had lost track of where they were going and was just enjoying the ride. Ben had jerry-rigged a disc player into the Jeep and had some kind of rap music blaring from the speakers dangling under the front dash. Tom didn't particularly care for rap, but between the effects of the alcohol and his newfound freedom, he was getting into the hard bass it was known for.

Ben drove off the main road and into a field, taking a dirt path that ran between the field and some woods. Not really caring, Tom reached into the back for another beer and almost took a nosedive out of his seat when Ben hit a dirt mound. Laughing, Tom unhooked his seat belt and decided to stand up, holding onto the top of the windshield for the rest of their journey. Ben slid the Jeep a little too close to the woods and a branch snapped Tom across the cheek, leaving a nice gash, but Tom was so far gone he didn't even feel it. He was having too much fun trying to hang on, drink his beer and holler at the top of his lungs.

Ben chuckled to himself. "Looks like Tom is ready to have some fun!" he yelled.

"Damn right!" Tom yelled back.

Coming up over the next knoll, Tom noticed a bonfire in the distance. Pointing, Ben motioned that that was where they were headed.

Pulling up, Tom was yelling hello to everyone there, barely hanging on inside the Jeep. Ben stopped the Jeep and got out, walking over to a couple of the guys who were watching Tom with great interest.

"Wasted?" one asked.

"Didn't take much," Ben replied.

"Jesus, this should be fun," the other guy replied.

"That's why we're here!" Ben exclaimed as he slapped the guy across the shoulder.

"You guys ready to party?" Ben screamed into the night as an array of whoops and hell yeahs rang out in the darkness.

"Let's ride," Ben yelled, pointing at the vehicles. By this time, Tom was so intoxicated he was pissing off the side of the Jeep without a care in the world.

Pulling up to the house, they did not bother to be silent. They were so far out that no one would hear them, and who would stop them anyway, they were the law, after all! Ben kept Tom back a bit as he let the other boys go on ahead first. He took care of his men. No one would ever say he took first dibs. Loading Tom up with some whiskey, Ben started talking to Tom about doing the deed. Teaching the woman a lesson. Who was the boss? Ben started talking to Tom about the tits on the whore down at the pub and how he would like to lay into her like a bull ready to ride. Tom hadn't felt like a man in quite a while, and a combination of his now hard penis and the effects of the alcohol had him wanting to pound the neighbor's dog let alone any nearby female.

It was time. Ben took him into the house and watched his face as Tom realized what was going on. The woman had been stripped down, her breasts now bruised and bloody from all the rough fondling Ben's men had been subjecting them to. She lay flat on the table, her face turned away from where Ben and Tom stood. Two men stood on each side of her, each holding one of her legs wide enough out that another man could stand in between them. Tom's dick grew harder as he watched a guy pound into the woman. Over and over he relieved himself in her until he was done.

"Go at it, son," Ben said, shoving Tom in the direction of the hostage. "Looks like she's waiting for you. I won't tell Emma. I doubt if she would approve. Come and get me when you're done," Ben said as he walked off towards the kitchen.

There wasn't anyone else there. No one was there to hear her screams. No one was there to pick her up after they were done with her. They left her discarded like a bag of empty chips. No one was there who cared. The demons danced around the bonfire that night, stealing souls and devouring lives.

"Load 'em up, boys!" Ben yelled. "Let's get on out of here."

"No evidence, Tom," Ben said as he handed the gun off to the other man.

"No evidence," Tom repeated as he aimed the firearm at the lifeless body of the unrecognizable female.

"Consider this your initiation into our little group, Tom. You man enough to handle this, or do you need to get Emma's permission?" Ben chided.

Pulling the trigger back, Tom destroyed her face with one shot. The adrenaline rush that Tom felt was exhilarating. It wouldn't be his last if left unchecked.

Walking outside, Ben had Tom get back into the Jeep. Taking a gas can from the back, Ben set the house on fire in multiple places. Climbing back into the Jeep, he gave Tom a rough shake. "Proud of you, man. You got what it takes to play with the big boys. You're welcome to ride with us anytime."

"What now?" Tom asked, thrusting his chin in the direction of the burning house.

"I think there's a new deputy in town. Let her clean up this mess," Ben said as he cranked the Jeep. Starting off down the drive, the burning house behind them, Ben reached into the backseat for another beer. Picking up the long-forgotten jacket, he tossed it into the air and watched in the mirror as it caught the waves of dust as they drove away. "Beer?" he asked, handing one to his new accomplice as he drove to dump him off at Emma's.

53

She heard him stumble into the house. Dixon was on alert, being the first one to hear the vehicle coming up the drive. Emma paused in the shadows, Mossy nearby if she needed her trusty five-hundred. For now, Emma just wanted to see who exactly was visiting her farm in the middle of the night, especially since her husband had not come home yet. While he had left a note that he would be back later, there was no additional information about where he had gone. Patience was not one of Emma's stronger virtues, and while she had no reason not to trust her husband, it was an odd place to be in within her marriage when her betrothed had no recollection of their union.

She could smell the alcohol before she saw the man. Beer. Making his way into the living room without breaking anything, Emma saw her husband turn the light on beside his recliner. Wondering who he was with, Emma, still in bare feet and her nightgown, crept back down the hallway and made her way back upstairs to their bedroom. Walking to the window, she melted into the curtain as she peered outside with her monocle.

"Ben," she muttered under her breath.

She wanted no part of whatever Ben was up to and she knew he had ulterior motives for bringing her husband home smelling like he had spent the night in the local dive. Whatever the reason, she needed to give Tommy his space. Assuming he would pass out downstairs, she crawled into bed, once again spreading her hand across the mattress to that all too familiar emptiness. Tears fell as she remembered all too clearly other nights in their marriage when their bed had not been so empty. When would all this craziness end? When would their lives get back to some sort of routine? Or was this their new normal? The thought made Emma sick to her stomach.

Drifting off to sleep, Emma was awakened by the arm reaching around her waist and the undeniable stench burning her nostrils. Startled, she tensed up as her mind fought to wake itself and make sense of what was happening. Or was her mind playing tricks on her, betraying her against her deepest wishes. The smell pummeled her senses. She felt his hand slide up over her breast, finding and fondling its target until it reached its objective, triumphant.

Emma stiffened her back against the man lying in her bed, her body responding to his promptings, her mind swimming in emotion. It would be so easy to just give in, but something felt wrong. This was her husband, yet he didn't remember her, and to make matters worse, he was intoxicated.

"Tom," she whispered as she tried to slide away. Trying to brush his hand away, she pushed down on his arm to get it away from her breast. He used the opportunity to seek pleasure elsewhere. His hand slid down her stomach, and she twisted away, the strength in his arm making it almost impossible to sit up.

"TOM," she said with a thread of fear drifting from her voice. "Tom, please. Don't do this right now."

Tom pulled her back to him with such strength that she slid against him effortlessly, his face now buried in her hair. The smell of him and the mixed emotions made her sick to her stomach. This was not how she wanted their reunion to be.

"Come on, baby. Let me have some fun," Tom stammered in his drunken state.

"Tom!" Emma squealed as she felt his hand reach up under her nightdress. "Stop this right now."

Awake now, Tom rolled over onto his back and flung his arm up over his head as the waves of nausea rocked him like a boat on the open ocean during a hurricane. Groaning, he barely missed vomiting on the bed as his head went over the side of the mattress.

Torn between emotions, Emma didn't know whether to try to save him or throw him out of her bed. This man she had known for years now had never acted like this before. Flashes of her new normal pulsated through her mind. NO, she would not accept this. There was no way she would allow her relationship with her husband to be built on false pretenses, or would she? What could she do? She just wanted her Tommy back, not this person he was becoming.

"Tom?" she said gently, trying to get out of the bed without rocking him off at the same time.

Groaning, Tom lay back on the pillow, his arm back over his eyes. "What?"

"What's going on here?" Emma asked.

"I'm sick. Can't you see that?" he shot back.

"There's a difference between being sick... and being drunk," Emma replied.

"Either way, it's none of your business. Leave me alone," he said in a dismissive tone as he rolled over into the middle of the bed, still fully clothed. Standing up straight now as waves of anger pulsed through her veins, Emma looked around the room that she once shared with her husband. Walking around the side of the bed, Emma made sure not to step into the mess Tomás had made. Grabbing the quilt that had been given to them on their wedding day, she gently laid it across his body, being careful not to wake the stranger now snoring in her bed.

Emma knew what he would require the next morning besides a heap of coffee and eggs with ketchup, he would need quiet. She had chased everyone away right after lunch, anticipating his late rising. He came stumbling into the kitchen looking like he had been beaten all night by Satan himself. Tom made his way to his usual chair at the kitchen table without looking at his wife and put his elbows on the table, his head gently resting on the palms of his hands. Walking over, Emma slid a steaming cup of coffee under his face and waited for its contents to waft to his nostrils. Groaning,

Tom slid one hand around the cup and lifted it to his lips, sipping the hot nectar of the near dead.

Resting the cup back on the table, Tom glanced over at his wife standing with her back to him at the stove. He could still feel the tension emanating from her body. He felt like a kid having to explain to his mom why and how he broke the window with the baseball that she'd bought him for Christmas. Damn her, if she hadn't bought the fucking ball, he wouldn't be in trouble!

Emma turned with his plate and caught him staring at her. "Tom," she said with a bit more chilliness than she had intended.

"I suppose you want to talk about last night?" he asked her.

"I don't even know what to say to you," Emma replied.

"Good. What I do is none of your business, and I sure as hell don't answer to you."

"Tom, I'm your wife! I worry about you especially after all that has happened!"

"Yeah, I forgot. I can't take care of myself before my heroic wife can come and save my stupid ass. Is that what you want to hear, Emma? How awesome you are? How I am so weak and feeble that I need you to take care of my every move? For Christ's sake, Emma, I don't even remember you!"

The words stung and he knew it. He meant them to drill right into her soul and kill any love she had for him so that it made things easier on him, except he realized it wouldn't erase the guilt. She was a good person, just not his person anymore. He didn't want to be here acting like this big loving family. Not when all he wanted to do was put his hands around her throat and strangle the last breath out of her. If it wasn't for her, he wouldn't be in this mess, of that he was certain. Her voice still haunted him even after he was pulled from the ditch, and with each word that left her mouth, he hated her even more. He had had enough of this conversation, that was one thing that he knew for certain. Slamming his arms down, coffee splashed across the table as he scooted his chair back and stood up a little too fast, swaying. Emma ran over and tried to prop him up before he fell.

"Leave me the fuck alone!" he screamed.

"Tommy, I was just try—" she got out before he interrupted her.

"Stop with the Tommy thing! You are not my mom! God, how I hate that!" he spat back.

"I'm sorry," she said quietly. "I've always called—"

"Just stop. That person is dead. This is me now. Live with it," he said as he walked to the doorway. Turning, his eyes bored right down into Emma's heart. "Oh, by the way, just so you know, I don't have your six anymore."

Emma stared at the shadow of the man she once knew. She understood.

54

They arrived in the middle of the afternoon, walking boldly up the little-used driveway straight to the farmhouse. Several dozen frozen faces clothed in tattered and dirty clothes, now immune to the smell of feces and unwashed body odors between them. Mostly adults, they did have a couple of younger kids thrown in the mix, who had no idea why they were there, they just wanted to be with the only people they had some semblance of familiarity with. Whether this was intentional or not, it didn't matter. They still outnumbered the people at the farm.

When no one answered the front door, the man who was taking lead motioned for a couple of the followers to head off around the side of the house while the rest of the party waited out front. The man pounded on the door this time, making sure that whoever might be inside heard him or his fist found its way through the door, whichever came first.

Marauders, they were called in certain circles. Folks who had banded together and went out to take what they needed, or simply wanted. The rules of life had changed. It was now a day-to-day survival scenario. These same people used to be someone's neighbor who took their children to soccer practice after school on Thursdays. These same people sat two pews up from you during Sunday worship. These same people bowed their heads and prayed to the same God that you did. They made fun of you when you brought up having a little extra food or water in the house, you know, "just in case." The experts called it normalcy bias, not wanting to confront the possibilities, or in some cases the certainties, because it shattered their misconceptions about what reality was. They read the same newspapers, watched the same news reports on the television, even read the stories you shared on Facebook, and still did nothing to secure their future. They didn't want to flirt with the idea that something could happen because it would shatter their false little world that they had built around them.

These same shells of a human had lived through the same small apocalypse that you had, and watched their children die of starvation or, worse, watched their child get raped while they were defenseless to help. Guilt is an overwhelming emotion. It can make a man go against his belief system that he has lived all of his life. To this caldron of shame, add in their own personal demons, who were making their stomachs eat them from the inside out, and you have your very own, homegrown zombie. It wasn't as melodramatic as they were used to seeing on the television with a mystery virus, but they were still zombies nonetheless.

Opening the door, the leader of the group was surprised that there was no one seemingly home. He had visited out here on occasion when he needed advice from the old man about his beehives, and had observed that the homestead seemed well stocked with odds and ends of supplies that would come in handy now that the electrical grid wasn't working. The old man liked to talk. He was easily led into giving away more information than he should to someone he barely knew.

The leader silently divided the group off into directions as he made his way into the kitchen, looking for anything they could use to survive or barter to someone needing the junk. Looking around, the leader looked at the pictures scattered around with no emotion. He was tired. Tired of having to fight to survive. Tired of wondering where his next meal was going to come from. Tired of the sights and smells he encountered as he took from others. Tired of feeling angry that he thought this would be easy. His plan had failed him, miserably. He should have been better prepared at his own house, but no, he thought he would just take supplies from others when and if the time arose. Now all he did was spend his time sneaking up on one family after another, looking for anything and everything that could earn him an hour of rest. He was tired of killing.

Hearing a noise, he walked boldly into the master bedroom. The old woman was there, her eyes as big as the plate she put the turkey on at Thanksgiving as the intruder entered. Demanding things had become easy for the leader, so had hurting the victim when they didn't give him what they wanted. He needed gold and she said they didn't have any. He said he needed opioids, and the woman had none. He needed guns and ammunition. The woman showed them where the safe was but was so scared that her hands shook uncontrollably as she tried to enter the code to unlock the vault door.

There was no alcohol in the house other than what the old woman had used to make her homemade vanilla with when she made Christmas cookies. There were no cigarettes and no lighters, but there was food the old woman had spent hours canning from her garden. They took all of that.

The leader dragged the old woman into the living room by her hair and asked her where the rest of her husband's medicine was, since he wouldn't be needing it anymore. They had shot him where he lay on the couch, destroying the lower half of his torso. Crying now, the old woman had become useless to the leader. Bashing her in the spine with the butt end of his shotgun, he tossed her into the chair. Being unable to move because of the damage the man had done, she had to sit there and stare at the man who she'd betrothed her life to almost fifty years earlier.

They left after they took what they wanted, leaving the old couple defenseless against the demons waiting in the shadows.

55

Emma's nostrils picked up the odor as she was walking up the driveway. Flashbacks of a time long ago again filled her thoughts. She knew that foul aroma. The air was thick with the miasmas of rotting flesh with a hint of sweetness. An odd smell, death was an aroma you will always remember.

Her pulse quickened as she stood at the doorway, her hand rising to knock. Pausing, she realized it was the first time since all of the recent drama started happening that she was scared. The bouquet of rotting meat mixed with the sweet scent of applesauce was starting to make her eyes water.

She wanted to take a deep breath to calm her nerves, but couldn't. She would surely gag. Digging around in her backpack, she pulled out a bandana and folded it in half. Placing it over her nose and mouth, she tied it behind her head. While it made the smell less noticeable, Emma's stomach was now flipping over and over.

Closing her eyes and breathing out, her breath caught as she knocked loudly on the door. Eternity passed while she waited.

Please, she begged her invisible God.

She jumped when she heard the floor creak as someone was walking towards her through the kitchen. Still standing outside, she tried to squint through the curtain on the back door.

"Aunt Amy?" she yelled. "Is that you?"

Waiting for a reply that never materialized, Emma reached down and grabbed the door handle. She gave it a twist.

"Sweet Jesus," Emma said under her breath as the door opened. Lifting her head, Emma paused, her eyes darting back and forth, looking for answers to what lay ahead.

"Aunty Amy? Uncle Randy? Are you guys in there?" she yelled, the stench overwhelming her as she started coughing up the foul fumes that were now attaching themselves to her tongue.

Turning her head, she positioned her ear in alignment with where the door was now cracked open. No sounds came from inside.

Pushing the door farther open, Emma looked around the kitchen. Dishes were piled in the sink, left unwashed with decaying matter crawling with small white maggots. Amy's dishtowel was flung over the back of the kitchen chair that she always sat at, waiting for her at any moment to step into the room and start cleaning. Her coffee mug sat on the table in front of her chair. Broken dishes were scattered around the room, with the doors to the cabinets that used to hold them now left open. Drawers of spoons and knives were dumped and then discarded among the chaos. Someone had obviously been looking for something.

The air was still. Too still.

Emma stepped inside and waited.

Please, God, she pleaded.

Waiting, Emma could not pick out any sounds within the house that indicated she would find any of the inhabitants alive. Making her way towards the hallway, Emma wished the house had windows that allowed some kind of light into the middle of the house.

The smell of death heightened as she made her way towards the living room. Catching a glimpse of the floral sofa, Emma remembered the delight on her aunt's face when she'd bought the hideous, nine-foot-long piece of foam and wood.

"It's glorious!" Amy had said with as much pride as the day her grandchild was born.

"Seriously?" Emma said, more of a statement than a question.

"We'll be able to get five people on this couch," Amy replied.

"If we can get it into the house! This thing is the longest, ugliest piece of furniture I have ever seen!" Uncle Randy shouted from somewhere behind the efflorescent monstrosity.

Laughter, starting at a low boil, escalated until Emma's cheeks hurt. Tears of happiness cascaded over her lashes as she looked back and forth from her aunt to her uncle. They were the only living relatives older than herself that still gave her a sense of being a youngster.

Now tears fell down her face, not only from the putrid smell but from the realization that both of her beloved kinfolk were the cause of the emanation.

She caught a glimpse of the top of the woman's head barely peeking above the back of the recliner as she entered the room. Pausing, Emma contemplated just turning around and running away.

It would be the easiest way to handle this, she told herself.

Scanning the room, all hope faded of finding her aunt and uncle alive as Emma saw the bottom of her Uncle Randy's work boot resting against the arm of that god-awful sofa. Couldn't she just lie to herself and say he was napping and she didn't want to wake him? Guilt flooded her as she realized that she should have checked in on them sooner, but with trying to find her husband and nursing him back to health, along with all the extra people at the farm, she'd just kept pushing it further down the list of things to do.

Deep in the pit of her soul, she just wanted to go home and forget that she was here, to live without the knowledge that they were gone, but an invisible rope was pulling her towards them. She needed to deal with this. She needed to bury them, but there was no way she could lift them herself. She could, at least, throw a cover over them so they weren't so exposed to the world as death ate at them. Kindness matters even after, it keeps us humane.

Tentatively, Emma walked over and gently pulled the afghan that her aunt had crocheted from the back of the sofa. Catching a glimpse of her uncle, she guessed he had been gone for a couple of weeks now, his face sunken and ashen in pallor. The small bottles and used needles on the table next to him told Emma that his diabetes was probably the culprit.

Grasping the edge of the sofa, Emma felt a need to say something over her family before she left. Taking the afghan with her, she walked to the small divide between where her aunt was sitting and the couch. Collecting herself, she hugged the blanket as she searched for the words as if hidden within the folds of the yarn.

A pressure on her knee startled her as her eyes flew open. Looking quickly down, she saw her aunt's hand was now outstretched. Jumping back, Emma screamed.

The hand bounced up once as if pulled by a string and then fell back to its resting place.

Emma blinked. Did that really happen? Maybe she hit it with her leg as she was walking by?

"Yeah, that had to be it," she said, trying to convince herself.

Gathering her wits about her, Emma waited until her legs didn't feel like jelly. Slowly, she approached the chair her aunt was sitting in.

"Aunt Amy?" she squeaked out.

The old, withered hand moved as the woman flexed her fingers in response to Emma's voice.

"Sweet Moses!" Emma exclaimed under her breath as she flew around the chair. Kneeling before her aunt, Emma cupped the woman's tepid cheek in her hand. "Aunt Amy? Can you hear me?"

The woman's eyelashes fluttered. "It's me! It's Emma!" Emma gently grabbed the woman's outstretched hand and brought it to Amy's lap. Turning it gently over, Emma felt for a pulse.

"Honey, it's Emma," she said as tears spilled down her cheeks.

With all the strength the woman had left, Amy opened her eyes and looked at her brother's daughter. Years of memories flooded behind the glazed look of Emma's aunt. "Emma," the woman whispered.

"Yes! It's me. I'm here!" Emma sobbed. "I need to get you out of here!"

The woman grabbed onto Emma's hand as if to try to stop her. "What?" Emma asked, confused.

Lifting her lashes, Amy looked into Emma's eyes, quietly pleading. "Leave me," she stuttered.

Dismayed, Emma shook her head. "I just can't leave you here!"

Amy didn't blink but held onto Emma's gaze with the force of heaven behind her. "Please," she whispered. Emma stood as the realization of what her aunt was asking her to do hit her. She wanted to die. She was done with this life. She had stayed with her husband, and now, now she wanted to join him here in this house that they had built together.

Emma could feel the emotions ripping at her as she looked around the room. Their Christmas tree always stood before the big picture window with plenty of presents each year for everyone. The dining room table, peeking out from around the corner, where the family would gather at Thanksgiving to enjoy the homemade noodles that her aunt had taught Emma to make. That big, damn, ugly sofa that now cushioned her uncle's decaying body.

Oh God, please no, Emma silently begged to the highest of heavens.

This was her aunt's home. Her husband was here. Was it crueler to make her leave? Her time was short, obviously. Should she leave her here to pass with her husband, surrounded by the warmth of her own home? Emma knew the answer, but it didn't make it any easier.

Walking over, Emma picked up one of the discarded needles lying on the table beside her uncle. Fumbling through the opened bottles, Emma tried to fill the needle with as much insulin as she could. Nothing. Tossing it aside, she walked back into the kitchen.

Opening the back closet door, Emma remembered her aunt keeping their dog's supplies in here. Blue was a Chow and had been in the family forever. In his later years though, Emma remembered her aunt having to give him insulin shots. Looking for one of the larger syringes, Emma knew what she had to do. She had one shot at this and didn't want to screw it up.

Walking back to her aunt, Emma picked up the discarded blanket and tucked it carefully around the woman she loved deeply. Kneeling before her, Emma took both of her hands into hers and prayed out loud. Squeezing her aunt's hands tenderly, Emma watched as the woman's eyelashes parted for the last time. "I love you so very much," Emma said as the tears flowed freely down her face. A hint of a smile lit across the frail woman's face.

Emma picked up the needle and found a vein in the back of the woman's hand. Inserting the sharp tip, the woman didn't even flinch. Once all the air was dispersed, Emma tucked the afghan over her aunt with her hands resting in her lap beneath it and she waited. Sneaking her own hand beneath the blanket, Emma held on as the woman passed over. Sitting there sobbing, Emma's heart screamed out in anguish over both of her family members along with all the stress that had been building within her over the last few weeks.

As the waves of emotions subsided, Emma wiped her face and stood. Could she just leave them like this, to rot here in this home, waiting for someone else to find them? These were their belongings, things that her aunt and uncle worked their entire lives to have. Just things now, for someone else to discover, to loot.

Walking out of the house, Emma found what she needed. Once she was done, she stood before the farmhouse and said one last prayer as she flicked the match.

56

"Psst!"

Shelby looked over in the direction the sound was coming from. Peering around the side of the door was Angie.

"Hey, don't want to bother you if you're tired, but I really could use some help," Angie said, looking sheepishly at her host.

"Sure! Come on in," Shelby responded, glad for the break from the madness her mind was spinning. "Pull up a chair over here," she said, motioning for Angie to sit beside the bed. "What can I help you with?"

Grabbing the only seat in the room, Angie picked it up and turned, looking at Shelby. "Are you sure? I don't want to cause you to miss a nap or anything," she said still standing as she set the chair down.

"Oh, please! I welcome the company! Anything to get my mind off my leg." Patting the side of the mattress, Shelby motioned for Angie to sit closer. "Seriously, what's going on?"

"Well, this is kind of embarrassing," Angie began, her eyes fixed on her hands in her lap.

"Spit it out! You're killing me here!" Shelby giggled in desperation.

"Okay, okay. Well... as you know, everyone has chores to do here, and I'm kind of out here like, oh, I can help, but—"

"But you don't have a lot of experience and have no idea how not to get in the way or ask a million questions while you're trying to figure it out?" Shelby blurted out as she interrupted the young woman.

Angie looked up at the woman sitting on the bed, relief written all over her face. "Exactly," she said with a sigh. "How did you—?"

"Know?" Shelby said quickly. "Because I was you once. I wasn't raised here; this is Jeremiah's home turf."

"Oh! I didn't know that."

"No reason for you to. It's not common knowledge and, heck, I've been out here long enough now for the elders to have forgotten and the youngsters to see only my roots, but no, I'm not from these parts," Shelby explained.

"Mind if I ask where you grew up?" Angie asked.

"Not at all. Chicago. Actually, south of Chicago in Gary, Indiana. Completely different lifestyle. It was hardcore gangs and very little reason to look forward to the future."

"How did you end up here?"

"How about we save that story for another day? Right now we need to stay on topic so that dinner gets on the table on time," Shelby stressed.

"Yes, this time crunch. I still can't get used to how things have changed. Before, I would just pop something in the microwave when I was hungry. Now, I have to think about being hungry three hours in advance!" Angie laughed.

"You'll get the hang of things sooner or later. I believe in you," the older woman said, smiling.

"Thank you," Angie said softly.

"For what?"

"For saying that. Not many people acknowledge how appreciative or grateful they are of each other. It's refreshing when it happens."

"I meant it."

"I know you did," Angie said, realizing how much trust she had in this woman she had only known for a short amount of time. "Listen, the issue I'm having. It's kinda along the same line. Winter is coming, and I know there are things that need to be done, but I have no idea what or when or how or—"

"Woah! Slow down!" Shelby said, laughing. "Once you get started, it all comes out at once! I promise, I will help, so take a deep breath. Second thing I want you to do," Shelby said, holding up two fingers, "is go out to the dining room and look in the bottom of the big buffet. There are binders in there. Grab the two black ones that are about three inches deep and bring them here."

"Okay? But how do you know—" Angie started to say before she was once again interrupted by Shelby.

"Just go get the binders!" Shelby said, now laughing.

"I've seen these before!" Angie proclaimed.

"Really? Where at?" Shelby asked as she laid the book across her lap and opened the front cover.

"Emma! She has books just like this!" Angie squealed as she opened hers. "Yes, even the sections look the same!"

"Well, quite honestly, it was her idea. Each farm, or Alpha Farm as Emma calls them, is pretty much set up the same way when it comes to management. That way, if something were to happen, farm folks could be integrated easily," Shelby explained.

"Integrated?" Angie asked.

"If something happens here and we had to leave and go to another farm or someone came here, say like Jack and Dee, others within the group would be able to slide right into our life and help without being a burden."

"Goodness, a burden," Angie whispered.

"You are far from being a burden, Angie. You also are not an outsider anymore. You are one of us, just new to this, so maybe it's time you learn a bit more. This… network that Emma has built is larger and more diverse than most people realize. Each farm is its own functioning entity but, grouped together, will be able to function as one, if needed. We can move supplies and people great distances without help from the outside. We even have our own language if needed."

"I had no idea. I saw the books at Emma's when she and the kids were talking about when the animals were bred and such, but I had no idea it involved other things besides that. It's like you all have your own little world going on!"

"You could say that, I guess. A lot of us saw the direction this country was headed and we were quite alarmed. Funny how God throws people in your path. Each member within our organization was vetted and has sworn an oath to each other. We know what's at stake here and plan to be a part of the solution, not the problem," Shelby explained.

"I just came in here to ask you how to can tomatoes!" Angie snickered. "Now I feel like I could take over the world once I finish reading this!"

Laughing, Shelby closed the book on her lap. "It's not quite that easy, and we won't need these for just canning tomatoes."

"Are you serious? I need forty YouTube videos and would prefer to have Martha Stewart here! This shit is like rocket science at times. Water bath can? Pressure can? Nah! But if you do green beans, you could create botulism and then kill everyone over Thanksgiving dinner! I mean seriously! How do you figure this all out? And then, how do you can without a stove? I mean, you have the woodstove, but can you actually process jars on there?" Angie said, now breathless and a faint flush across her cheeks.

"Breathe, girly girl! We got this! You are going to have to trust me on this. You can do this, I believe in you." Shelby giggled.

"Thank you," Angie said, looking at the woman on the bed with great admiration. "I'm going to go start dinner, but seriously, I cannot thank you enough. I have felt so helpless here. Ridley's mom, Dee, seemed to slide right in when she got here. Now I know why and how. I want to learn everything," she said as she bent down to give Shelby a hug. "Thank you again," she whispered as she stood and walked out of the room, a skip in her step from the excitement.

Watching her leave, Shelby nestled back against her pillows, a broad smile still spread across her face.

No, girly girl, thank you!

57

Even in a down grid, it didn't take long for news to get around. People were both just naturally nosey and gossips at heart. Not only were they talking about Emma becoming a deputy but also about Doc Scott's house catching fire. With no working tankers, the fire had to just burn itself out. Emma happened to be leaving her Aunt Amy's house when the news came in. Going straight to Ben's office to see if he had gotten word on what had happened, she was surprised to see him just sitting at his desk, feet on his desk with his boots kicked off, relaxing.

"What happened out there?" Emma asked, mortified. Jane had been staying out there since Scott was gone, and Emma couldn't get any information on if she got out okay. All Emma knew was that Jane had not shown up at her farm.

"No idea."

"You haven't gone out there yet to investigate?"

"No, Emma, no I haven't. Could you pipe down a bit? I have a massive headache."

"When are you even planning on going out there? We could have a real issue going on here. With all the other break-ins, who's to say this wasn't intentionally set?" Emma asked so many questions so fast that Ben thought for an instant his head might explode.

"I'm not going. I have other things I need to do here in town. Hell, I don't even think Scott is in the state. My time would be wasted out there. It's gone. I can't bring it back."

"What?" Emma stared at Ben in disbelief. "People need to know what's going on around here, Ben, and they need to know that the person that they elected into a position that was sworn to protect them is actually doing his job and not hiding behind his desk!"

Tossing an empty file folder across the desk at her, Ben groaned as he swore he felt his brain shift in his skull. "Deputy, go fill this out during your investigation."

"What?"

"Emma, get the hell out of here and go do your job. NOW!" he screamed.

Emma looked at the most pathetic excuse for a sheriff she had ever seen. Reaching down, she not only snatched the file off his desk but grabbed the keys to his Jeep and, yelling, "Yes, sir!" walked out. She would get to the bottom of this.

58

"Mom! What's wrong? I've been standing here for ten minutes talking to you with no response. Are you even on this planet?" Lauren said, walking around to face her mother.

"I'm so sorry, my love. I've got a lot on my mind with this whole deputy role that's been shoved in my face and a couple other things," Emma replied. She had no intention of telling her about what was going on with Tom. If anything, her new job title could be used as a distraction.

"You know you don't need to accept that package, right?" Lauren asked.

"Package?" Emma asked, a bit confused.

Lauren gave a bit of a giggle. "Wow, you are out of it! MOM! You don't have to accept anything anyone dumps on you unless you want to. You taught me that a long time ago when I was getting buried at work! It also includes emotions that someone is trying to deflect onto you to bring you down. Sounds like you have a bit of both going on with this. Don't accept this balled-up piece of crap that the sheriff is trying to dump on you because he doesn't want to do his job. Return the package of crap and move on."

Emma reached out and touched her daughter's cheek. "Oh, wise one, sounds like you had a great teacher. Beautiful and brilliant, you are a lethal combination."

"Funny, Mom. But no, this is obviously bothering you. What would a Prepper Chick do?"

"Huh?"

"It's kind of like what would Jesus do, but since we're in a down-grid situation, I thought it would be more fitting."

Emma laughed. "Did I raise you?" Emma asked with a giggle.

"Seriously, Mom, think about it. Play out the Conflicted scenario like in your card game. It's a down-grid situation. You have been offered a position within what's left of the local law enforcement to help resume law and order. Do you accept the position? Why or why not?"

"I see what you did there. Okay. Well, let's work through all the pros and cons," Emma replied.

"Okay, pro is that it gives you connections and an inside view of what is going on out there. Even though we don't live in town, they still affect us out here," Lauren started.

"Yes, agree. I wish there was a way to get information out to the masses though. Some have no idea what is going on and no idea what to do to make their lives better."

"Well, could the new position help with that?"

"I don't know. I couldn't possibly go around and talk to every single person individually. I mean, I could, but it would take forever," Emma shot back.

Emma was silently watching the wheels spinning in her daughter's head. *Come on, Lauren, you can get this. You know what needs to happen. Step up.*

"What about a newsletter that can be distributed?"

YES! Emma felt the first wave of excitement wash over her. "Well, yes. Like the newspaper?"

"Yeah, but not as large. We don't need the sports section anymore, but the comics could come in handy," Lauren chimed.

"I love it!" Emma shot back.

"Let me work on a few things," Lauren replied. "But it looks like we both might have new careers?"

"Yes, yes, it does," Emma said with a smile creeping across her face. "I need to head over to Scott's to see what happened and see if I can find out where Jane is at. You want to ride along?"

"Ride?" Lauren asked.

"Well, I kinda borrowed the sheriff's Jeep," Emma replied with a sly grin.

"I could investigate and find fodder for my newsletter!"

"Your newsletter?" Emma asked, already knowing the answer.

"Yes, Mom. We have a lot to do to save this town. You have the knowledge that I don't have to save these people, but I know how to get it out there. Let's be a team!"

"Oh, honey, we have always been a team. But right now, people need us."

"I get it now," Lauren said with a whisper.

"Get what, luv?" Emma asked, genuinely confused.

"All these years, what you do. How we had to share you with others. How that ate away at you and made you feel inadequate as a parent. How you were trying to save the world but felt like you lost your family in the process," Lauren said bluntly, looking into her mother's eyes.

"Yeah. That's pretty much it in a nutshell." Tears formed in Emma's eyes. "Forgive me."

"A million times over. Forgive me for being so selfish when you were born for the universe," Lauren said as she wiped a tear from her mother's cheek.

"Universe or not, I will always be your mom, and I had a duty to raise you to the best of my abilities. Right now, hearing you, sounds like I did an amazing job. I love you, Lauren."

"I really know that. I know you love me. I've never doubted that," Lauren said as she hooked her arm through Emma's and steered her towards the door. "But right now, this dynamic duo has a job to do. Off to save the world!" she said as she thrust her fist into the air and giggled into her mom's shoulder. "We need to get capes. Maybe tights too…"

"Now, Lauren!"

"Okay, Mom, just capes."

59

Emma and Lauren drove the sheriff's Jeep over to Doc Scott's veterinary farm. While it wasn't far with the Jeep, Emma thought about the tunnels that ran between her farm and what was now the remains of a once thriving local business. Dr. Scott Smalley was a much-loved member of the local community and a much-needed resource, one that was sorely missed now that he was off in Tennessee with Angie.

Emma hadn't thought about them for a while. She needed to get word to them about what had happened. With all the commotion going on recently, she hadn't thought about communication since most of the commotion was going on at her farm and she didn't want to let her hand be seen. OPSEC was an important part of a prepper's life. One aspect that could tilt that hand between life and death. That being said, she knew she needed to get word to Scott, but she would wait until she was done looking at things out here.

Taking the bend in the road a little too fast, Lauren gave a squeal as they came into view of the homestead. Smoke was still whipping up from what used to be the house. Glancing around, the outhouses and barn all seemed to be fine, just the house had been destroyed. Columns of sandstone peeked from beneath the rubble where they had once held the wood structure.

Parking the Jeep a distance away, Emma motioned to Lauren to lie low for a bit. They exited the Jeep and made their way over to an area that would afford them a bit of line of sight protection but allow Emma a chance to glance around a bit before they approached.

"What do you think happened?" Lauren asked her mother.

"Not sure yet, but I'm wondering where Jane is at," Emma responded.

Taking her pack, Emma tossed it into a shallow ditch and motioned for Lauren to follow. Giving her mom a sideways glance, Lauren reluctantly climbed down and lay prone in the trench. Emma squatted on her haunches beside her daughter and flipped open a side pouch on her Expedition bag, removing a pair of binoculars. Resting her forearms on the edge of the recess, Emma slowly observed the area before her from one side to the other, looking for movement of any kind.

Motioning to Lauren, Emma followed her out of the recess and they made their way quietly, skirting the edge of the property towards the barn. Pausing occasionally, Emma showed Lauren how to check for tracks and, most importantly, to just listen and look for something abnormal.

Lauren spotted it first, lying along the drive. A piece of clothing discarded? Something that had blown from the house? Emma made a mental note to check it out when they were done but had the vaguest recollection of familiarity in the color.

60

Megan gave the child a bounce on her knee like her granddaddy did to her when she was little. She had heard that it worked to distract a child from whatever was ailing him. This wasn't working though. She had bathed him and changed him into a new diaper and put him in a onesie. She had fed him earlier, so she really didn't think he was all that hungry. Tired, maybe. No one seemed to be sleeping right anymore since the blowup. She knew for certain she hadn't. Maybe he was feeling her? Feeling her raw nerves not only about having to leave her home but also about not dealing well with her husband's death and all this responsibility now dumped into her lap.

Bastard took the easy way out, she thought to herself.

Flashing back, the hurt was starting to turn to anger as she thought about her husband. She could see him in her mind, driving the coast of California with a cute little blonde in the car with him, toying playfully with each other, giddy with excitement about where the road ahead was taking them.

Irritated by her own imagination, Megan snatched the baby off her knee and stood up. Walking over, she tossed him onto the bed with a short little thud.

"Well, that got your attention," she said out loud.

Robbie lay there staring up at his mom. His long eyelashes stood at attention against the rim of his widened eyes, the curiosity of their new adventure in life apparent on his face. She had to give him credit. He was taking everything in stride and not fussing a lot.

Is this what he needed? Megan thought. All she had really been doing was focusing on his survival, which had now become a full-time job for herself and the kids. Emma had made it easier since they had all been at her farm, but Megan also knew she didn't want to become dependent once again on someone and then have that person get ripped away from her also. Lying down on the bed beside little Robbie, Megan placed her hand on his belly and gave a brisk rub with enough pressure it moved his entire body back and forth a bit. His small fist curled up as he inserted it into his mouth, cooing at his mother as bits of slobber started to seep from around his hand.

Megan smiled at her child as waves of apprehension enveloped her. Could she get her kids through the days, the weeks ahead? Hell, it could be years before everything returned to normal. And then what? She had left her home behind. She would have to start all over again rebuilding their lives. She had no furniture, no transportation and barely any money, not that it mattered right now. She had stashed some bills, but most of her cash was locked in someone's computer, and she had no way to access it and no way to spend it for things they needed, as everyone else was in the same predicament. The days of walking into a store and swiping your ATM card were long over as far as she could tell. Listening to the little bit of chatter that the other houseguests had inadvertently let slip, she doubted they had any hope either of things getting back to normal.

"Now what?" she muttered under her breath.

For now she would stay put at Emma's farm. Actually, Emma had made sure with no doubt that she understood she was more than welcome here. But what about after? Would she continue to stay here?

What if things just didn't get better? Then what? Megan's demons advanced full force into her mind, overwhelming her with so much emotion that she doubted her own ability to handle all the what-ifs that her mind generated. Tears started to fall from her eyes as she stared at her small responsibility. This wasn't his fault, but she felt he would pay the cost for all the stupid in the world. She couldn't bear the thought of seeing him hungry or hurting. What would happen to him if she died?

Cradling him against her body, she continued to rub his stomach briskly, her chin now resting on the top of his head so he couldn't see the tears. Letting her left arm fall from holding her head up, her hand met the pillow that she had slept on last night. Turning her hand, she stretched her fingers out and grabbed the softness beneath her palm and squeezed it tightly. The thoughts playing in her head paralyzed her as she let them play out.

61

Lauren skimmed over the page of her newsletter. "Still needs something," she mumbled to herself. "But what?"

Bringing her hands up to her face, she covered her mouth with her fingers and let out a long forceful breath. What can I give people that will help them survive but also teach them what to be looking out for? What do they want versus what they need to know?

Running the tips of her fingers over her eyes, she gave a gentle massage to try to work out the stress of sitting at her desk for hours. She wanted this newsletter to be awesome. Correction, she needed this newsletter to be awesome. She knew the importance of the communication that needed to get to every household in the countryside. Without electronics, that had to be done the old-fashioned way, with paper and pen. Then she had to duplicate the information that she had gathered together. Not so easy. She couldn't just write out several thousand of these. There had to be a simpler way. Making a mental note to talk to her mom later, Lauren was hoping the woman had some information in the thousands of books Emma had in her library.

Those books! Goodness. Lauren hated those books more than anything. Remembering back to when her mom moved them all to the farm from Indiana to Ohio, Lauren thought her arms were going to fall off from all the boxes of books. And those boxes were also packed first out of everything in the house that Lauren had grown up in. Books. Not clothes, food or fun stuff. It was all about the books with her mom. Lauren smiled as she remembered that half of the moving truck was nothing but books. She would admit, she had made fun of and was pissed about them at the same time, but now she was glad her mom wore the tinfoil that she had back then.

Picking her pen back up, Lauren grabbed a blank piece of paper and started making notes to herself. First she wanted some feedback from her siblings about what they thought a newsletter should contain. Then she wanted to talk to her mom about any information she might have about mass producing the letters. Then she wanted to go into town and look around.

As she jotted down the last notation, her stomach twisted. She hadn't left the farm since everything went haywire. She had heard some things as the others were talking, what Mike and Chloe and her mom had seen, but this would be the first time for herself, and she admitted, it made her a little anxious. She would definitely need a plan, as her mom and some of the others would have concerns about her safety. She wasn't necessarily a gun fanatic like some of the others, but right now she wished she had listened. Maybe it was time to do something about that. She should be able to protect herself, and just like when she went to Doc Scott's with her mom, Emma was the only one with a gun. What if something had happened?

Making another notation, she would pop in on Uncle Mike and see about a gun training class. Maybe some of the others on the farm would like to attend and Lauren could do a piece for her newsletter on what went on. Heck, Unk might start teaching all over if people wanted to learn! Feeling like this was a big contribution for the newsletter, the bubble burst when she realized she had better actually ask her uncle if he would teach the class before she started spreading the news. Being as private as he was, he might not want to. She would save that for conversation over dinner tonight, hoping to get some backup on that from everyone else.

What else?

Pictures? Were they an option or a waste of valuable paper space? Good question, Lauren congratulated herself. Looking up from her paper, Lauren looked out the window above her desk. Fields of corn stood ready to be picked. How would that happen now that there was no power? So many questions!

"Jesus!" she exclaimed. "I may need to borrow some of my mom's tinfoil after all. And this talking to myself? Is this how people lived before electricity was invented?" Funny thing was, she was actually enjoying the time away from Facebook and her cell. Yes, she missed catching up with her friends and what was going on at work kinda scared her once things came back around, but she was happier, calmer, definitely less stressed even with all the challenges ahead. She might not feel the same way if she were still at her apartment in town, but being out here on the farm with her family definitely had its advantages and rewards. She was getting to spend some sweet time with her nieces and nephews, and she was seeing her mom in a whole new light. She wasn't just her mom anymore but an intelligent adult who really cared about other people and spent the time to help them. Growing up, Lauren had felt distanced sometimes from her mom, who was always so busy. Now, she was starting to actually understand the dynamics of the woman's life.

Okay, I really need to get a move on besides sitting here just talking to myself.

"Why yes, yes, you do, Lauren!" Lauren said in a predominate mimic. Lauren gave a chuckle. It was one thing to talk to oneself, but to answer yourself back brought a whole new dynamic to the conversation.

Walking into the kitchen, Lauren was surprised to find Jessica and Megan fixing lunch instead of her mom.

"Hey, what are you two doing here?" she asked.

"Emma had to go with Uncle Mike, so we volunteered to put the grub together. Go figure!" Megan explained.

"It's nice to give her a break once in a while," Jessica continued. "Besides, I can show you my mad cooking skills!"

"I'm not sure I'm up for all that. I was just going to grab an apple and head into town," Lauren said nonchalantly.

Jessica caught the foul ball in Lauren's comment, but it flew right over Megan's head. "You're going to town, huh? Your mom know about that?" Jessica asked.

"Is there a reason why she needs to know? I'm just going in to get a few things from my apartment and snoop around town a bit," Lauren responded as Megan started to pay attention to the conversation.

"You have an apartment in town?" Megan asked, looking at Lauren.

"Yes, she does," Jessica responded before Lauren could get a word in, "but Mom convinced her to move right after the power went down."

"Yes, I have a rather nice apartment in town," Lauren agreed, giving her sister-in-law a sideways glance. "I've been thinking about heading back in and picking a few things up that I think will be useful for my newsletter. Besides, I want to talk to some neighbors and see what's been going on. We've been so isolated out here and I need firsthand knowledge of things if I'm going to put together a credible newspaper."

"Mom's not going to let you go by yourself!" Jessica shot back.

"Well, first off, Mom can't stop me!" Lauren replied, now obviously annoyed.

"Ask Uncle Mike. Maybe he'll go along to keep an eye on your back?" Jessica suggested.

"Nah, he's too busy here on the farm and keeping an eye on Miss Chloe," Lauren said with a wink.

"All I know is Emma will be beyond pissed if you go into town by yourself," Jessica replied.

"How long are you planning on being gone?" Megan asked.

"Not long, maybe a couple of hours at most. I just want to grab a few things and see for myself what's going on out in the world. We're pretty sheltered out here on Mom's farm," Lauren explained.

"Take me," Megan said.

"Oh, now wait—" Jessica started to voice her objection.

"Emma is keeping the kids for a few hours. We'll be back before she even knows, and I'll keep an eye on our resident journalist here and make sure she sticks to the plan. Grab some things and we're out of there. Besides, I need an adventure to break this mind bend I've been on. Please, Jess, you don't even have to tell her because we'll be back long before she even realizes we're gone!" Megan begged.

"Oh my god! And if you're not? My ass is grass right along with you two! I don't want to piss that woman off! Are you insane?" Jessica squealed, knowing she didn't stand a chance against the two girls in front of her, but equally scared of the wrath her mother-in-law would rain down if she found out. "Okay. Two hours. Get there and get back. Understood?"

"It's a solid forty-five-minute jog there!" Lauren exclaimed "That doesn't give us enough time!"

"It will if we take the horses," Megan stated matter-of-factly.

"Oh! Now you're stealing Emma's horses too! Sweet Jesus in heaven, if either of you screws this up…"

"Nah! We got this," Lauren said with a grin, appreciating the quick thinking on Megan's part. "Let's get saddled up!"

The ride into town was uneventful until they rode past Lauren's aunt and uncle's house. Emma had told the kids what she had found on the way in to see the sheriff, but it didn't make it any easier to see the house burnt to the ground.

"Think they felt anything?" Megan asked as she pulled the horse she was riding up alongside Lauren's.

"Mom said they were already gone, so I doubt it. I'm looking at it like more of an on-the-spot cremation," Lauren explained.

"Or a Viking funeral for a farmer," Megan said, her voice barely above a whisper.

"What?" Lauren said with a half laugh.

"You know, Vikings? They put them on a boat and send them out on the water. Once they're out in the middle, someone shoots an arrow and lights them on fire. Very heroic."

"Indeed," Lauren said as she reined her horse around. "We better get going." She didn't want Megan to see the tears about to bust out over her eyelashes. Megan had hit a nerve when she said it was heroic to die in a blaze of fire. It made Lauren angry that her aunt and uncle had to die this way. They deserved to be around family and friends, not burnt up like a chicken on a barbeque grill.

The closer they got to town, the more nervous Lauren felt. Most of the scattered houses along the way were boarded up, with any vehicles shoved in front of the houses as an extra barricade. There was none of the familiar—no kids laughing as they sailed down the slide on their swing set, no laundry hanging outside on the clothesline, no neatly mowed lawns with manicured flower beds or any decorations on the homes showing signs of the upcoming holidays. It was at that moment that Lauren realized she didn't even know what day it was anymore. Could be Thursday, but was it November yet? Was Thanksgiving coming soon? What happened to Halloween? Did anyone get dressed up and go trick-or-treating.

Lauren looked over at Megan riding a bit of a distance from her. Megan's kids were losing a huge part of their childhood. The newsletter could help fix some of that if Lauren could get it up and running. Making a mental note to figure out the date and keep better track, Lauren also wanted to talk to her mom when she got home about celebrating some of these just to keep some kind of normalcy for everyone.

Reining her horse in, Lauren closed the gap between herself and Megan. She was excited about getting back home. She would put together an impromptu Halloween party for the kids to get some excitement going. After all, Lauren had many fond memories of the holiday herself. Why not help contribute to her nieces' and nephews' social development with some ghost stories and apple-bobbing contests?

"Hey, Megan, what do you think about throwing the kids a party when we get back home?" Lauren asked her companion.

"I think they would love it! What kind of party are you thinking of?" Megan asked.

"Maybe a Halloween party? I'm not even sure what the date is anymore, but I know it's about that time of year. Whether it's actually October thirty-first or not, we can still have a party and have some fun," Lauren explained. "The kids could use it."

"I could use it! Are you kidding me? I don't know which way is up anymore, and this could definitely take my mind off everything for a while. Think we could put some costumes together when we get home?" Megan caught herself. Home. Home used to be with her husband and kids out west. Funny how she didn't even hesitate to call Emma's farm her home now.

"I'm sure Mom can figure something out. I've seen her make paint before so why not face paint? Besides, if she doesn't know, I'm sure she has a book for that!" Lauren giggled.

"Yeah, your mom loves her books, doesn't she?" Megan agreed.

"Yep, sometimes I think she loved them more than us," Lauren responded, not thinking.

"What? No way! It's obvious how much your mom loves all you guys. I only wish I had that growing up."

"It wasn't always what you see now. Her work and her prepping stuff took up a lot of her time. None of us kids played sports or anything because no one was able to get us there. It sucked," Lauren tried to explain.

"And all those kids that did get to play sports are probably wishing they had your mom right about now," Megan said.

"I know. I've been thinking a lot about that lately. I gave Mom such a hard time back then. She tries, in her own way, but her way isn't something I know how to handle. I've always wanted that cookie-cutter mom, and she isn't even close to being that."

"I know, but she is awesome even if she doesn't fit into your perfect mold. You ever get the impression she wanted you to be different?" Megan asked Lauren.

"Actually no, not even during my emo stage. I remember coming home with my hair shaved around the sides and dyed pitch black. I was waiting for her to bitch, but nope, all she did was tell me she loved me. She even went with me when I got my first tattoo. It was a birthday present from her," Lauren said, remembering it all too well.

"Maybe it's time to cut her some slack like she did for you?" Megan asked.

"Yeah, maybe." The guilt had gotten to Lauren hard and fast. It hit her right in the middle of her stomach. She had an overwhelming need to go home and give her mom a big hug and tell her how much she loved her. "Let's get going so we can get home."

His hands were on the bridle of the horse before either girl knew what was going on. "Woah!" he commanded as he tried to steer Lauren's horse away from Megan's.

"What the fuck!" Lauren screamed as she kneed the gelding, trying to get him away from the stranger. "Let go of my horse!"

The horse, confused on what command to follow, started to bounce his head in defiance.

"Megan?" Lauren screamed.

"I'm here!" Megan responded as she rode around to the other side of Lauren. She guided her horse in to try to get close enough to kick at the man.

"Stop it! Let go!" Lauren was now getting highly agitated. Where did this guy come from?

Megan gave the hijacker a swift kick in his back, sending him straight to the ground. "Come on! Let's get out of here!" she screamed as she kneed her pony hard. Lauren looked down at the man as he was trying to get back on his feet.

"Josh?" she said, stunned.

"Give me your damn horse!" he yelled up at her as he reached for her stirrup.

"Lauren! Let's go! Now!" Megan shrieked.

Lauren walked her horse away from the man and looked back, pity written across her face. Turning the horse's head towards Megan, Lauren clicked her tongue and rode off silently, her mind in a whirlwind as memories flooded in of the boy who asked her out on her first date.

"No, I was born close to here. My youngest brother was born just south of Cleveland. We moved from here to Indianapolis when I was, like, I don't know, maybe twelve?" Lauren was saying to Megan.

"Then how was he your first date?" Megan was confused.

"My grandparents still lived here when they were alive. When I would come back to visit for the summer, I didn't exactly stick around their place. Josh was a neighbor kid back then, and we hung out a lot together before my grands died," Lauren explained.

"Oh! Makes sense now," Megan said. "I can't believe he acted like a crazed lunatic with you if you knew him! That's just nuts!"

"We'd probably better start paying better attention now that we're getting closer to town. There's a couple more houses, and then we hit the city limit. I'll be honest, Megs, I'm kinda concerned about what we'll find, but I need to get to my apartment. We'll be safer there," Lauren continued.

"If you think so. I know one thing, we get into trouble and your mom is going to kill us."

The two rode in silence as they neared the town's outskirts. They had ridden past a few abandoned cars, but now that they were entering town, the streets had been cleared. The residents had pushed them across the main entrance to block anyone traveling. Men and women were stationed at the outpost as the two rode up, naive to the sights locked on their positions.

"Ladies!" a big burly man yelled out from behind a Ford LTD. "What brings you out this fine day?"

"I-I live in town here," Lauren stammered, fear setting in as she surveyed the scene before her. Never before in her life had she ever had a gun pointed at her. "Have an apartment up on Hickory Street. Was wanting to get back in so I could pick up some of my stuff."

"Sorry, ma'am. All abandoned properties have been confiscated by the sheriff."

"Ben?" Lauren asked, confused.

"You know Sheriff Olan?" the man said, now a bit interested in who this visitor was.

"Well, my mom does more than I do, but yes, he has been out to the farm a few times," Lauren clarified.

"What farm? What's your name, little girl?" the man gruffed.

"Emma Montalvo is my mom. My name is Lauren," she replied.

Commotion behind the barricade got the two girls' attention as the whispering increased. A lone man ran off towards town from somewhere within the barricade where he had been hiding.

"I'll be with you right quick if you could just sit still for a bit." The man's tone had obviously changed to a more neighborly one instead of the snide, vexing demeanor of just a few moments ago.

Megan knew they were in over their heads. She had no idea things were going to be like this, especially this close to the farm. Now what? If they turned to leave, they would be shot, that much was clear. Hopefully the fact that Emma was Lauren's mom would pull some weight here. Looking at each of the faces behind the barricade, Megan was wondering when the last time they bathed or had a hot meal was. Cigarettes were not in short supply, as every face except two carried the glow of lit ash, and the aroma of cheap whiskey meandered over to Megan like a drunken cowboy at a rodeo, making her stomach want to hurl its contents. Glancing over at Lauren, Megan prayed the girl could get them out of this mess.

"So the sheriff said to let you two in since your daddy's here," the big man said, looking at Lauren.

"My dad? Is here?" Lauren said in confusion. She knew he had been taking off for lengths of time but had no idea he was coming into town. Feeling a bit relieved that her father was around, Lauren watched as the tall, skinny kid wound his way out of the obstruction until he was standing between the girls, holding out his hand. Lauren finally figured out that he wanted one of the reins from her horse. Tossing the leather rope over, the boy caught it with his left hand as he slid his hand behind the cheek piece of the bridle. Lauren glanced over at Megan and tried to give her a reassuring smile.

"Get off the horse," the boy instructed Lauren.

"I..." Lauren began before a hint of anger crept in. "Why do I need to get off my horse? Just let me get through!"

Dropping the rein of Lauren's horse, the kid turned and shot Megan's horse in the breast. The horse tumbled forward onto the ground, flipping Megan over its head.

"I told you to get off!" the boy screamed at Lauren now.

Lauren, still in shock at what she just witnessed, threw her hands in the air as she lifted her leg over the saddle's horn and slid off. With her arms still raised, Lauren made her way over to where Megan still lay on the ground.

"You okay?" Lauren quickly asked.

Megan only nodded, as the deafening sound of the wailing horse was too much for her. Rolling over, Megan started gagging as the horse defecated on the ground mere feet from where she lay. Grabbing the distraught girl by the arm, Lauren pulled her up and away from the tortured beast.

"Get the other horse over to Ed's so we can have fresh meat," the big guy directed the skinny kid.

"Wait! What?" Lauren started screaming at the man. "What do you mean, fresh meat?"

"I mean exactly what it sounds like. That horse will feed a lot of people in town," he shot back at Lauren.

"I've had that horse since I was little! You can't just cut him up and let people eat him like a cow!" Lauren said, now bewildered at the conversation she was having with this man.

It was too much for Megan, who turned and vomited. Losing all control of body function, she could feel the warm flow of urine down her legs.

"Yes, we can," the man continued with a slight grin creeping over his face. "Just like a cow."

Lauren was stunned. Was this how life was now out here away from her mom's farm? How much had she been protected by the woman who just a bit ago she had been complaining about?

"Where's my dad?" Lauren screamed at the man.

"Your daddy is down at the pub. Joey, you want to escort the princess over there along with her friend here?" the man asked the skinny kid. "Don't let them out of your sight," he said, turning to dismiss his association with them. He had other business to attend to.

Lauren walked over and helped Megan to her feet.

"Lauren, I—" Megan began before the other girl shushed her.

Holding her close, Lauren and Megan walked into the opening of the barrier, with the skinny kid close behind them. Once on the other side, the boy pointed his chin in the direction the girls were expected to go. Once on the other side, the girls saw the reality of what could have been their deaths. At least a dozen bodies were on the ground with rifles aimed outside the roadblock. It was sad to think these people probably shopped at the same grocery store and had kids in the local grade school. Now they were ill-trained mercenaries. Any twitch and they could have been dead. Glancing back, Lauren couldn't even fathom the outcome for the two horses she'd left behind. This was her fault. If she hadn't gone off on a whim once again, they wouldn't be in this predicament. Thinking about how her mom would react to any of this was a road she didn't want to think about right now. Now, she just wanted to get to her dad.

The girls paused outside what was not much more than a hole in the wall. Candlelight flowed from the windows as the smell of cheap cigars and dime-store perfume moseyed from the open doorway with more class than the cheap prostitutes who stood at the entrance. Megan yanked back on Lauren's arm to get her to slow. "I don't want to go in there!" she said, trying to get Lauren to stop.

"I'm not leaving you out here by yourself," Lauren whispered back in a huff. "Here, stay right behind me," she continued as she shoved the other girl to trail her into the pub.

It was hard to see as Lauren followed the skinny kid into the bar. With the lights down and a thick haze of smoke, Lauren squinted until her eyes started to water. The boy led them through the crowd of locals towards a room in the back, where a pool table was visible through the doorway. He thrust his chin out towards the room as he turned and walked to the bar. Lauren stood there with an uneasy feeling starting to swell in her stomach. The room around her started to melt away as her vision narrowed to the doorway of the alcove.

She saw him sitting in the corner, smoking the short stub of a cigar. His arm was wrapped around the waist of a woman that Lauren had never seen before as she teetered on his knee. Laughter erupted through the small room as the woman looked back at Lauren's father with a smile broad enough to show her rotten teeth behind the bright red lipstick.

Lauren could feel the coldness of the room as it crept across her skin. None of this was making any sense. Why was her father in this place? Who was the woman? Feeling an intense need to run away, Lauren turned to find the exit when she ran square into Ben's chest.

"Well, hey, little lady! Fancy meeting you here," he said with a mischievous grin.

"I-I shouldn't be here. I need to leave," Lauren stammered.

"Ah, no!" The excitement was evident in Ben's voice. "We're all family here! Find a seat and stay a while," he said as he gripped Lauren's elbow to spin her back around. "Now, who do we have here?" he asked as he spotted Megan still tight behind Lauren.

"Hi! I'm Susan," Megan said, thrusting a hand in Ben's direction. "Lauren came into town to have a little fun with me. We haven't seen each other since we went to college together."

"Oh really? College girls, aye? Where do you live here in town?" Ben asked.

"Over on Hickory. I have an apartment over there," Megan explained as she remembered what Lauren had said earlier. "You should stop over later! A couple of other girls are coming over, and we're going to have a small party for old times."

"Hickory, why yes. I know where that is. Funny, I don't remember seeing you around town before now," the sheriff stated, giving Megan the once-over.

If there ever was a time that Megan was glad she was still breastfeeding, it was now. Hitching her shirt lower, Megan let the sheriff have a look at her rather robust cleavage. "I keep out of trouble, or at least I don't get caught," she said as she shot a quick wink at Ben.

"Well now!" Ben exclaimed. "Maybe I will stop on over after I take care of some business here. Give me a chance to get to know you girls a little better."

"Sure thing. We're heading home now. The rest of the girls should be there soon, but I needed a bottle, ya know, and I knew I could get what I needed here," Megan cooed. Grabbing Ben's collar, she gave it a salacious tug. "I'll see you in a bit, then."

Pushing Lauren behind her towards the front door, Megan did not take her eyes from the sheriff until she rounded the corner of the exit. Turning, she grabbed Lauren's hand and pulled her into the bushes beside the bar. Keeping the two moving, Megan put as much distance as she could between the pub and themselves until they were both out of breath and had to stop.

"What the fuck just happened back there?" Megan panted.

Lauren dropped her head onto her knees as she slid down the outside of the building to the ground. Her head was spinning in a thousand different directions. "I don't even know." She moaned.

Picking Lauren's chin up with the cusp of her hand, Megan looked at Lauren's now tearstained face. "We have to get out of here and fast."

"Let's get to my apartment," Lauren suggested.

"Are you crazy? There is no way we are even going close to your apartment! That asshole of a sheriff will be all over that area soon, and we need to be out of town before he realizes he got played. Lauren, think! How do we get out of town without going back through that barricade?" Megan pleaded.

Running her hands through her hair, Lauren blew out the rest of the pent-up breath she had been holding inside. "I guess, through the ball fields? We used to play little league there, and there's train tracks that run alongside that if we follow them, will bring us right to the western side of the farm."

"Can you get us there without anyone seeing us, and fast?" Megan asked.

"Oh man, I'm trying to remember. It's been a while now since I've been on that side of town," Lauren said, fighting through her memory.

"You have to! We need to get out of here fast!" Megan was all but screaming now.

"Megan, my dad?" Lauren finally said, the tears filling her eyes.

"I know, honey. We'll figure this all out when we get home. Let's get going before they start looking for us."

Standing, Lauren peered around the side of the building they had been sitting beside. Taking Megan by the hand, the two girls disappeared into the night.

62

He watched her as she sauntered towards the chicken coop. He had her schedule down to the nearest minute, as he had spent weeks following her every move. Even though things were in a chaotic state with the condition of the electric grid, there was some normality to people's daily tasks starting to creep back in. He had waited patiently, and now it looked like that patience was about to pay off.

Her spikey blond hair was a little longer than when she first arrived, but she still had a hard edge to her that drew his attention. Maybe it was the "go fuck yourself" attitude that perked up his manhood or the freedom with which she allowed her body to strain against the borrowed T-shirt she got from his wife, but she definitely got his attention and held it. Just thinking about her taut nipples pressed against the back side of a Def Leppard concert tee made his dick hard. Reaching down, he slid his hand down the front of his jeans and squeezed. Feeling the blood looking for a release made his breath catch in his throat as thousands of nerve endings screamed up his throat, his eyes fluttering shut against the addictive sensation.

He hadn't been sure his pecker would even work again after all the shit he had been through, but after a night out with the boys, well, let's just say that he had never felt more pleasure than in the abuse he had put it through that night. Grasping harder, he bowed his head as a muscle cramp crept up his back, sending him into spasms. Resting his hand on the wall, he braced himself so he didn't fall to his knees as his manhood oozed into the inside of his briefs. Keeping his eyes closed, he focused on getting his breathing under control as perspiration broke out across his brow.

He needed to feel the inside of her. To take control of her. To make her submit. It was all he could think of lately. Some would say he was consumed, but he looked at it more like conquering an adversary. She wanted him. He could tell by how she acted when they were together, but she was just too weak to allow herself the pleasure. He could change that. Hell, he would change that whether she wanted him to or not. He could see her face afterwards, the surprise at the amount of pleasure he would give her. Grabbing himself again, he fought back the urge to give in again.

Chloe bounded towards the Barn of Torture, as she called it. It had become her chore to gather the eggs every day and keep an eye on all the chickens. Everyone had a duty, and this seemed like the safest thing for the city girl to do to immerse herself into her new way of life. It wasn't like she would be helping to birth a calf anytime soon, so starting small was a good step for her. It also got her out of the house and away from some of the chaos that swirled around in there like autumn leaves in a winter breeze.

She had resolved that her life would not return to her known normal, but she was okay with that. After all, she was tired of turning tricks for rich assholes who treated her like a commodity. Here, she had a fresh start. She was Chloe, someone's friend and sister instead of just a piece of ass.

Opening the door to the small building, Chloe waited for her eyes to adjust to the dimness within. She understood why pirates wore eye patches! Left eye was above deck; right eye was below. That way they could see at all times without having to lose valuable seconds without being able to see when an enemy could instantly thrust a blade into their torso. And here she had spent most of her life just thinking that all pirates were blind in one eye!

"Ahoy, wenches!" she yelled as she made her way inside, the chickens squawking at the intruder. "Oh, just calm yourselves. It's just me," she responded, rolling her eyes at her intended victims. "Now, hand o'er yer bounty before I off yer heads!" Chloe said in her finest pirate talk, giving herself a giggle.

"Aye, I'm glad no one is in here with me! They would think that I had lost my bloody mind!"

Picking up her little lathe basket that she used to collect eggs in to transport them safely to the house, Chloe timidly walked over to her first gudgeon. Licking her lips, she sized up the chicken sitting on the nest.

"I don't suppose you'll just hand over that egg and no one will get hurt?" she half sniveled.

The chicken just looked at her. "God, I hate this part." Chloe moaned as she timidly stuck her hand out towards the chicken's underside. "Just sit still and don't peck at me," she commanded of the yellow-feathered poltroon.

Chloe turned her hand over, palm down and gently slid her hand beneath the hen, feeling around for the much-valued gratuity.

The door slamming behind her jolted her so much that her hand came flying up, knocking the chicken off its nest. Spinning, Chloe faced the insensitive intruder with the basket in front of her for protection.

"Mike, damnit! You should knock first!" she screamed.

"Before I go into a chicken coop?" he asked with a sly grin creeping across his face.

"Yes, well. We wouldn't want to disturb the girls while they're working, now would we?" she stammered.

"You the madam of the coop now?" he shot back with a laugh.

Chloe felt the comment cut deep before she realized it was just a joke. He knew nothing of her past, and she intended to keep it that way. But Mike caught the sudden change in her demeanor.

"Hey, you alright?" he asked, reaching out to run his hand down her arm.

"Yeah, so what brings your bloody self out to my lair?" she asked with a grin.

Maybe Mike had misread her, but he didn't think so. He had caught her off guard a few times that she tried to recover quickly, but he knew something was there. Something she was hiding.

"I came to see if you want to go on a picnic down by the creek?" Mike chuckled. "I had no intention of scaring you this bad."

"You didn't scare me!" she shot back a little too fast.

"Oh no? Then why is your heart beating a mile a minute?" he asked.

"How do you know—?" she started to say as her hand went to her chest, verifying what the man stated as fact. Before she could utter her next denial, his lips covered hers.

She melted. She melted straight into the man who was sweeping her off her feet, and there wasn't a damn thing she could do about it. She wouldn't even know how to begin to stop the tidal wave of emotions he caused in her soul.

Letting her come up for air, he didn't miss a beat. "So, about that picnic?"

"You expect me to talk after that?" she half muttered, wiping the spittle from her lips.

"Finish what you're doing. I'll meet you in the house in say, an hour? We can go from there."

"You're not going to help me so I can get done faster?" She pouted.

"I have my own thing to do," he said as he smacked her playfully on her rear. "An hour."

Michael walked out the door, letting it bang closed behind him, and Chloe exhaled for the first time since he walked into the room. Damn if he didn't have a way of messing up all her senses!

Turning back to the business at hand, Chloe boldly slid her hand beneath her next couple of victims, knowing the sooner she got done, the sooner she could go on this picnic Mike had planned.

Chloe's pulse increased again a she heard the door open. This time, though, he let the door fall gently back instead of the loud bang just minutes earlier.

"Forget something?" she asked, not turning around. She didn't want him to see the enormous grin growing across her face that she couldn't hide.

He didn't respond.

"Oh, want to play some games instead?" she cooed playfully.

Her head snapped back as the hand grabbed a handful of her champagne tresses, the basket she was holding so delicately just moments before forgotten as it tumbled to the floor. She could feel his breath on the side of her neck, the faint smell of beer wafting beneath her nose.

"Mike!" she screamed.

"Is that who you really want right now?" he whispered in her ear.

Every nerve within her body was now at attention. How could she have been so stupid?

"What do you want?" she said slowly, yielding to the pull he had on her hair as her body fell back against him.

"You," he breathed out, the air tickling the small invisible hairs on Chloe's ear.

Her stomach wanted to heave, but dealing with johns for so long helped her keep her cool.

"Me? Why do you want me? What is it that you want from me?" She spoke so softly that she barely heard her own words over the beating of her heart.

The man's other hand wrapped around and covered her breast, looking for her stiff nipple. His knees buckled slightly as he found his intended target. He had wanted to touch, to taste her for so long now.

Chloe's mind was racing a mile a minute as she tried to wrap her head around what was going on. She needed to stay calm and not panic, no matter what the man was doing to her body. In another life she had learned to turn off her emotions and use her assets to get what she wanted. Why was this any different? Could she play this out and not get hurt? Could she suppress all the emotions that she had been freeing recently with Mike, like a girded bird finally finding freedom? Why was this happening?

"You like this?" the man whispered as he squeezed.

God, Chloe, think! she screamed silently.

Chloe pressed back against the man even more. Closing her eyes, she turned the imaginary lock that closed the door to the outside world. "Hmmmm," she moaned.

She felt his lips against her neck. Reaching down, she twisted her hand around behind her and grabbed his crotch. Putting slight pressure on his groin area, she waited for the intended response.

"You like that?" she moaned.

Murmuring something unintelligible against her neck, the man was becoming more and more engrossed in his own lust. Gripping again, she slid her foot back between his legs at the same time. Making one more intense massage, she immediately reached up with both hands, securing his hand on her head. With a tip of her hip, she sent the man crashing around and against the nesting boxes in front of her. Trying to catch himself, the man let go of her hair long enough for her to step back away from him.

"Tom!" she screamed, her eyes wide in horror.

Tomás Montalvo gathered himself together and stood up facing his prey. Bending down slightly, he brushed off the bits of straw that had stuck to his jeans when he had fallen.

"Chloe," he said nonchalantly without looking at her.

"What the fuck are you doing?" The murderous look on her face fielded the emotions spewing from her mouth as any sense of escaping evaded her now.

"Giving you what you've been asking for," he replied as if he were doing her a service. His eyebrow rose slightly as the grin crept across his face.

"Like hell I've been asking for it! You're fucking insane!"

"You played too, but another time, then. I will leave you to your chores," he said as he walked to the door. Turning to leave, he looked at Chloe with such an intensity in his eyes that Chloe could not break the hold. Raising his index finger before his lips, he simply and quite effectively sent her world into a tailspin before he let the door slam behind him.

She waited until she thought he was far away, trying to compose herself, her mind still trying to wrap itself around what had happened.

Tom?

The thought made her sick as she remembered what had happened. She'd thought it was Mike coming back in. She'd thought he had forgotten something, forgotten to tell her something maybe. Never in a million years did she think it was anyone else but Mike. He was a part of their group, their pack. Damn it, he was a part of her new family! Now what was she going to do? How was she going to face Emma? Her fight-or-flight instincts were in overdrive as her mind spun around in all different directions. Good god, she didn't know what to do!

Placing her left hand on the edge of the door, she reached down and grabbed the doorknob with her right. Bowing her head and closing her eyes, she took a deep breath. She had to get out of this room before she suffocated. Gripping the handle with a fear of what was on the other side, she transferred her energy into running away as fast and as far as she could.

Opening the door, she didn't wait to see if anyone was out there, she just took off at a pace that would surprise any professional sprinter. Up over the small knoll and down the lane to the house, she was not going to stop until she felt she was in a safe place. As fast as her legs could go, she ran past the house and took off along the tree line to the back field. Following the path that she and Emma had walked, she found the entrance into the deep, dark woods. Slowing a bit, she ran too close to the raspberry patch that Emma had planted years ago and spun around as the thorns dug in and held on to her clothes. Ripping her arm away from the prickly captors, she felt the skin beneath her clothing sting from the deep scratches the bushes left.

Running deep into the open arms the forest offered, she slowed long enough to jump over a couple of fallen logs and take a quick turn off the path.

Her mind screamed as she stood and circled around, looking for a place to hide.

Where would she go?

Around and around she turned, trying to find the magic door to get her out of here and back to her life in Los Angeles.

She saw the cabin almost hidden behind the thicket of evergreens and underwood. Taking off, she ran into the building, slamming the door behind her. Pressing her back against the door, she slid to the floor as she tried to catch her breath.

Damn it to hell and back!

She had no idea what to do. Tell Emma? That would destroy her. She loved that man beyond reason, which was apparent since Emma used such love and grace to deal with her husband's odd behavior since the accident. Ignore what happened? Then what? What if he attempted to pull the same shit on one of the other girls? She almost laughed out loud as she thought of Tiffany and Johnisse, but Megan. Innocent Megan. Was that why she was acting so weird lately?

Oh please, no! Not Megan. Megan wasn't eating lately, and even though no one had caught on, Chloe had. She had watched her move her food around on her plate, acting like she was eating and then hurriedly cleaning up all the plates, hers mostly still full of rearranged sustenance.

Chloe wrapped her arms around herself as she thought back to Tom's hand on her breast. Shuddering, she tried to shake off the feeling of his fingers manipulating her body. She wanted to forget that she used her prior experiences to outwit the man who had just changed so many lives if she talked. She had to say something, she just wasn't sure who she should talk to. Definitely not Emma.

Oh God, she felt the pain that would Emma would be wrapped in if she found out her husband had betrayed their marriage. Emma was a good woman and did nothing to deserve this!

It was just too much for Chloe to keep bottled up inside. The tears started to flow down her cheeks and her body was rattled by the sobbing that overwhelmed her small frame.

"Damn it!" she screamed. "I was supposed to be able to trust you! How could you do this to us?" Over and over she felt his hands on her, his breath on her neck... "Fuck you, Tomás Montalvo," she screamed into the void the forest provided her. Lying on the hard wooden floor, Chloe wrapped her arms around her knees, trying to comfort herself as the tears continued to slide down her face. Time slipped by as her mind numbly replayed the past hour over and over and left her empty trying to find answers. The sun continued to fade as Chloe's breathing started to level out and picked up a familiar rhythm as exhaustion finally overcame her.

"Hey, have any of you seen Chloe?" Mike asked of the group as he walked into the kitchen.

Emma was sitting at the table sipping a cup of tea as her husband sat across from her, eating a bacon, lettuce and tomato sandwich. Tiffany was busy cooking another batch of bacon for the rest of the group while Jay was looking through the side drawer below the counter, trying to find a pencil.

"No, hun. She hasn't been in here since I've been here," Tiffany replied.

"I just got here myself." Jay shrugged.

"I think Tiffany has some bacon ready if you want a sammich there, Mikey boy," Tom said as he chomped down on his own BLT.

"No, thanks. Listen, if anyone sees her, tell her that I'm looking for her," he said as he started to walk out of the room.

"Mike? Everything okay?" Emma asked.

"I hope so," was his quick reply before he disappeared.

The shivers from the chill that had settled on her skin woke her up. Wrapping her arms around herself as she sat up, she blinked her eyes in confusion as to where she was.

"Mike!"

She had forgotten about their picnic with all the crap that had just happened. An all too familiar uneasiness returned to her stomach. She had to go back to the house and face what had happened. Drawing her knees up to her chest, she rested her head on her knees. What was she going to say to the only woman who had ever watched out for her? *Hey, your husband's a slimeball? Hey, can't trust him, so let's string him up in the nearest tree. Isn't that what you end-of-the-world people do to the creeps who betray your group?*

Picking her head up, Chloe ran her hands up the sides of her head to fluff her assumedly flat hair. She needed to get this mess cut. If she had it shorter, Tom would not have been able to control her so easily. She had learned that lesson early on in her chosen profession. Never give a john the advantage. Slamming her head back against the door, she realized she could never escape her past. What was the use? It haunted her around every corner she took, sticking its tongue out and making her feel like a thrown-away rag doll that no one wanted anymore.

Standing up, she turned and opened the door to the outside world. Where did she go from here? Back to Emma's? There was nothing left for her there.

Mike found his sister alone in her office. Giving a gentle knock, he walked in and shut the door behind himself.

"Sis, I still can't find Chloe anywhere. Have you heard from her?"

"No! Why didn't you say something before now? I figured you had found her since I haven't seen either one of you since lunch," she said as she pushed her chair away from her desk and stood up. "Where did you see her last?" Emma said, visibly concerned.

"Out in the chicken coop. She was gathering eggs."

"Odd. I don't remember seeing any new eggs in the kitchen. Have you asked Tom? I know he was out and about before lunch," she asked.

"No to the Tom part. I poked my head in the coop earlier but didn't see much since it was kinda dark in there."

"Come on. Let's go have a look around."

"Wait," he said as she started to walk past him. "The reason I came in here. I…" He started to stammer.

"Spit it," Emma said.

"I may have scared her off, and she just doesn't want to see me," he explained.

"Why would you say that?"

"Well, she and I have been spending quite a bit of time together. I kissed her."

"You think your kisses have magical powers to make all the girls run away," Emma asked.

"No, damnit."

"I'm sorry. I know you're worried, but I'm not following."

"I kissed her. Like, I made it known that I like her and want to spend more time with her. Like, maybe have a relationship." Mike barely choked out the words to his sister.

"A relationship? You?"

"I know, right?"

"It's not that. You deserve someone special. I was just giving you a hard time, so relax. Listen, if there is any one thing I know about our Chloe, it's that she can take care of herself and that she knows what she wants. I wouldn't worry too much about scaring her off."

"Speaking of, what do you know about her? She doesn't like to talk about herself and I'm getting tired of trying to pry information."

"A little. She lived in LA, obviously. Had a day job and stalked my site at night. She has a good heart, Mike, if that's what you're asking. She's just a little misunderstood. I trust my Spidey senses, as you like to say. Bro, we're wasting time here. We need to get going if you're done with my Dr. Ruth expertise."

Following his sister out the door, Mike had an uneasy feeling in the pit of his stomach.

Mike hit the door with the tip of his boot, hoping someone was in the kitchen to open the back door. He did not want to put his bundle down for an instant. Kicking the door again, he finally heard shuffling on the other side as the door slowly opened. Pushing it fast with his foot, Mike forced in past Tom, who was still trying to figure out what was going on.

"Go get Emma!" Mike said to the bewildered man, who was standing and staring at him and the woman he had in his arms.

"What's going on?" Tom stuttered.

"Please! I asked you to go get your wife! Chloe needs help!" Now shouting with frustration, Mike walked into the living room still carrying his bundle.

"Chloe? What's wrong with her?" Tom asked, following after his brother-in-law.

Laying Chloe on the sofa, Mike turned and was about ready to punch Tom square in the face but stopped short. It would hurt Emma more than it would Tom, he realized.

"Can you please go get Emma?" Mike said, now seething through his teeth.

"Go get her yourself," Tom replied. Staring at the man in disbelief, Mike wasn't about to leave the woman but saw no other choice. He could stand there and argue with the imbecile of a man his sister was married to or go get his sister himself. Turning to leave, Mike would deal with Tom later.

"Don't let her move if she wakes up," Mike demanded of Tom. "I'll be right back. Emma was headed back towards the barn when we split up, so I'm guessing she's around there."

"Sure," Tom replied, looking at the long form of the helpless female lying on his sofa, his eye wandering to her breasts as he felt his groin harden.

Mike was already out the back door and headed to the barn before he heard Tom's reply. Walking back out into the kitchen to make sure the man had left, Tom clicked the lock on the door. It might buy him some quality time with the little blonde by the fireplace and would definitely alert him when anyone came back to the house and fumbled around to find a key.

Walking back to where his victim lay, Tom closed the curtain to the outside. No distractions. His mouth now salivating from excitement, he grabbed his crotch and gave a light squeeze.

"Soon," he said as he walked over to the helpless woman.

"Chloe?" His voice was barely over a whisper as he jabbed the woman in the cheek with his finger. Satisfied that she was unconscious, he ran his hands over her breasts, watching her eyelids for any movement. Satisfied, he slid his hands up under her shirt and slipped this fingers under her bra.

"Ah, yes," he moaned as he fondled her nipples. Flipping her shirt up, he wanted to see what she kept to herself. Groaning, he hesitantly touched the rosy buds that were exposed. He needed more.

Kneeling beside her on the floor, his tongue now teasing her nipple, he let his hand travel down her stomach until he felt the silky strands of hair. A gush of warmth flowed over him as he ejaculated in his pants, his eyes rolling backwards as his muscles seized during the episode. Chloe moved.

Damn it.

He had been clenching her nipple between his fingers during his climax a little too intensely. Backing up, he was starting to stand as her eyes fluttered open.

"What the..." she started to say as she tried to sit up. "What the fuck are you doing?" she screamed at Tom as she ascended more out of the fog she was in. Startled, he looked down at her chest, her breasts still exposed. Chloe clutched at her shirt, trying to cover herself.

"Don't touch me!" She was now sitting up and trying to swing her legs off the couch. "Don't you ever touch me again!"

"You might want to keep it down," Tom said as he gained control over himself.

"Or what? Get the fuck away from me!"

"Or what? How about I hurt someone you love? How about you won't know which one of these assholes it is until it's too late!" Tom now spat through clenched teeth.

Both of them jumped at the pounding on the back door. Walking to the doorway, Tom turned and once again placed his index finger over his lips. Leaving the room, he strode through the kitchen to the back door and unlocked it, letting Mike and Emma in.

"Sorry," Mike said. "I didn't think I locked it when I left. Habit, I guess."

Mike rushed past Tom and headed into the living room with Emma right behind him. Tom stood and watched them for a minute.

How would this play out? Would Chloe spill their little secret, and if she did, then what? Mike would be angry, that was a given. And Emma? She wouldn't do anything except gasp and look at him like he ran over her puppy. This was so tiring, living in this house with these people. He wasn't ready to leave just yet, but maybe it was time. Grabbing his jacket from the coatrack, he needed to get to the cabin and pick up his supplies. But first, he needed to get those two damn kids of Varga's.

63

Glancing around the room from the corner table he had chosen, Tom felt a sense of belonging that he hadn't felt in quite some time. Getting out and away from the farm and spending time with the boys had brought a newfound confidence and some new hobbies to his life that Tom was finding quite uplifting. It was better than lying around under Emma's thumb anyway.

Picking up the empanada, Tom sprinkled some hot sauce on the end and bit into it. Oh god, he could have died and gone to heaven. He hadn't had food like this in forever. While Emma could cook, it wasn't with the authenticity he had found in town at the tavern. These women could cook over an open fire like he had never experienced before. Why he had never come into this joint before now was beyond him, but he was finding it fast becoming like a second home to him. So much so that he had found it quite pleasurable to flirt with the owner's daughter, a homely little twit with thick glasses, but being thirteen and wanting to do nothing but fuck, Tom found it his obligation to help her out. He owed her one more romp before he headed out of town, not just for old times' sake but for keeping those brats of Varga's busy so he could enjoy his dinner. It was easy as pie to get the kids away from the farm, so easy that Tom felt edgy. He'd picked up on Mike being out with Emma looking for Chloe, but where was everyone else? He felt like he wasn't invited to the party! Oh well, made life easier for him, and now, being in town, there wasn't a whole lot anyone could do. Besides, Emma would never think to look for him here. No one would.

He would stay here tonight, safely tucked away within the confines of his newfound cabal. Ben was stopping by in a bit to discuss the plan for the next few days, but he knew they needed to get on the road at the ass crack of dawn if they were going to make it to DC by nightfall. Tom was looking forward to the trip. He needed to get away from his wife. He would deal with his kids later. Hell, if they knew he was leaving, they might want to tag along just to get away from their mother, but he had no way to take care of them right now. They definitely would be safer and better taken care of with Emma. A flame of guilt hit him in the gut. He was walking away from his family. No, he was just walking away from his wife. His kids would understand, they had to. He would make it up to them in the future after he had time to get his life together. He had big plans. Get his own house and begin building his own life instead of having every inch of his vivacity imprisoned by one woman.

Looking around, he wondered what was taking Ben so long. Deciding to kick back with a cup of coffee after his meal, Tom scooted the chair next to him out and rested his foot on it. He had to admit, he was still feeling a little off-kilter from the previous months.

A few weeks on the beach would do wonders for these old bones, he thought.

Right on cue, his little playmate appeared. Dressed in a pair of jeans and a T-shirt, the girl reminded him of one of his own kids.

Jesus, he muttered, wiping the thought from his head.

Her hand outstretched, Tom's eyes followed hers to the booty she offered. Tom picked it up and placed it tenderly beneath his nostrils as he inhaled.

"My favorite! How did you know?" He beamed.

The girl giggled as any young, enamored female would when she pleased her sweetheart.

"I stole it from my papa," she responded, quite proud of herself.

"I'll remember to thank him later," Tom said as he bit the end off the cigar. "Come, sit," he said as he pulled the adolescent onto his lap, wrapping his arm around her tiny waist.

Tom was so engrossed with his pleasures in life that he didn't see Ben walk up. Resting his hands on the back of the chair at the table Tom was sitting at, Ben looked at the sight before him. Here was the husband of one of the most honorable woman on the planet with a young twit on his lap, acting like he was a teenager. He could kill Emma himself sometimes, but even this was a low for Ben. It was why he stayed single.

Kicking the chair, Ben watched as the two untangled themselves.

"'Bout time you got here!" Tom said to Ben as he scooted the young girl off his lap and sat up straighter.

"Yes, well, this town doesn't run itself," Ben replied, clearly agitated.

"Looks like things are starting to really fall apart around here. You sure you're going to be able to leave to go to DC?" Tom asked.

"Don't worry about what goes on in my town. You need to worry about who's going to be on your ass shortly," Ben replied.

"No worries there. No one knows where I am, I made sure of it."

"Oh really?" Ben asked, turning his head to look around the room.

"Yeah, besides, we'll be gone in the morning, right? Plan still the same?"

"We'll see." The tone in Ben's voice was now barely above a whisper. "You sure no one from the farm followed you into town?"

"Why?" Tom asked with concern. He had picked up on the tone in Ben's reply. Ben didn't hear Tom's question as he stood up to get a better view. Motioning to a kid at the bar, Ben started to shift uncomfortably back and forth.

Before the young man made it all the way to the table, Ben's voice boomed across the room. "Where are our guests?" he asked, his arms flung out to encompass the room.

The kid stopped in his tracks, looking around the room. Running back, he climbed onto the bar as he further scanned the room.

"Joey! What the fuck!" Ben thundered across the distance.

"Ben! What's going on?" Tom asked, now on his feet.

"You, my friend, might want to get our bundles of joy ready for a trip. We're leaving tonight."

"What? Why the change of plans?" Tom asked, concerned but annoyed that Ben wasn't giving him any real reason for the modification. "Ben! Fucking answer me!"

"Your daughter is in town looking for you."

64

Emma listened to Chloe as she told the two what had happened. She listened but couldn't comprehend why anyone would do this to another human. She also was trying to figure out how this lowlife got onto the farm without sending off all kinds of alarms.

"You said you were in the chicken coop when this happened?" Emma asked, perplexed.

"Yes," Chloe said, looking at Emma. Her heart was breaking, but she knew she owed Emma the truth.

"Mike, we need to go out there and have a look around. Honey, are you going to be okay for a bit? I can have Tom come back and sit with you, but I really want to see if we can track who this was before he gets too far away," Emma explained.

"Good idea. Let's stop over and see if Kevin is done at Jonathan's. He can come with us," Mike agreed.

"Emma," Chloe whispered, her lashes lowered so she wouldn't have to look at the woman as she shattered her world.

"Honey, I'm right here. Everything is going to be just fine. I promise."

"Emma." Chloe tried again to find the words, but they evaded her conscience like rats after the sun comes up.

"Chloe, what's wrong? Is there more?" Emma asked.

Emma could hear the words, but they sounded like they were coming through a tunnel a million miles away... Tomás... her Tommy. Did this?

Mike looked at his sister. Judging from the pallor of her skin, he was afraid this was too much for her to comprehend. The anger within him had to be controlled until he wasn't with Chloe or his sister, neither knowing his capabilities as a trained mercenary.

"Emma, sit down," he said as he tried coaxing her to the chair he had placed behind her.

Emma looked around the room, frantically opening and closing her eyes to try to reset the moment.

"Emma," Chloe breathed as she reached for the woman's hand, "I'm so sorry."

"I don't even know what to say," Emma muttered, her thoughts scrambled.

She heard the Jeep crank over as she looked at the disheveled girl in front of her. "Mike?" she asked, looking around.

"I'm right here," he replied.

"Shit! Then who is outside taking the truck?"

"What?" Mike asked.

"Someone is outside taking the Jeep! Can't you hear that?" Emma now screamed as she jumped up to look out the window. "I can't see anything from here!"

"Where's Tom?" Mike asked.

"No idea other than he was in the kitchen when we came in!" Emma said as she realized it was a real probability that Tom was taking the truck to get away from what he knew Chloe was about to tell them all.

Mike pulled the curtain back from the window at the front of the house and peered outside. There he saw his brother-in-law backing the Jeep away from the garage. "It's Tom," he said as he watched his niece outside helping Tom load two children into the vehicle.

Let him go! The words thundered in her head. "Just let him go for now," Emma responded.

"He has Matheo and Alicia," Mike said as he turned towards Emma. "I'm going after him!"

"No. You need to stay here with Chloe. He's still my husband," Emma said.

"He's fucking crazy!" Mike screamed at her.

"I know he hasn't been acting normal, the normal we remember. I've seen pieces of him come back when we're together. Let me deal with this!" Emma shouted as she turned to leave.

Jessica walked into the kitchen as Emma tried to go after Tom.

"Jess, why did Tom take the kids? Did he say where he was going?" Emma asked frantically as she tried to get her coat on.

"What's going on?" Jessica asked, quite concerned at the confusion she walked into. "All he said was Mom needed the kids and took off towards town. Why?"

"Chloe will explain. Can you sit with her for a bit?"

"Sure, no problem," Jessica replied as she started to walk into the other room.

"Mike!" Emma yelled. "Let's go!"

In the barn, Emma started to saddle her horse when she noticed two were missing. As Mike came in, she asked him if he knew where they were.

"No, but I haven't been out here all day."

"What is going on around here?" Emma asked no one in particular, her world shattering around her.

Both riders now mounted, they took off down the drive.

"Mike!" Emma shouted into the wind. "Let's go this way," she said, pointing off down the railroad tracks that ran through her farm. "It will get us there faster."

Mike reined the stallion he was on around and followed his sister.

If there was one way Emma liked to clear her head, it was on a long drive with loud music blaring on the radio and the windows down so that the wind could blow through her long hair. It was the closest thing she had to describe what freedom felt like. Tonight, Emma rode with the horse's cleats beating against the iron and stone beneath its hooves. Her hair was a tangled mess behind her as her thoughts returned to her husband and the danger ahead.

Emma held up her hand as she slowed her horse. They were a short distance from town and Emma felt comfortable enough to stop here and walk the rest of the way in. An overpass across a creek allowed them a natural marker to find when they would head back to the farm. Directing her horse, Emma guided him into a group of small trees a couple of yards deep into the woods that ran alongside the tracks. Jumping down, she tied the reins to a branch hanging low and waited as Michael did the same.

"We can sneak into town from here and avoid the idiots manning the barricade," Emma explained.

"They have a barricade now?" Mike asked.

"Yeah, something Ben wanted to keep people out."

"Or in. More people he can control, less work he has to do."

"True, but I'm pretty sure we can get in behind the old ball field."

Mike reached over and grabbed his sister's arm, using his other hand to motion her to get down. He quickly gave her a hand sign to listen and be quiet. Waiting in the dark, Emma could hear the horses' heavy breathing but couldn't make out much more other than her own heartbeat, but she waited, trusting her brother.

The footsteps approaching slowed as they reached the overpass where Emma and Mike were hiding.

"Lauren, slow down!" Megan said breathlessly.

"You okay?" Lauren asked her companion.

"Yes, just need to catch my breath." Megan wheezed.

Emma looked at Mike as they both recognized the voices from above. Standing, Emma wasn't quite sure how to address the two runaways above her without scaring them to death. Looking at Mike, she shrugged her shoulders and winced.

"Lauren! Megan!" Emma yelled.

"OH MY GOD!" Lauren screamed.

"No, it's just your Uncle Mike." Her uncle's booming voice echoed from behind the trees. "God will be arriving shortly after I tan your hide!"

Emma and Mike hiked back up the short distance from the woods and gave both girls a hug.

"What are you two doing out here?" Emma asked.

"We… um," Lauren stammered.

"We went into town because I wanted to see what it was like in there now," Megan said hurriedly before Lauren could continue.

Lauren looked at her companion. "No, Mom. We went because I wanted to go to my apartment. This isn't Megan's fault. I also wanted to see what information I could get for my newsletter," Lauren explained.

"And did you do either?" Mike asked.

"No. Mom, Dad's in there," Lauren said, trying to soften the blow.

"Yes, we know. It's why your uncle and I were heading in. Some things have happened at the farm that your dad is involved in, and I'm afraid it's not good."

"I'm going back with you, then. I need to tell you some other things we saw that you need to know about," Lauren said.

"I think you girls need to go back to the farm. Take the horses," Mike said, pointing down into the woods.

"No, I really need to talk to Mom."

"Megan? You want to come with us too?" Emma asked. "I really don't want you to ride home alone since you haven't been on a horse much. I also don't want to just leave you here, but I don't want to force you into anything you don't want to do."

"I'm coming with you all!" Megan shrieked.

"Let's get going, then," Emma said as she grabbed onto her daughter's arm. Wiping Lauren's bangs out of her eyes so she could look directly at her child, Emma smiled. "I love you, but I am upset that you didn't tell me you were coming to town. This isn't the same world you remember, either of you." Emma continued as she looked over at Megan. "We can talk about that later, but right now we need to get into town."

"Mom, I really need to tell you some things, and I'm afraid that it's going to hurt you."

"Honey, listen. Life sucks sometimes. Right now is one of those times, but hiding from the truth hurts no one but yourself and the relationship you have with the ones you love. I'm tougher than you think, trust that. Talk. We need to quiet down soon the closer to town we get." Turning her daughter towards town, Emma started walking. She needed to get to her husband and the two kids he had instead of standing out here debating how much whatever information Lauren had was going to hurt her feelings.

Is that even possible? Emma thought. Her life had already been turned upside down. She might as well get all the bad out of the way in one big gulp.

65

She walked boldly into town, not caring who saw her. Her fury pushed her beyond reasonable thinking, blinding her sanity to the importance of safety. She had a burning desire to see the man she had just spent the last thirty years of her life with, and she knew exactly where to find him.

Ben saw her first, walking with a purpose towards the bar. The woman had an aura about her that none could deny. She defiantly commanded attention, even more now with the savagery of her emotions clearly painted across her face.

God, she's beautiful, Ben thought. Shaking his head, he kicked out any emotions he had towards the woman who made his life a hot mess sometimes. Turning, Ben maneuvered himself and Tom so that the woman's husband didn't see her approaching behind him.

"Tom," she said.

Turning, the look on his face was pure, unfiltered repugnancy.

The three adults stood there staring at each other, waiting for one or the other to make a move. Emma slowly pushed the two children behind her and started to back up.

"What the fuck do you think you're doing?" Tom asked her as he grabbed the little girl.

"You are not taking these children. Neither one of you," Emma stated with an uncanny boldness.

"Listen, I was just taking them back to their home in DC, or Miami. Wherever the hell they lived. I loved their mom, and it's my duty to get them home. There are people, their family, waiting for them there," Ben explained, his arms outstretched to his sides.

"That's bullshit and you know it, SHERIFF," Tom yelled.

"Don't get me started on what you seem to be dealing in here, Tom. Selling these kids? For what, a few measly dollars so you could take off and leave your miserable life? Really?" Ben spat out at Tom. "From the look on your wife's face, I'd say you haven't communicated your plans to her yet!"

"Shut the fuck up!" Tom screamed.

"Watch your tone with me, spic."

Tom shook his head, trying to clear the fog. "What did you say?" he asked Ben.

"I said don't use that tone with me."

"No, you called me a spic," Tom said matter-of-factly. Tom shook his head again, the fog lifting quickly as memory after memory came flooding back.

"It was you!" he screamed at Ben.

Emma backed the children up farther, trying to figure out from the exchange what exactly was going on. She knew Lauren was behind her somewhere, and she needed her daughter to get these kids out of here, and fast.

Ben didn't flinch. He knew from the look on Tom's face that he remembered what had happened the night in the cellar.

"It was you! You were behind all of this shit! You killed that girl because she wouldn't shut up after you nearly fucked her to death."

"Tom, shut up," Ben said with an icy calm.

Emma looked back and forth between both of these men she had known for a very long time, one of whom she'd been married to for over thirty years. It was like staring at two complete strangers.

"No! You might be the sheriff, but you aren't going to tell me what to do. Maybe it's time for a new sheriff to take over all the sick twisted shit you and your boys do!"

"You want to keep talking? I know what you were going to do with these bastard kids here, Tom. You think I don't know what you've been up to? You gonna sell these kids for a pretty penny, now weren't you? You think those people operate here in my town without me knowing about it? Oh, please!" Ben chuckled. "You can't find all that damn gold your wife has hidden, so you thought you would use the next best and easiest way out, well, besides that whore you've been sleeping with."

"You're just pissed off because you won't get a cut before they leave. I know what you've been doing in the next county over. I know what you did that night in the basement."

Emma blinked, trying to stay calm. Piece by piece, the puzzle was coming together. These two vile creatures before her, their conversation was making her desperately sick. Emma's mind was spinning in several directions at an unfathomable speed. Finding a way for her to get these children behind her away from these demons and to safety was her top priority.

"Do you think running your mouth like this in front of your wife is going to save you, or her for that matter?" Ben asked Tom.

"Fuck her, all she has done is make my life miserable," Tom replied before he could stop himself.

Looking at Emma, he figured he might as well continue his barrage. He had nothing to lose now anyhow. He wanted out, away from everything that was being force-fed down his throat as usual. He hated his life, Ben was right about that, but he just didn't want to get away, he wanted to see the woman standing there before him pay for his misery. "By the way, if you can't figure it out, I don't have your six anymore," he said with a smirk.

The words cut to the core of Emma's being. She knew it was going to be bad, but to stand there and basically wish her dead was something she wasn't ready for. Blinking, she just looked at him in disbelief. This man before her, whom she'd vowed to love till death, just told her she was on her own. The cord of three had been cut.

"Wow, you didn't know?" Ben asked Emma with a faint sense of sympathy.

Emma lowered her eyes first and then lowered her head so neither could see her fighting the tears, the kids behind her starting to pull on each hand that she held tightly. Turning, she yelled to Lauren to come get them.

"Tell her to stay the hell away from here," Tom spat at Emma.

"She's just gonna..." Emma trailed off as Tom screamed over her.

"If she comes near here, I will shoot her!"

"What? She's your daughter!"

"No, not really. Not anymore. She can be just as easily discarded."

"Tom, what are you saying? This is crazy!" Emma pleaded. Lauren had known no other father figure besides Tom. He had been there for Lauren's first boyfriend and her first heartbreak. He had watched as she learned how to drive and when she graduated from high school. He was there when she learned how to ride a bike and when she had gone to her first day of preschool. He was there when the monsters under her bed scared her so bad that she cried.

Emma had no idea what Lauren had seen that night and had no idea the danger she was placing her daughter in. Backing up, Emma scooted the children behind her a little bit closer to safety, wondering what was taking her daughter so long to get the kids.

As she was rounding the corner of the building, Lauren was within sight of the scuffle but could not hear exactly what was being said. She saw what she thought was an argument between her parents and the sheriff, but something was off. Her gut was trying to warn her to be cautious, but Lauren kept moving towards the group. She saw her mom trying to keep the kids behind her to try to shield them.

"Mom?" Lauren called out.

"Lauren, stay where you are," Emma said without losing eye contact with Tom. Backing towards her daughter, Emma kept pushing the children behind her towards Lauren.

"Emma, stop now before I shoot you," Tom said, his voice now unrecognizable to his wife.

"You wouldn't dare," Emma replied with a newfound boldness. This nonsense had to stop. She knew her husband had been through a lot, but it was no excuse for turning against his own family.

"Mom?" Lauren yelled out as she saw Tom raise the gun towards her mom. Every muscle in her body was now on fire as the adrenaline pumped through her. Lauren was both in as much shock and disbelief at what she was witnessing now as she had been the night she had seen her dad in the field. She couldn't let him hurt her mom the way he had that other woman. Reflexes taking over, Lauren started to run towards her mom, screaming for Tom to stop.

Swinging the pistol in Lauren's direction, Tom pressed the trigger. The bullet found its intended target, right in Lauren's thigh, toppling her straight to the ground like she had hit an invisible wall.

"I told you to tell her not to come over here!" Tom now sounded like a wounded animal fighting for its life.

Her eyes watching Tom's pistol as it moved from herself to the direction behind her, Emma had observed her husband sighting in the muzzle as his finger pad slowly pressed the trigger. She saw a flash as the projectile erupted out of the firearm. She knew the deafening sound would be coming, expecting it to ring in her ears as her head looked towards her daughter in horror.

"NO! What have you done?" Emma screamed.

It all happened so quickly. Tom brought the hilt of the pistol back with as much force as he could and clocked Ben forcefully across his nose. Ben was caught off guard, caught up in the pain Emma was going through with what her husband had just dumped on her. He spun around and fell back against the wall, sliding down into a slump on the ground as blood spurted from his face. Emma pushed the kids backwards as she turned to try to get them away as fast as possible. She figured the commotion between the two men would be the perfect time. If there was anything she had learned over the years, it was to notice the signs a person gives off before they do anything physical. She saw it in her husband, the clenched jaw, his shoulders clinching, his hands balling and unballing. She knew something was coming and was glad she was ready for it.

She felt the pull on the back of her skull. It felt like all of her hair was being yanked out of her scalp. Her head jerked backwards as her arms flew up.

"Emma, give me those fucking kids!"

Reaching up, she grasped her hands around the base of her hair being pulled, securing it from being pulled any harder.

"Tom!" she screamed.

She heard a gun go off as the hand holding her hair released its grip. Spinning around, she saw Ben with his firearm aimed at Tom. Looking quickly at Tom, Emma saw where the bullet had grazed his arm, making him drop his gun.

Tom lunged towards Emma, pulling her in front of himself as Ben centered his muzzle once again.

Emma raised both of her hands towards Ben, her eyes wide with horror. "Ben!" she yelled.

Tom pushed her towards the unsuspecting sheriff. Emma stumbled forward, falling onto the sheriff, barely missing the pistol.

"Get off me!" Ben yelled at Emma, throwing her like a rag doll off to the side.

Emma bounced around and finally got turned back towards the two men.

"Don't even think about it," Tom was saying.

Emma gasped in horror as she saw Ben's gun pointed towards Tom. Tom stood in the doorway; in his arms he held the little girl in front of himself like a rag doll to block the path of any projectile.

"Ben, please don't shoot her!" Emma begged.

"Yes, Ben, please don't shoot the little girl. She's worth a lot of money to someone!" Tom taunted, his voice unrecognizable to Emma.

"You're a sick fucker, Tom," Ben said calmly.

"You can talk," Tom sneered back.

"You know, I've done a lot of stuff I'm not proud of, but to hide behind a child is a low I would never go to. You're a fucking coward."

Emma stood as her gaze never left the child's frightened face. "Tom, please, just give her to me."

"No way! She's going with me. Stop me and I'll make sure no one gets her. I'll break her fucking neck just to make you sick. And it will all be your fault, once again," Tom snarled.

Emma felt the faint, cool breeze on her face before the terror snuck in. It was enough to keep her from being overwhelmed with the realization of it all. In one fell swoop, all was revealed to her heart, and she had minimal time to sort through it all. The evil that she had been feeling in her own home now was personified before her. The devil walked and talked on her land. He had been sleeping in the very bed in a room below where she spent hours praying to her own God. He called her by name. She called him husband.

"Aren't you proud, Emma, how you've made me into the man before you. How you cut my balls off so that you could get your way. All these years, ALL THESE YEARS, all I have done is live in your shadow, and I'm tired of it. I'm tired of you and your shit! If I had a gun right now, I would shoot you myself. I've never wanted to hurt anyone as bad as I do you. You have made my life miserable, and I hate you for it."

"Oh! A little trouble in paradise?" Ben smirked.

"Shut up, Ben!" Emma shouted.

A switch went off in Emma's head. She had preached it a million times, but now it was her turn to live the words. Each of us, in our lifetime, will have to make a decision. The bad guys already lived in the reality of death. They trained for it. This mental fuck would be the downfall of a lot of good people in a life-or-death situation, as it would take them too long to join the dark side. There are no rules in love and in war. It would be a lesson hard learned for many; some would only learn it with their lives.

Time slowed as Emma's reality became clear. She was here in the present between a corrupt small-town sheriff and the man she had been married to for the last thirty years. Two innocent lives hung in the balance of her decisions going forward.

"I'm taking these children with me, and I'm leaving, so don't try to stop me."

"Like hell you are!" Ben returned.

Tom moved the child in front of him again to block any shots that Ben could get off. Emma's heart now beat in her chest so loud she couldn't hear the exchange of words going on between the two men. Her eyes looked from the young boy and back to the little girl dangling like a rag doll in her husband's hand.

"Ben," Emma said, "put the gun down and let him leave."

"What?" Ben asked, surprised.

"Do what I told you," she begged.

"Yeah, Ben, listen to the bitch."

"Ben, please!" Emma pleaded, this time with such intensity it shut Ben up.

Emma stepped in front of Ben's gun, blocking it in case he decided to shoot her husband. She could die here, but it was a chance she was ready to take. Without a doubt in her mind, Emma knew her Tommy was gone. The shell of the man standing before her was a stranger. Actually, no, he wasn't completely foreign to her. She had picked up on the energy this being had been emitting for some time now and had spent countless hours praying for its source to be revealed. It had. It stood before her now.

"She'll pussy whip you next, you fucking asshole," Tom said, laughing at Ben. "I'm leaving with these kids, and no one better try to stop me again." Tom was now spitting out the words toward Emma as his arm snaked tautly around the little girl's waist.

Emma could hear Ben shifting his weight from one leg to the other behind her. He was getting restless and, with that, stupidity would not be far behind. She would deal with him later, but for now, there was no way she was taking her eyes off the circumstances before her. Tom had her full attention and deservedly so. He was the wild card in all of this.

Emma could feel the boldness rising within her soul. The warmth spread across her chest and across her shoulders, snaking down her arms, empowering her fingers. Like the women who walked before her, she wondered briefly if she was placed here on this earth for this time, for this moment.

"These lives are innocent." She calmly spoke directly to Tom, not losing eye contact.

He blinked and his eyes traveled to her mouth.

"Let them go," she whispered as he watched the movement of her lips.

Like a slow-motion movie, Emma's hand slid around to the back of her hip.

"Let them go," she mouthed, her eyes watching for any sign, any change in his face.

Tom felt himself being swallowed by her eyes, by the slow methodical movement of her fleshy lips. His vision slowly receding inward, he was losing all peripheral vision as his concentration was fully on her face. He blinked.

Emma saw it, the black fog that drifted over his pupils, devouring what was left of his essence.

"Nooo!" His high-pitched scream was backed by the personification of evil that had been haunting Emma for weeks now. Emma's eyes quickly diverted to his throat as his arm flung the little girl away from his body and he reached for Emma.

"Not this time," Emma said calmly as she turned slightly. Raising her pistol, she centered the sights on the heart she had known intimately and gently pressed the trigger.

66

Demons. We all have them. They play in the dark recesses of our mind. They tap-dance across our heart and leave it bruised and damaged. They make us believe untruths and scatter our emotions to the winds like freshly changed leaves in a fall breeze. Demons manipulate us to a point that we become our own worst enemy, sprinkling self-doubt and unworthiness upon our souls like grandpa would layer salt on his mashed potatoes at Christmas dinner. We have given them, might I say willingly at times, unnecessary power over our lives. How do we take that back? How do we break free from these invisible bindings that they have placed around us, or have we bound ourselves, placing blame on them? It's easier that way, to blame something outside of ourselves. To not take hold of our own destinies and just go with the flow. But a time will come when we each must make a choice. Circumstances will be life changing, that fork in the road, so to speak. You will either step up, or step aside, but either way, your life will not be the same. We each carry this fate at least four or five times during our time here. Is it God? Do you believe in a higher power? Is it not the balance that nature craves, that good versus evil?

Emma had demons who had taunted her all of her life. "You aren't good enough!" "You are stupid!" "No one could love you." Over and over the demons sang to her and pushed her harder to become someone she might not have become if she had learned how to handle the demons earlier. She lived to make others happy, to take care of their wants and needs because that was what she thought she was only good at. She chased her own dreams away just so she could support those she loved because that was the only time she felt like they loved her. But Emma ended up losing herself in the charade she played. Who was she? Why was she here? To make someone else rich? She missed most of her children's lives because she worked. She worked because she wanted to give them a better life than she had, and the funny thing was, all they wanted was her time, something that couldn't be bought.

Something that she gave grudgingly to someone else in exchange for a monetary benefit. How could she be so confused about what love wanted?

Mike's demons trailed him like the wake of dust behind his motorcycle. He ran so far and so fast, he did not allow the demons to settle. He had been hurt. Hurt by a man that was supposed to be there to show him the ropes. To show him, teach him about life. But Mike had to learn the hard way as the old man left. He left to go fulfill his own selfish desires, and Mike had to not only figure things out but also fill in the gaps where the old man left deep wounds. Mike would listen, night after night, to the demons surrounding the old woman as she cried uncontrollably as her heart longed for the old man. But the old man left anyway, and Mike vowed to never cause anyone so much harm. Love was a joke.

Megan's demons surfaced when she faced the challenges of raising a child with a handicap. Life threw a curve ball and she didn't get the big house with the white picket fence, the doting husband and 2.5 perfect children who excelled at everything and were loved by teachers. She didn't even get the dog. Oh, she got the big house alright, that seemed immense when she was beyond tired from taking care of a newborn alone because her so called "doting husband" was doting on his secretary. How many nights had her head hit the pillow, so tired that she couldn't even cry herself to sleep? Scared that she would sleep so soundly that she wouldn't hear the baby cry if he woke. Her demons, poking at her after she turned the light off and stretched her hand out across her bed to feel the cold emptiness of space. Is this what her life had become? Was she not worthy to be loved?

Shelby's demons chased her minute by minute into her normality of servitude. Her job was to make sure everything was alright. With everyone. All the time. She woke before the sun to make breakfast for everyone and was the last one to lay her head on a pillow at night. She worked hard. She found her worth in others' notion that "That Shelby, she's a hard worker." She wore it like a badge of honor. She never asked for anything from anyone. If she needed, she did without, as she didn't want to be a burden. A liability. An obligation. Wasn't love supposed to be free? Or did she need to earn it? It was all very confusing when your demons wanted it to be.

Ben's demons kept him awake at night, figuring out the next move on the chessboard. Power and control fed his soul after the fiends had their way with him. It was the only two things that could quench the hunger deep within him. Day by day, Ben moved his life around until he had everything and everyone under his thumb. Money wasn't his only motivator. He wanted complete domination over everything that touched his life, and if he didn't get it willingly, he took it. He took it from those around him, his family. He took it from his employees. He took it from the people who lived in his town. And he had plans to take "influence" even further. But he also took it from his own heart, from his own soul. Feelings were a weakness that Ben couldn't afford. Love was a distant memory.

Chloe tried to make excuses for the demons she allowed to play in her life. A horrible childhood, a need to make money, or just not wanting the attachment that another human whose heart you were melded with were all doors that open to the netherworld. When did you stop, turn around and face the succubus that you yourself were becoming because of the choices you had made?

And Tomás… He had it all, one would think. Doting wife and kids, a secure home and the ability to live out the rest of his life in comfort and peace, watching his grandchildren grow up. But the demons of greed and pride visited, and they could bring even the most honorable men to their knees. Jealousy, if left unchecked, could destroy a person's life.

No matter how perfect someone's life seems, once you look beneath the masquerade of denial, you will see   that we all face our own demons.

We are in this life together.

Love is the key

to unlock the chains that hold us down.

<u>Published Books</u>

Alpha Farm Series

The Beginning

Facing Your Demons

Coming Soon!

Book 3 of the series coming in early 2018!

INFIDEL coming in 2018!

Two Nations Under God coming in 2018!

SWARM coming in 2018!

Thank you and please consider leaving a review for *Alpha Farm, Facing Your Demons* at Amazon.
Please visit Annie's website at www. AnnieBerdel.com
The author welcomes any comments, feedback or questions at
AnnieBerdel@yahoo.com

ABOUT THE AUTHOR

Based in Indianapolis, Annie Berdel is a self-proclaimed advocate of educating women in the art of personal protection and self-reliance.

As an aspiring writer, Annie took her advocacy and dove into the dystopia genre with strong female lead characters.

A passion for firearms, herbal medicine, knives, slingshots, home canning, Kali street fighting, Kempo karate and furry animals fuels the fire and adds countless stories to be told beginning with her inaugural book "Alpha Farm, The Beginning".

Mother, business professional and bibliophile, in her spare time, Annie likes to stretch the boundaries of survival in a post-apocalyptic scenario.

Wanting to leave the Big Blue Marble better than she found it for her children and grandchildren, Annie is always learning, always loving and always looking for ways to help people become self-reliant and better prepared for whatever may come.

Made in the USA
Lexington, KY
03 March 2018